SOLAR

SIEGE

ARGO'S ASCENSION

Jim and James Hurley

PRAISE FOR SOLAR SIEGE

"I was completely blown away by this book! The story is sharp and well researched. The characters are relatable and had me invested in their struggles/victories from start to finish. This book has it all—action, suspense, shady space politics, a dash of romance, and just the right amount of sarcasm courtesy of Captain Eckhart and his crew. He quickly became one of my favorite characters—a tough, straight-shooting space miner with a messy past and an old grudge against the Federation, but with a surprisingly soft heart. If you love fast-paced sci-fi with a twisty plot and a cast of characters you can really root for... *Solar Siege* is a must-read!"

Muselife

"*Solar Siege: Argo's Ascension* pulled me in right away. The story takes place near Jupiter, where an old broadcast and secret logs reveal something dangerous that could put humanity at risk. From there, the action takes off and doesn't slow down. The world-building is detailed but not overwhelming, and the science feels believable without getting boring. If you liked *The Expanse* or *Project Hail Mary*, this book has the same mix of big ideas and suspense.

What I enjoyed most was how the characters felt real. You can tell the authors, a father and son, put a lot of heart into the story. Their teamwork shows through in the moments of friendship, loss, and courage. Overall, this was a fun and exciting read. It's the start of a trilogy, and I'm already looking forward to seeing what happens next.

Bobby Minor

This book grabbed me from the very first page and never let go! It's equal parts thrilling and thought-provoking, with that perfect blend of science fiction and heart. A must-read for any sci-fi fan!

Jersey Shopper

There's danger, conspiracies, and high-stakes action—but what really stood out to me were the relationships between the crew. Made the suspense hit even harder. A must read for any sci-fi fan!

Purple Girl

CONTENTS

PROLOGUE

A Whisper In The Dark

T he Federation science station drifted undetected in the shadow of a giant asteroid, swallowed by the endless sea of space. Far off in the distance, beyond the Trojan asteroids loomed Jupiter; its giant, swirling storms now centuries old. The reinforced outer walls reflected the cold glow of the station's floodlights. Hidden deep within those walls, something far more consequential was unfolding, an event that would shape the fate of the entire solar system.

A single red light pulsed in the darkness, the only sign of life inside the dimly lit command center. The station's automated systems hummed quietly, monitoring the facility's core functions with cold precision. At one of the main terminals, Dr. Elijah Ember, one of the last true visionaries of humanity, stood with his hands clenched behind his back, his gaze fixed on the flickering holographic display in front of him.

Lines of data scrolled endlessly across the screen, alien symbols interwoven with human DNA. The Federation had no idea what Ember had uncovered, and he intended to keep it that way. He had to, if humanity had any hope of surviving what was to come.

He switched to a second screen and watched the recording of McConnell's ship approaching the Argo for the hundredth time. All the while, scanning a file on Jim Eckhart, the Argo's captain, that he purchased with a small fortune. It detailed how Jim punched then Lieutenant McConnell in front of the press, earning an "honorable" discharge only after signing an NDA. The Federation's crimes remained hidden and unpunished.

On his screen, McConnell's shadow loomed larger than Jupiter itself. Ember didn't need old files to know the truth, only that Jim Eckhart's hatred of the admiral was the one card left to play.

＼＼＼＼＼

Two weeks prior, Elijah had sent Mariana his last secret message right before Admiral McConnell's ship, the F.S.S. Ferrell, intercepted the Argo. He had buried the message deep inside a Federation transmission bound for the Ferrell. Mariana downloaded the anonymous message and received the instructions. His message had been simple: Escape from the Ferrell at any cost.

He believed that his plan to help Mariana escape from McConnell using Captain Eckhart's mining vessel had worked. His logic held. Why else would they have severed his lab from the communication systems and locked him inside? For all intents and purposes, he was under lab arrest, with no explanation from Admiral Kepler.

After weeks of failed attempts, he finally found a back door into their system. Ember now controlled the emergency protocols for the facility. He sealed the doors, essentially barricading himself inside long enough to accomplish his mission.

For all his genius, Dr. Ember had miscalculated. Gideon's betrayal left him with no good options. There was no other way to get his discovery to Mariana. She was the only one who could stop the Federation's plan to seize control of the entire solar system.

He activated the first of three transmissions as the guards hammered the entrance. His secret message was buried deep within a fake emergency SOS broadcast, which he sent across all Federation channels. His encryption would slip past the techs unnoticed who would blindly follow protocol and forward the message to Mars.

> *Mariana, if you are seeing this,*
> *it means I have failed,*
> *and that I am most likely dead.*
> *They are coming for you next.*

Dr. Ember typed slowly, watching the words appear on the terminal for his second message. He knew the risks but never thought it would end like this. The Federation's ambition had exceeded even his vivid imagination.

The system once called him a billionaire, a pioneer, a madman. Now he was only a man out of time, trying to save a future that might already be lost. He had to act fast.

The console's hum seemed louder in the silence after the transmission. Ember straightened, knowing that they would never let him live for his betrayal.

The research—his research—had to remain hidden from the Federation at all costs. He had spent years unlocking the secrets of the organic compound beneath Ganymede's ice. Its properties defied logic, reacting with human biology in ways he couldn't explain.

This second phase required Mariana to recover the plans needed to stop the Federation. She couldn't do it alone, which was why the Argo was central to his plans. The size of the files made it impossible to smuggle them inside the SOS message, even with advanced encryption. His fingers moved over the console, sending the transmission.

The second file's destination was the only location within a hundred million miles that offered any hope of success: the abandoned Federation base on Ganymede. It was desolate, remote, and forgotten, but also full of the horrors they left behind.

Captain Eckhart's crew was elite, one of the few belt crews strong enough to handle deep space travel. With Mariana's help, there remained a sliver of hope that they could recover the data needed to stop the Federation.

He prepared the third message, its destination far beyond the outer planets, deep into the unknown. He wished he could do more for Mariana; all that remained was to pray for a miracle. So, he sent it.

꘎꘎꘎꘎꘎

Ember had uncovered the Federations plan to use the compound to build futuristic warships and weapons for conquest. After their catastrophic failure on Ganymede destroyed their primary supply, only a tiny deposit remained here in the Trojan Belt.

Ember had uncovered a message hidden deep within the compound, something far beyond human comprehension. The Federation saw a means of conquest; he saw a dire warning etched in its DNA. If he was right, humanity wasn't standing at the edge of a golden age of expansion. It stood at the brink of annihilation.

※※※※※

The locks disengaged with a hiss as the station's pressure doors slid open. Heavy boots struck the floor. Ember didn't turn. He already knew who it was.

"Dr. Ember."

The voice was cold, clipped. Federation Admiral Gideon Kepler entered the lab, flanked by two armed guards. His uniform was spotless, the Federation Security Division insignia gleaming beneath the command room's muted lights.

"It's over."

Ember exhaled through his nose. "You have no idea what you're dealing with, Kepler. You never understood the consequences of my research."

Kepler's lip twitched. "Spare me the theatrics. You've wasted enough of our time. The Federation is done with your delay tactics."

Ember turned at last to face the man who had once stood at his side, now his most dangerous enemy. He studied Kepler's face, hunting for hesitation, any flicker of doubt. But he found none.

"They won't stop, you know," Ember said, his voice calm. "McConnell. The High Council. They'll keep pushing forward. They don't understand what they're tampering with. They never did. You know that, Gideon."

Kepler didn't blink. "You had your chance to cooperate. But instead, you betrayed everything we've built. The damage you've done to Federation operations is beyond calculation."

"I betrayed you?" Ember said. "You mean you stole my research and distorted it into a perverse weapon of destruction. That compound wasn't designed for war. It was meant to give humanity a way to avoid the same fate of those who created it."

Kepler stepped forward, slow and deliberate. "Then you should have followed orders. Because of your defiance, Admiral McConnell had to erase Mariana's memory.

"Do you think I wanted this, Elijah?" Kepler's anger rose. "McConnell may strut around as the High Council's weapon, but he's just a pawn. When you sent Mariana that message, you forced my hand."

The room went still. Ember felt his pulse quicken but held his ground. He had prepared for this.

"She's already escaped with the Argo," he said, bluffing. "You really thought I'd let the Federation hold the key to my research?"

Kepler's expression soured. He gestured to a guard, who raised his rifle, the barrel trained squarely on Ember's chest.

As the soldiers took aim, the control panel beeped. Ember smiled.

"You're too late," he said.

The last of his transmissions had already launched into the void, well beyond the Federation's reach. Its target lay in the outer solar system, where it would remain dormant until Mariana discovered the trail he had left for her.

Kepler's gaze snapped to the screen. His face twisted in rage.

"Stop that transmission!"

The guard fired.

Pain erupted in Ember's chest. The shot slammed him backward against the console. His vision swam. The taste of blood filled his mouth. Even as his body failed, he managed a faint, defiant grin.

"She will stop you," he whispered.

He didn't mention that Mariana would need to access a Federation system before the message could reach her. That was a detail worth dying to protect.

Ember reached for the self-destruct protocol. His fingers found the switch. He triggered it. Alarms shrieked throughout the station.

Flashing lights stuttered across the corridors. Smoke curled through the vents. Distant rumbles shook the foundation.

Kepler stormed forward and grabbed Ember by the collar, hauling him upright. "What did you do?"

Ember coughed, blood spattering onto Kepler's spotless uniform. "I gave her a chance to live her own life. She's more than a Federation experiment. She..."

He slumped against Kepler's chest. The admiral stepped back and let him fall. The guards rushed to the consoles, scanning for any scrap of data to salvage.

Elijah's plan had worked. He destroyed the station to give Mariana the smallest of chances at freedom, giving his life for his granddaughter without hesitation.

The ceiling groaned. Beams crashed through the control panel. Guards at his heels as the command center crumbled. Dr. Elijah Ember died as the station collapsed into silence. His final transmission passing through the void, a whisper carried to a destination he would never reach.

Sparks danced across the shattered console. The final line on the broken screen glowed for a moment before vanishing:

Project Chimera — Subject Twenty-Two — Classified as "Stable. Experiment successful."

The screen went dark.

Far across the solar system, the exterior hull of the *Argo* was in shambles as it limped through space. Its destination: Mars. Somewhere in the vastness, an encrypted signal relay came to life.

Elijah's instructions, buried in the SOS transmission, triggered a silent command, an undetected breach dispatched the message, humanity's last vestige of hope. No one could decipher it except Ember himself and one other.

They are coming for you next.

Mariana stood in front of the display in her room. Her green eyes reflected the screen's dim light as she stared through the viewport. Still seething at the captain for denying her request to investigate the Federation Black Site, she said nothing. No emotion. No movement.

Then, after a long silence, she pressed the comms button.

"Captain, how long until we reach Mars?" she asked from her bunk in the living quarters.

"We're inside four weeks now," came the reply through the ship-wide comms. "And twelve hours since the last time you asked. Find a hobby, or it's going to be a long ride."

She already knew. The question had only served as a distraction. A way to keep her thoughts away from the inescapable truth: they were coming for her. The real question was whether she'd be ready.

LIFE IN THE ASTEROID BELT

The *Argo* hung in the asteroid belt like a lone watchman, its hull catching the faint glow of a distant sun. From this vantage point, the asteroid below looked deceptively tranquil, a jagged mass of rock and metal adrift in space.

Jim Eckhart, captain of the Argo, knew better. This was a delicate mining operation, and they were already behind schedule. He sat in his captain's chair, his tall frame rigid as he scanned the data feed. His graying hair was disheveled, the sign of too many hours juggling logistics, politics, and the nagging headache of dealing with the Federation.

"Diane, report," he said, steady but firm.

At her console, Chief Geologist Diane Patel's eyes flickered between the holographic projections of the asteroid's surface. "Our palladium vein lies about 300 meters from the surface," she said. "High yield. Stable ground for now. But if we dig much deeper, we could destabilize the site."

Jim contemplated. This was the game. Pulling treasure out of floating death traps while keeping your crew alive.

"Bucky," Jim said, toggling the comm to the surface. "How's it looking?"

Bucky Buchanan's confident voice crackled through the speaker. "Drill depth is 290 meters, Captain. Five minutes from contact. Chief Samuel's got the crew ready for ore collection. Should still meet our quota."

"Good. Keep it that way. No shortcuts."

"Stable positioning with the asteroid's orbit," Lisa Cross confirmed.

As he turned back to his display, Grace Hernandez, the chief engineer, appeared in the doorway. Petite, with sharp eyes that carried more weight than her frame.

"I assume you've seen the engine readouts?" she asked, stepping forward.

"I have," Jim said. "Everything within limits."

"Barely," Grace countered. "The containment unit on the FLS drive is running hot. If we need a fast crew extraction, let's not find out the hard way that it's compromised."

Jim sighed. He and Grace had tried being more than colleagues once, but life on the Argo made it impossible. Still, he trusted her advice, even when her words chafed.

"Let's get a maintenance crew on the containment unit," he said. "But keep the Argo focused on the mining operation. We hit our quota and get out before McConnell finds something else to gripe about."

Lisa slid a new set of data onto the forward display. "Heads up, our thermal window closes in three hours. When the asteroid rolls into solar shadow, comms will go noisy and hull temps spike three percent."

Grace added, "And the FLS containment margin is already concerning. A fast temperature drop in the shadows is where things crack."

"You'd never let that happen," Jim shot back.

Her laugh lingered after she disappeared down the corridor.

The comm chirped again. Karl Dresden, the robotics specialist, reported from the drone bay. "Captain, drone units are in position. Ready to assist with the ore extraction." He was more comfortable with machines than people, and he spoke with nervous energy.

"Good work, Karl," Jim said.

He leaned back, watching the feed from the asteroid. On the surface, the mining team moved with practiced rhythm. Bucky stood over the rig, barking orders while Chief Ryan Samuel directed the ore into containers.

And then there was JT. This was his first operation with the crew, and his first real chance to prove himself to his father.

Jim's eighteen-year-old son stood near the shuttle, arms folded, frustration written across his face. He had his mother's blond hair and blue eyes, and his father's size, already broad-shouldered and tall. He wanted to be with the crew, working the rig, proving his worth. But he was stuck with the least glamorous assignment: shuttle watch.

Safety protocols demanded that one crew member stay aboard in case things went south. But Jim knew it wasn't the responsibility JT wanted.

"James," Jim said over comms. His father was the only person who didn't call him JT.

"Yes, Captain?" His son's reply was stiff, formal.

"Everything look good?"

"Yes, Captain," JT said.

"Shuttle is secure. Tether's anchored."

Jim hesitated for a fraction of a second. "Good work, James."

JT didn't respond, but Jim could feel the tension in the silence. Before he could dwell on it, Diane's console beeped.

"Uh... Captain?" Diane said, her fingers flying over the holographic interface. "McConnell's moving."

Jim's stomach twisted. "What do you mean, moving?"

"He's positioning his ship closer to us," BK confirmed. "Locking a geoscanner on the asteroid. Looks like he wants a clearer read on our progress."

Jim's grip tightened on the armrest. "He's looking for problems. We're doing everything by the book," Jim said. His tone was calm but edged. "Let's see what he does next."

The mining operation carried on, but with one eye on their unwelcome observer. Jim suspected McConnell was angling for something, and it wouldn't end well for Jim and his crew.

Beneath the harsh starlight, the asteroid looked like a sleeping giant not wanting to be disturbed. Commander Matthew "Bucky" Buchanan stood atop the main mining rig, one hand gripping the safety rail as he scanned the rough terrain. He had the confidence from years of working the toughest dig sites in the asteroid belt.

"All right, people," Bucky called into the crew's earpieces. "Let's crack this rock open and earn our paychecks."

Chief Ryan Samuel, a veteran miner with a permanent look of skepticism, waved his crew forward. Ten miners moved with trained precision, securing the rig, activating the drill, and setting up ore containers.

The ground shuddered as the drill came to life, boring into the asteroid in search of the palladium vein Diane had flagged.

Above, Karl watched through his drone interface. His glasses reflected the display as robotic arms stretched from the hovering drones, assisting with ore collection. "All mining and spy drones are in position," Karl said. "Ore extraction should be optimal, provided we don't get any sudden—"

A tremor rocked the asteroid.

"—instabilities."

"Hold steady!" Chief Samuel barked, bracing himself. "We expected some shaking."

Inside the shuttle, JT followed everything on the monitors, his hands locked on the controls. He hated it. Stuck in here while everyone else did the real work. His comm buzzed.

"JT," Bucky's voice cut through. "You're our safety net. If this thing turns ugly, reel us in. Understood?"

JT took a deep breath, forcing down his frustration. "Understood."

Across the surface, the drill bit deeper, spitting rock and metal. Chief Samuel's team worked fast, filling the first ore containers. Real progress at last.

Jim turned to BK Colony at the comms station. BK, big as a bear, had a protein bar in one hand while fine-tuning the console with the other.

Bk squinted at the comms feed. "McConnell just sent a Binding Ops Directive to our channel. Move drilling sites in under ten minutes or face a contract penalty and license review."

Jim's muscles flexed. "What is this jerk pulling now? He knows we're trying to meet our quota before the thermal window closes."

McConnell's voice cut in, cold and deliberate. "Captain Eckhart, your operation looks like it's in danger of being shut down."

Jim tensed. On the bridge, BK's fingers hovered over the controls.

"McConnell," Jim answered evenly. "Something I can do for you?"

"You can tell me why you're mining outside the approved zone," McConnell replied. "This sector of the Belt belongs to the Federation, and I don't recall authorizing this site."

"We're within the approved zone. Check the coordinates."

"Oh, I have." McConnell sounded smug. "And I'm telling you to move. Immediately."

Silence stretched between them. On the asteroid, Bucky's crew froze mid-task.

"You want us to move?" Jim asked, voice hard.

"I insist. I'd hate for there to be... consequences, like your mining license being revoked, Captain."

Jim muted the comm and leaned toward BK. "Tell me you're pulling something from his ship."

BK tapped his console, already eavesdropping on McConnell's channel. "He's not alone. Federation patrol nearby."

Jim shut his eyes for a beat. Damn it. From bad to worse.

"Captain," Diane said, "the new site is risky. My scans show minimal palladium. If we move, we'll come up short of our contract. We're barely meeting our quota as it is."

"Yeah, I know," Jim muttered. His fingers drummed the armrest, mind racing. They couldn't risk a confrontation, but staying put meant giving the Federation an excuse to shut them down.

"Bucky," Jim said into comms.

"Yeah, Cap?"

"Pack it up. We're moving. Federation orders."

Bucky sighed. "You got it, Captain."

Chief Samuel gave the word, and the crew scrambled, locking down equipment, pulling the drill, and stowing ore containers in the shuttle.

From the pilot's seat, JT watched them climb aboard. His jaw tightened. "That's it? We're just letting McConnell push us around?"

Bucky clapped a heavy hand on his shoulder as he passed. "Welcome to working in Federation space, kid."

JT gritted his teeth. The shuttle thrusters engaged, and the vessel lifted off the asteroid, leaving behind the empty borehole as they repositioned to the new Federation-approved site.

An ominous feeling stirred in JT's chest.

The second site was far worse than their first selection. The terrain was jagged and uneven. Rocks of every size littered the surface. The ore deposit was thinner, making it impossible for them to meet their quota. But it was Federation-approved, and that was all that mattered to McConnell and his goons.

The shuttle touched down again, thrusters kicking up a swirl of dust and grit as it settled onto the asteroid. Bucky, Chief Samuel, and the rest of the team stepped out, securing their boots to the metallic walking planks bolted to the rock around the new site.

"All right," Bucky said as he adjusted his helmet. "Let's get this over with."

The rig's stabilizers punched into the surface with a deep thunk. Chief Samuel and his crew wasted no time. They moved fast, assembling the drill. Karl's drones hovered overhead, sweeping the terrain with tight scan patterns.

Inside the shuttle, JT sat with both hands on the controls. The fact that he wasn't allowed outside ate at him.

This is a waste of my time, he thought.

Jim sat on the bridge, eyes on Diane's geological report. Data scrolled across the monitor. Composition, thermal gradients, structural risk, location of the deposit. Diane had a gift. She didn't miss anything.

After several hours of digging, "Captain, this isn't good," Diane's voice came through the comms. "The site's losing integrity."

"What's the issue?" Jim asked.

"There are soft pockets forming near the deposit." Her hands moved quickly across her console. "Bucky's going to need a light touch. If we break through the wrong layer, the whole thing could collapse."

Jim sighed and rubbed his temple. "Bucky, give me something we can work with."

Bucky crouched at the drill site, inspecting the fractured terrain. "I've got nothing, Jim. This place is a disaster. One wrong move and we'll open up a fissure or drop straight into a void."

"How much time do we have?"

"We're taking a big gamble by digging here. We keep this up much longer and we risk losing the rig or worse if we don't take precautions."

Jim paused. McConnell was watching. If they aborted now, he'd twist it into justification for pulling their license. He was itching to tighten control. Jim gritted his teeth.

"Keep digging. The moment the surface shifts, the team evacuates immediately. The contract isn't worth losing lives."

Bucky didn't answer right away. "You sure about that, Cap?"

"Not even a little," Jim said. "But if we leave now, McConnell shuts us down. He's forcing us to take the loss. He knows that if the surface gives way, we'll have to jettison the rig and cargo to save the crew."

Jim leaned forward and continued. "Prep the miners. Make sure they're ready to disengage mag locks fast so they can float free. JT pulls them back in. Run the evacuation protocol. No heroes today. The goal is survival. We take the hit and regroup later. We've still got the backup rig. Once McConnell leaves, we go back to the first site. We'll finish the job and hit quota. That's how we get through this. Understood, Commander?"

Bucky muttered, "You should've punched him twice. Once for you, once for me."

A quiet laugh passed through the team. Chief Samuel gave a nod and went to work.

The drill roared to life. Karl's drones dropped into position, aiding the extraction. Machinery thrummed through the suits, a pulsing vibration that normally meant progress.

JT sat rigid, his gut telling him that the rock had only seconds left.

Just as they reached target depth and prepared for extraction, the asteroid groaned beneath them. The surface buckled. A violent tremor cracked the ground, splitting the site wide open. The drill jerked and sank as the rock gave way under it.

"Abort!" Bucky shouted.

The crew bolted toward the shuttle as the ground shook beneath their feet. Karl's drones tried to compensate, but the terrain was failing too fast.

JT's headset exploded with voices.

"We're losing the rig. There's no pulling it free."

"Save what cargo you can."

"We've got half the load, Commander."

"Move. Move. Move. Release the mag locks now!"

"Shuttle, drop the rig and pull us in," Bucky ordered.

Through the viewscreen, JT saw Bucky grab Chief Samuel and shove him forward, barely avoiding a chunk of flying rock. The ore containers slid. The tether snapped taut under the weight, keeping them from falling into the abyss.

Frustrated with McConnell's ridiculous orders, James flipped the controls to engage the shuttle's tether system, locking all three to the winch instead of releasing the rig. The magnetic winch ground upward inch by inch, but the weight was too much for the shuttle.

"Come on," JT said, pounding the thrusters. The shuttle lurched, thrusters firing to stop the entire load from vanishing into the collapsing asteroid.

The crew began drifting back down toward the surface wreckage as Bucky slammed into the side of the shuttle, one arm grabbing the emergency release. He pulled the handle to cut the equipment tether loose and keep the shuttle from snapping in half.

"Haul us in!" he barked.

JT gritted his teeth and yanked the lever. The winch groaned as it reeled in the crew, dragging them away from the crumbling surface. JT fought to hold the shuttle's position as the asteroid beneath them gave way.

The last miner had just cleared the cargo bay door when Bucky pounded a fist against the hatch.

"JT, pull in the cargo containers. We need to salvage whatever we can."

Once the final container locked into place, Bucky turned toward the cockpit. "We're secure. Let's go!"

JT obeyed. The thrusters roared, lifting the shuttle free just as the asteroid's surface collapsed completely, swallowing the mining rig, empty containers, and any hope of recovering their bounty. But they had survived. That was the only thing that mattered to the captain.

As the shuttle climbed back toward the Argo, JT looked once more at the fractured landscape. His chest felt tight. The mission was a failure. And McConnell had just been handed the excuse he needed to take control.

He hated that his father was right. Survival came before pride. But deep inside, the hunger to prove himself burned hotter than ever.

The Argo's cargo bay hissed as the shuttle's struts locked into place. The ramp lowered, and Bucky stormed out, helmet in hand, his face contorted with frustration. Dust clung to his suit, sweat streaked his jaw, and he let out a long breath.

Chief Samuel followed, shouting over the noise. "Secure the cargo! Lock it down. Karl, assess the drones. Full inspection."

JT unstrapped and ran a hand through his sweat-soaked blond hair. His pulse still raced. That was too close.

Before he could step out, Bucky's voice echoed through the bay. "JT!"

JT froze. He turned, shoulders tensed. Bucky's palm slammed into his chest, pushing him back a step.

"What were you thinking?" Bucky shouted. "You could've snapped the winch and killed us all! That much weight could've torn the shuttle in half. With you in it!"

JT opened his mouth, closed it, then tried again. "I had to do something."

"Had to?" Bucky's blue eyes blazed. "What if the tether failed? What if we had to explain to Jim that his kid got sucked into that asteroid? You're not here to be a hero, kid. Sometimes we take the loss, follow orders, and live to fight another day."

JT clenched his jaw. "We still got them out."

"We were lucky," Bucky snapped. He cursed under his breath and rubbed the back of his neck. The fight drained from his face. Luckily, everything worked out okay. Just don't try something like that again. You follow orders and never question them if you want to earn the crew's trust."

Before JT could respond, another voice cut in. "All right. All right, clear out before I start throwing people out the airlock."

BK Colony leaned against a stack of crates, arms crossed, amusement tugging at his face. His voice was sharp, but his eyes had the glint of someone who had seen much worse.

"I've got miners who need food and engineers who need to service the shuttle. Unless you're volunteering to clean out the air filters, move it."

Chief Samuel muttered something under his breath and turned to guide the crew toward the mess hall. JT turned on his heel and made for the upper decks. He was wound tight from the confrontation, and he needed a moment to breathe.

But it didn't last. The captain's voice came over the ship-wide comms, calling everyone to the mess hall.

Fifteen minutes later, the mess hall sat packed. Half the crew ate without tasting their food. The other half stared at the walls in silence, their eyes hollow and unfocused.

JT dropped onto a bench. He picked up a protein ration, peeled it open, and stared at it. He didn't feel hungry. Bucky eased into a seat next to him with a groan. His tray over-flowed with whatever the galley crew could scrounge up.

"Heck of a way to start the day," Bucky said, stabbing his food.

JT exhaled. "Is it always like this?"

Bucky huffed out a tired laugh. "No. Sometimes it's worse."

JT shook his head and rubbed his temple. His head buzzed with the aftershock of the adrenaline dump.

That was when Diane appeared. Her dark eyes locked onto Bucky. Worry covered her face. Bucky glanced up, and for a brief second, the tension drained from him.

"Are you okay?" she asked quietly.

Bucky's charm came as second nature. "Better now that you're here."

She rolled her eyes but winked before walking toward the kitchen. JT didn't miss the way Bucky's eyes followed her until she disappeared around the corner.

"You two really think you're clever, don't you?" JT raised an eyebrow.

Bucky grinned. "I don't know what you mean, kid. You're too young for that kind of stuff anyway. Go train on your simulations."

JT smirked but didn't press the point.

Before the conversation could go any further, the overhead comms cracked to life. "All senior crew to the bridge. Captain's orders."

Bucky set down his fork. "Well. That can't be good."

JT stood with him, both heading for the exit. The day wasn't done with them yet.

⸺⸺⸺

The Argo's bridge sat mostly empty. Jim stood alone at the command console, hands braced on the smooth panel, his eyes fixed on the flickering alert. The transmission waiting on the screen pulsed like a ticking time bomb about to go off. Admiral McConnell. Here we go, Jim thought.

The senior crew filed in. Lisa, Grace, Karl, BK, Diane, and Bucky moved to their stations. JT hovered near the back, still unsure where he belonged in moments like this.

Bucky stepped up beside Jim, arms crossed. "Think he's calling to congratulate us on a job well done?"

Jim exhaled through his nose. "Let's get it over with." He accepted the transmission.

McConnell's face filled the screen—thin, lined, eyes like sharpened blades of ice. His uniform looked freshly pressed, the gold trim shining like he had dressed for an award. His posture gave nothing but contempt. "Captain Eckhart," he said with that flat smile, the kind a man wears when he believes he already knows the outcome. "I trust the operation was successful?"

Jim didn't flinch. "I'm sure you've already seen the complications. That was your Federation-approved site."

McConnell's mouth twisted, something between a smirk and a sneer. "Yes, I saw. Quite the show."

Jim's fingers tapped the console. His patience was wearing thin. "What do you want, McConnell?"

The Admiral leaned forward, feigning concern. "I'm disappointed, Captain. We gave you simple orders. You ignored them. That sort of behavior can raise... concerns."

Grace, under her breath, said, "Here we go again."

Jim stood his ground. "We followed safety protocol. We pulled out when the site became unstable. That was your site, Benjamin. You knew the risks. You made us drill there anyway."

McConnell ignored the comment and shook his head slowly. "The yield from your operation came in well below the contracted quota. That's unfortunate."

Jim saw where this was going. He drew a slow breath. "We do the best we can with what the Federation gives us, Admiral McConnell."

McConnell cut him off. "Your best isn't good enough."

The transmission cut out. Silence filled the bridge.

Karl snorted. "Anyone else want to punch that guy in the face?"

"I'd like to take a mining drill to his precious flagship," said Grace, leaning forward.

Jim rubbed his eyes, exhaustion creeping in. "He's trying to paint us as incompetent. But why?"

BK, who had been silent, spun his chair toward him. His brown eyes sharpened. "That call wasn't just for us."

Jim turned. "What do you mean?"

He tapped a few keys, pulling up a data feed. "McConnell's ship broadcast that transmission through multiple relays. He wanted other ears on it."

Bucky cursed softly. "Great. Now we're the gossip of a Federation group chat."

"We need to figure out his endgame," said Diane, frowning.

Jim looked toward BK. "Talk to me."

BK's fingers flew across his console. His thick hands moved like a pianist's. "Already digging. If he thinks his channel's secure, he's never met BK Colony. I'll find a way in."

Jim nodded. Then he turned to the rest of the crew. "Get some rest. We've got a long cycle ahead."

One by one, the bridge cleared. Only JT stayed behind.

Jim looked over. "Something on your mind?"

JT hesitated. "Back on the asteroid... I know I could've handled it better, I should have followed orders."

Jim studied him before speaking. "It's honorable of you to admit it. What matters is you got the crew out. Everyone messes up. The important thing is to learn from your mistakes and not repeat them. That's how it works out here. We survive; we adapt, we learn to do better."

JT searched his father's face. "Do you trust me, Dad?"

Jim's posture softened. "I wouldn't have put you on that shuttle if I didn't."

JT swallowed and nodded.

Jim clapped him on the shoulder. "Go get some sleep. Tomorrow is another day." Jim smiled. "We can start fresh."

JT hesitated, then turned and walked off. He exhaled slowly and glanced back at the empty bridge.

Outside the viewport, the asteroid field drifted past, silent and endless. One bad mining operation was all that it had taken for McConnell to tighten his grip. Jim's gut told him that McConnell was playing a deeper game than anyone realized. And Jim's instincts rarely failed him.

He stood at the head of the room. The holographic display hovered above the table, a cross-section of the fractured asteroid flickering in pale light. The image showed just how close he had come to losing everything and everyone he cared about.

As the crew dispersed at the end of a long cycle, their footsteps heavy, weariness clung to them. Jim remained at the bridge console; eyes fixed on the display. He tapped a few commands, switching to a new stream. BK had managed to decode fragments from McConnell's intercepted transmission.

Among the garbled lines, a few terms stood out: "Ganymede," "Project Chimera," and "reclaim source." The words chafed his nerves. This wasn't about minerals. The Federation had other goals, and Jim had only seen a fraction of their plans.

Dr. Raegan Inoue appeared at the doorway. Those closest to her called her Rae Rae, much to her annoyance. She stood barely five feet tall, lean as wire. Sandy brown curls framed her face, streaked with green highlights that shimmered under the bridge lights.

"You all right?" she asked, voice low.

Jim didn't turn. "Just thinking."

"McConnell?"

Jim frowned. "He's up to something. If we don't figure it out, next time he's going to pull our license."

Raegan leaned against the frame with arms crossed. "You'll figure it out. You always do. You've got a strong crew. And, Jim, your son's smarter than you give him credit for."

He glanced at her, lips twitching at the corners. "He's got the talent, but he's not ready to join the crew. Not yet."

Raegan shrugged. "We all have room to grow. Even you, Captain." She pushed away from the frame. "Get some rest. Tomorrow isn't going to wait."

Jim watched her leave, then turned back to the display. The asteroid sequence was behind them, but it haunted them like a shadow in the void. He shut down the console but couldn't shake the feeling that this was only the beginning of McConnell's torment.

O2

CHAPTER

THE COST OF OBEDIENCE

O nboard the F.S.S. *Ferrell*, Admiral Benjamin McConnell, the officer in charge of Federation Mining Operations in the Asteroid Belt, sat smugly at his desk as he reviewed his plans for the *Argo*. The door to his office whispered open, and Chief Science Officer Dr. Mariana Kade strolled in, her eyes locked on her datapad.

She spoke without looking up. "As our models suggested, we've found trace residue that likely originated from the compound. But we can't isolate the signature without access to the Argo's maps and data logs. Say what you want about Captain Eckhart, but he knows the belt better than anyone. If the data exists, it's on his ship."

McConnell steepled his fingers, his eyes never leaving her. "So, you're telling me that without boarding the Argo to access their systems, we have no way to find what we're after?"

Dr. Kade looked resigned. "Unfortunately, no. There's no other way."

They shared an uneasy moment. "Then we have no choice." His gaze was unreadable as he studied her face.

As she turned to leave, McConnell's voice followed her. "One more thing, Dr. Kade. I'll be sending two Federation guards with you for safety. You'll install a program in the Argo's systems. Quietly copy their nav, map cache, and crew rosters. If Eckhart resists, trigger the tracking device."

Mariana's thumb paused over her datapad. A half-beat of hesitation, then, "Understood." And he was gone.

In the doorway's reflection, McConnell watched her slide a thin memory device into her sleeve instead of her pocket.

Six hours after the collapse, the crew gathered in the mess hall in an unusual hush. The sound of the engines filled the space, a constant low vibration that reminded everyone just how fragile life was out here. The crew sat scattered and silent. The asteroid disaster still hung over them. Its remnants drifted through space behind them, a ghostly trail of failure.

Jim stood at the head of the room, both hands resting on the back of a chair. He scanned the faces around the table. They wore the same drained look as he felt in his bones.

Dr. Inoue leaned back with her arms folded, her face drawn. Grace leaned on her elbows, lips pressed into a thin, bitter line. JT sat farther back, silent, his shoulders tense. Only Bucky still looked composed, though a flicker in his eyes betrayed how serious the situation had become.

"All crew are accounted for," Jim said, breaking the silence. "In spite of McConnell's games."

"Barely," Grace replied. "That dig site was a death trap. What was the Federation thinking forcing them to mine there? If we'd stayed another minute—"

"We didn't stay another minute," Bucky cut in. "The captain pulled us out when he had to. That's what matters."

Grace narrowed her eyes but didn't argue. She turned to Jim. "What's McConnell going to report to the Federation? You think they'll be thrilled we came back shorthanded?"

Jim straightened. "McConnell isn't my priority. This crew's safety is. From this moment, every dangerous order gets logged and countersigned," Jim said. "We document, we escalate through the union channel, and if they push us past a redline again, we walk.

"That's the problem, isn't it?" Raegan's calm always made people pause. "The Federation is all about profit and output. If we fall short on our contract, they'll side with McConnell."

"So, what do we do then?" JT asked. His fists were clenched on the table. "Keep saying yes until they get someone killed?"

Jim looked at his son. "We have stay one step ahead of McConnell. He doesn't get to decide how we protect this crew. That's our responsibility."

JT shook his head. "That's not a plan. That's waiting for them to get us killed."

The silence that followed was uncomfortable. Jim met his son's eyes, unmoving. Then he turned away. "If McConnell won't let this go," Jim said, now addressing the full room, "then we make damn sure the Argo is ready for whatever. I want the maintenance schedule current, every system triple checked. We don't want any surprises on our trip back to Mars." He turned toward Grace. "Get me a status update from engineering."

He continued down the line, assigning tasks to each senior officer, one by one. Finally, he faced Dr. Inoue. "Doctor, keep me posted on anyone still in the med bay. I'll check in with the patients there shortly."

"Don't worry, Captain. We were fortunate the collapse caused mostly minor injuries with only a couple broken bones." Dr. Inoue gave Jim a concerned look, then spun around and marched off to the med bay.

Jim finally turned to JT. "James, you'll help Bucky with the stabilizers."

JT opened his mouth to argue, but the look on Jim's face made it clear the smart move was to let it go. He nodded reluctantly. "All right."

"Make sure all status reports are turned in by the end of today's cycle. It's going to be a long day, but that's what we signed up for. Time to get to work."

The crew began to disperse, the scrape of chairs and the sound of boots on the deck plates breaking the silence. Jim stayed behind, watching them go. JT was the last to leave, casting a glance back at his father before disappearing through the door.

The mess hall felt emptier now, the engines louder in the absence of people. Jim sank into a chair, his elbows resting on the table as he ran a hand over his face. The weight of command settled over him, heavier than ever.

He couldn't deny that JT had a point. The Federation wasn't going to let this failure slide. McConnell's report would surely reflect the incompetence of the crew, whether true or not. They would demand more, push harder, and sooner or later, the Argo would run out of luck. The thought sent a chill down his spine, but he pushed it aside. Worrying wouldn't help. Only unearthing McConnell's true objectives would.

The hiss of the door opening pulled Jim from his thoughts. Raegan stepped back into the room with a datapad in hand. She paused when she saw him, her posture softening slightly. "You look tired." She crossed the room to stand next to him.

Jim let out a low chuckle, though there was no humor in it. "Not at all?"

Raegan conceded. "Sure, Jim." She set the datapad on the table and slid into a chair across from him. "The crew's vitals look fine, by the way. Physically, at least. Mentally... well, you know the strain of asteroid mining."

Jim nodded. "I don't know how much longer I can keep this crew together, Rae Rae."

"You've been saying that for years," she said. "And yet, here we are." Jim's lip moved up slightly, but Raegan continued, " You're right about McConnell. He's pushing us into dangerous situations. There's more going on here than they're telling us."

Raegan studied him for a moment, then eased forward, her elbows on the table. "So, what's the play?"

Jim met her stare. "We figure out what he's really up to, and make sure we're ready for whatever's coming."

As if on cue, the aging comms system came to life and BK Colony's voice blared from the speaker. "The captain is needed on the bridge."

Jim flicked on the mess room comms and replied, "I'm on my way." As he climbed the ladder to the bridge portal, he began to wonder what fresh new hell was about to drop.

Before Jim had entered the bridge, BK was already speaking. "It seems like we're popular today, Captain. A Federation shuttle is approaching the docking bay and requesting permission to come aboard."

"Hail them back and tell them permission granted. Then have Dr. Inoue meet me at the docking bay," he added, his voice flat as he turned to leave the bridge. "Security Officer Power, come with me," Jim said, looking over his shoulder at Liam.

"Yes, Captain," Liam Power replied in a thick Irish brogue. He followed the captain in stride off the bridge.

The docking clamps whined as they latched onto the Federation shuttle, their metallic groans cutting through the Argo's faint hum. In stark contrast to the utilitarian, battle-worn Argo, the Federation craft's hull gleamed like a knife's edge. Its sleek, angular design screamed technical superiority, as if it had no business mingling with a ship like the Argo.

Jim waited at the airlock, arms crossed and shoulders squared. Behind him, Liam and Raegan stood in tense silence, their postures echoing the unease spreading through the crew. No one liked unannounced Federation visits, and this one felt more calculated than most.

The hiss of the airlock filled the corridor as the door slid open. A woman stepped through, flanked by two Federation security officers in crisp black uniforms. She moved with deliberate grace, her pristine white coat trailing behind her. The insignia stitched on her chest, a gleaming Federation emblem inside a gold circle, identified her as a high-ranking Federation science officer. Jim thought the image clashed with her age. She looked very young, early twenties at most. Her striking green eyes stayed focused, and her red hair was pulled back in a tight ponytail. She tapped the screen of her datapad, the serious expression almost enough to mask her youth and beauty.

Liam leaned toward the captain, voice low. "Is she for real, Captain? She looks like a kid dressed up in her parents' uniform."

"Captain Jim Eckhart," she said, her tone measured, with just a hint of formality. "I'm Dr. Mariana Kade, here on behalf of the Federation Science Division."

Jim reluctantly extended his hand. "This is an unexpected visit, Doctor. We weren't told to expect anyone from the Science Division."

Mariana didn't flinch at the cold welcome. Her lips curved into a practiced smile that never reached her eyes. "I'm here to investigate why the Argo abandoned a critical Federation mining operation. Considering your recent failure, Admiral McConnell sent me to deliver your updated mission parameters in person. You understand how important this operation is to the Federation?"

The crew stared at her. Dr. Inoue shifted, arms folded. Liam's fingers twitched near his belt.

"We had to pull the crew off the asteroid because the surface was unstable. Like it says in my report, that wasn't our fault," Jim said, voice calm but firm. "Risking their lives wasn't worth any amount of palladium. That's in my report too."

"Don't underestimate the value of those minerals," Mariana said as she stepped farther into the corridor. Her gaze swept across the Argo's worn walls with detached curiosity. "These resources are vital to Federation colonies and station expansion. They aren't cheap or easy to come by."

"Then you should find another crew to mine space rocks while flying thirty thousand miles an hour," Jim said, his tone hardened. He held her gaze. "You sent us because someone told you the Argo is the best mining crew in the belt. So, deal with it."

Mariana studied him. For a moment, her pleasant expression gave way to something colder. "The Federation values results, Captain Eckhart. Not excuses."

Before Jim could respond, Dr. Inoue stepped in, her voice even. "If this is about minerals, why send a Federation scientist? Palladium is rare, but it doesn't explain why a high-ranking science officer is here in person."

Mariana turned toward Raegan. Her stance relaxed just enough to suggest respect. "Because the Federation's latest advances depend on these materials, and this region of the belt has some of the only known concentrations large enough to justify deployment."

"For palladium or something else?" Raegan followed up, clearly doubtful. "Are we helping develop new stations or new ways to control the solar system?"

Mariana gave a small shrug. "That depends on your perspective. From mine, it's about scientific progress."

Jim stepped forward, breaking the tension before it flared. "Doctor, you've made your position clear. Now tell me what you're really here for."

Mariana tilted her head, weighing how much to share. At last, she said, "I need access to the Argo's maps and data logs. Specifically, anomalies in the bio-scans and geo sensor readings from this sector."

"That information is off limits," Jim snapped back.

"Not to me," Mariana replied, unfazed. She nodded toward the officers behind her. "I have clearance for any data relevant to Federation interests. Your logs qualify."

Jim's hands clenched at his sides. "If you want access, you'll review everything under my supervision."

Mariana gave another faint smile, polite but unyielding. "Of course. I wouldn't dream of bypassing your authority, Captain," she said flatly.

❚❚❚❚❚

Minutes later, Jim stood on the bridge with Mariana at his side, scanning the data on the consoles. The bridge crew worked silently at their stations. Their annoyance was visible as the Federation guards moved among them like silent predators.

Mariana leaned closer to one of the monitors, her brow furrowed. "Your scans are remarkably detailed for a civilian vessel. Did you study at the Academy?"

"No, years of experience," Jim said curtly.

"And yet... you missed this." She tapped the screen. An ill-defined cluster of anomalies lit up, their patterns glowing faintly against the asteroid field. "These readings suggest trace signatures of something far more interesting than palladium."

Raegan frowned at her comment then squinted at the display. "How could Chief Geologist Patel miss a rare mineral?"

"That's because I didn't," Diane said, her voice sharp.

Mariana looked at her, shook her head, and gave in. She had no choice. "What I'm about to share is classified. Normally McConnell would never approve me telling you, but he authorized limited disclosure to expedite your compliance. I'm not sure where this falls."

"We aren't just looking for a simple compound. We're tracking a non-human organic lattice—older than Mars—so far, we've only been able to find it in remote locations beyond the belt."

Jim's brow furrowed. "Are you saying there's organic life out here?"

"Not life exactly," Mariana replied. "But we've found residual remnants of something much older than humanity."

The room fell silent. Even Grace turned toward the screen, her skepticism replaced by interest.

"You expect us to believe the Federation found some ancient molecule buried in the rocks out here, and they hired us to dig it up?" Diane asked."

"I expect you to follow orders, Chief Geologist," Mariana said. "The Federation believes these compounds could lead to something far beyond our current understanding of life in our own solar system. Something that could change what we know about humanity's origins."

As they moved off to their tasks, Mariana stepped closer and lowered her voice. "Captain, you may not trust me, but this is bigger than either of us."

Jim didn't turn to look at her. "You're right, Doctor. I don't trust you."

＊＊＊＊＊

JT sat alone in the maintenance bay, perched on the edge of a workbench cluttered with tools and spare parts. The steady hum of the engines filled the room, the pulse of the ship beneath his boots. His gloves rested nearby, frayed at the edges. Despite the physical grind, it was the weight of his father's words that sat heavier on him, pressing him down like the ship's artificial gravity.

He twisted a bolt in his fingers, lost in thought. His father's voice from the meeting, the crew's sidelong glances—it all churned inside. No matter how hard he worked, he felt one step behind. Always close to being seen as a liability.

The bay door hissed open. Bucky strolled in, easy as always, his relaxed air clashing with JT's silence. "Figured I'd find you here," he said, leaning against a support beam. "You've got that 'I'm thinking too much' look."

JT didn't look up. "Not overthinking. Just thinking."

"Right," Bucky said with a grin. "And I'm the Federation's poster boy for following orders."

JT set the bolt down and ran a hand through his hair. "Why does it feel like I'm not doing enough for Dad? I work just as hard as anyone else."

Bucky walked over, picked up a spanner, and turned it over in his hands. "Your dad carries a lot of burdens. It's not about you not being good enough. He's just waiting until you're ready. He's protecting you."

JT shook his head. "It doesn't feel like protection. It feels like I'm just in the way. Like I'm not part of the crew. Just a kid he's stuck watching."

Bucky set the spanner down and met his eyes. "You've got more to prove than most. That's just how it is when your dad's the captain. But he trusts you, JT. Whether he says it or not, that's what matters."

"Trust doesn't mean much if I'm not allowed to do anything that matters," said JT, staring at the floor.

"Then make yourself matter," Bucky said, clapping him on the shoulder. "Show him you're more than just his kid. Don't worry about screwing up. Everyone does. What you do about it is what counts. Work harder than everyone else and don't complain. Learn everything you can about mining. If you want to be captain one day, you've got to know the whole ship."

Later, JT found his father in the observation room, standing by the wide viewport that framed the endless expanse of space. The bright glow of distant stars reflected off the glass, casting soft light across Jim's weathered features. He didn't turn when JT entered, but his posture shifted slightly, a silent acknowledgment of his son's presence.

JT cleared his throat. "Got a minute?"

Jim glanced over his shoulder. Concern etched on his face. "What is it, son?"

JT hesitated. Bucky's words still echoed. "I want more responsibility. I want to be treated like any other crew member. I don't need protection."

Jim turned, folding his arms across his chest. "You've got responsibility. You handle the stabilizers. You assist on drill sites with Bucky—"

"That's not what I mean," JT said, firmer than he expected. "I want to learn how to be a leader. Like you. I want to make decisions that matter and actually contribute to the crew."

Jim's eyes narrowed. "Contributing isn't just about giving orders. It's knowing when to lead and when to listen. You lead by example. Follow when expected. You earn trust."

"How am I supposed to learn that if I'm never given the chance?" His frustration slipped out. Years of feeling overlooked forcing their way into the open. "You treat me like I'm always one mistake away from being a liability."

Jim paused before saying, "This crew relies on each other to stay alive. Every day. This isn't about doubt. It's about trust. I need to be sure the crew trusts you like I do."

"They don't trust me?"

"They don't know you," Jim said. "Not like they know each other. Trust comes from consistency. Show up. Be reliable. Do your job every day. That's how it starts."

JT looked away. "So what am I supposed to do? Just wait?"

"Work hard. Earn your place. Learn what it takes to be captain. You've got the heart. You've got potential. Now prove you can be counted on when it matters."

The words hung between them. JT knew his father was right, even if it stung. His pride hated it, but something deeper had already accepted it. "I will, Dad," he said.

"Good. Then start with the stabilizers. Bucky's got his hands full. We can't afford downtime."

JT started to argue, then stopped himself. He nodded and left, his mind already racing with ways to show what he could do.

As the door hissed shut behind him, Jim turned back to the viewport. The stars burned cold and distant. He let out a slow breath, his shoulders sinking under the weight of command. And fatherhood.

In the lower corridors, JT walked with purpose. The talk with his father had bruised his ego, but it had also sparked something deep inside him. He wasn't just going to prove himself. He was going to make himself indispensable.

When he reached the maintenance bay, Bucky looked up from a mess of wiring and smirked. "Back already? Thought you'd be off brooding another hour."

JT grabbed a toolkit from the wall and dropped it beside him. "Brooding doesn't fix stabilizers. Let's get to work."

Bucky grinned. "That's the spirit."

A few crew members glanced over, nodding in quiet approval as JT and Bucky got to work.

As they focused on repairs, the constant hum of the ship surrounded them. Every bolt, every recalibration meant survival. For JT, it wasn't just maintenance. It was forward motion.

*   *   *   *   *

The command deck buzzed with quiet activity. Console lights cast a pale glow across tense faces. Mariana stood by one of the monitors, reading the data as it scrolled past. Jim stood nearby, arms crossed. He had spent years reading people. Her posture felt studied, like she was performing a part she knew too well.

"This is what you dragged us into?" Grace said from the navigation console. She pointed at the screen where organic anomalies blinked against the asteroid belt's edge. "A bunch of blips that might look like a rain cloud if we squint hard enough?"

"Thank you, Chief Engineer," Jim replied, a little more weight than necessary on her title.

"Organic signatures from what, though?" Raegan asked. "You said there wasn't life out here."

Jim stepped forward. "You're talking about the Federation's Project Chimera on Ganymede, aren't you?"

A flicker of surprise flitted through Mariana's eyes, but her polished smile held firm. "You've been doing your homework, Captain."

"McConnell's not as clever as he thinks. We intercepted one of his ship's transmissions. It mentioned Ganymede," Jim said. "I doubt that's a coincidence." He watched her face closely.

She gestured to the screen, where a map showed the moon's positions relative to the Argo. "It wasn't," Mariana admitted. "Ganymede is the Federation's main focus. We believe the organic compound came from there, scattered by a cataclysmic event millions of years ago. If we can trace its path, we might find more than just its origin."

"Like what?" Jim asked. Suspicion colored his tone.

"That's classified," said Mariana, glaring at him.

The silence that followed was dense. Grace gave a short, sharp laugh. "Of course it is. Let me guess, this is one of those 'do as the Federation says moments?"

"If that's how you want to see it," Mariana said, "then yes."

Jim raised a hand to stop Grace from firing back. "That's enough. The Federation is making the calls right now."

He turned to the display, his mind racing. The Federation's interest in the Galilean moons wasn't new. He'd heard whispers of hidden facilities and deep-level projects for years. But this felt different. These were dangerous revelations. The kind of information the Federation wanted to control and bury.

"Why now?" Jim asked. "The moons haven't changed. What's made this so urgent?"

Mariana's mask cracked for a moment. "We found something on Ganymede. A structure. Buried beneath the ice. It's emitting low-frequency signals. The Federation believes it's the source of the compound."

"A structure? Built by who?" asked Jim, his head tilted.

Mariana didn't answer.

"If the Federation already found something on Ganymede, why involve us?" asked Raegan.

"Because the signatures don't stop there," Mariana said. "Trace amounts are scattered across the asteroid belt. If we map them, we might reveal a network. Something linking Ganymede, the belt, and possibly more."

"And if we can't?" Grace asked, arms crossed.

Mariana held her gaze. "Failure isn't an option for the Federation. Look at what they're risking."

Jim let out a slow breath, his thoughts turning. This wasn't about minerals. It was about power. Something buried and forgotten, older than history itself, and the Federation wanted it badly enough to gamble with their lives.

"Diane," Jim said. "Can you reconfigure the geo sensors? Focus on isolating these signatures."

Diane sighed but nodded. She slid into her seat and began pulling up data. "I'll need a few hours. This isn't basic science."

"Do what you can," Jim said. Then he turned to Raegan. "Keep tabs on the security guards. I don't like them roaming around unchecked." He thought for a moment. Have BK set up a happy hour after shift. They've earned it."

"You've got it," Raegan said.

Jim turned to Mariana. His eyes stayed cold. "And you... you're going to tell me everything you know about this compound. No more half-truths. That'd be a decent way to start earning trust."

Mariana's smile softened. "I'll share what I can, Captain. But some of this... you'll have to see for yourself to believe."

Jim wanted answers, but he didn't press. He turned back to the data, the glowing patterns on the screen reflected in his eyes. The signature formed a fragmented trail, compelling and unimaginable. Whatever it was, the Federation wasn't going to stop until they had it first.

Hours passed as the crew worked in tense silence. Diane's fingers moved across her console, isolating patterns and tracing signals, while Jim reviewed the repair reports. JT had taken over monitoring the stabilizers, his focus locked in, shutting out the doubts that never seemed far behind.

In the observation room, Jim stood beside Mariana, her escorts nowhere in sight. The stars drifted past the viewport, their light flickering across the metal walls. The tension between them hung in the air.

"And if we do find it, then what?" Jim asked, his voice flat and direct.

Mariana didn't answer right away. She stared out into the void. "That depends on what we find."

Jim started to reply, but the comms crackled. Diane's voice cut in, tight with urgency. "Captain, you need to see this."

He and Mariana exchanged a look, then left for the bridge.

On the screen, new data flickered in sharp contrast to the earlier noise. The organic compound is nearly undetectable signatures now formed a loose but unmistakable path, winding through the asteroid belt. The trail split. Two diverging paths reached out toward the belt's edges and beyond before dissipating into the void.

"This changes things," Mariana said, eyes scanning the data.

"Not for the better," Jim replied.

The bridge had shifted into a blur of movement. Crew members worked to process the information, voices low but quick. On the main display, Diane's map showed a string of faint points stretching from the Argo's position through the belt and into deep space. One path curved toward the orbit of Ganymede. The other faded near the Trojan Asteroid Belt. Data breadcrumbs scattered through the darkness.

Jim stood in the center of it all, arms crossed, staring between the map and Mariana. Her silence pressed hard.

"This doesn't make sense," Lisa said. She gestured toward the map. "It's like the asteroids are being pushed away from this region. Why would the pattern bend like that?"

Mariana stepped forward and studied the highlighted zone. "Gravitational anomalies," she said. "The Federation's been studying that region for years. Our probes can't penetrate the field. Some vanish, others get pulled into the center. Whatever's in there, it's powerful. Ships stay clear or risk being torn apart."

"What caused the anomaly?" Raegan asked.

Mariana pulled up a new overlay. The map shifted, revealing a faint energy pulse from the anomaly's center. "We don't know," she said. "But it's there."

Jim frowned and turned to Cross. "How far from our position?"

"Four days at cruising speed," she replied. "Assuming we want to avoid asteroids and the stabilizers hold."

"Four days," Jim repeated. His mind reeled. The Federation had always controlled the belt mining operations, but now it made sense why. They were seeking something important enough to risk lives to acquire.

The comms lit up. BK Colony's voice cut through the silence. "Incoming transmission, sir."

McConnell's voice followed a second later. It was sharp, cold, and practiced. "Captain Eckhart. I trust you've made some progress."

Jim stepped toward the console. "We've got a lead, but the operation will take time."

"Time is a luxury we don't have," McConnell said. "Follow your orders, Captain. Find a dig site or we'll find someone who can."

Jim's fists clenched. "You're welcome to try. But this isn't a simple dig. What you're asking for is—"

"What we require," McConnell cut in, "is competence. You've been given access to information far beyond your crew's clearance. I suggest you start acting like it."

Jim bit back his reply. He knew what McConnell really meant. The Argo was useful for now. But once the Federation got what it wanted, they'd be expendable.

Around the bridge, the crew exchanged uneasy looks. Mariana tensed.

Jim leaned in slightly. "And if we say no?" His voice was quiet but sharp.

"You already know the answer, Captain Eckhart," said McConnell.

When the transmission ended, silence settled over the bridge. Grace whistled sharply and shook her head. "That guy's a piece of work. What's next, he sends a hit squad to babysit our dig site?"

"He doesn't need to," Raegan said quietly. "He knows we don't have a choice. The Federation controls the trade routes, the space stations, and our mining license. They could shut us down with a few keystrokes."

Jim turned to face the crew. The lines on his face had deepened. "We're not going to be shut down. We've been through worse, and we'll get through this too. Let's finish the job, buy some time, and figure out how to get them off our backs."

"But at what cost?" Grace asked. "Every time we play their game, we give something up. Next time, it might be our license."

JT, who had stayed silent, finally stepped forward. "What if we don't play by their rules?"

Heads turned.

JT stood near the nav console, his posture rigid, his voice unwavering. "What if we use what we've found and act before they do? We don't need McConnell breathing down our necks to finish this. Let's get ahead of the Federation for once."

Jim studied his son. A mix of pride and dread rose in his chest. "That's a big risk. What happens when they come after us for ignoring a direct order? There are still two Federation guards in the mess hall."

"We're already on thin ice," JT said. "Maybe it's time to stop pretending like we're not. Let's be honest. Everyone here thinks the Federation will arrest us once we're no longer useful."

The room went still again. Jim could see it in their eyes: Grace's quiet rage, Raegan's restrained concern, Bucky's distant focus. Even Mariana seemed shaken, though she wore her usual mask.

"We're not making that call now," Jim said. His tone was final. "We follow the signature to its source. We treat it like another mining job. If McConnell tries something like last time, then we take matters into our own hands."

As the crew began to disperse, Jim pulled Mariana aside. Her gaze met his, and he saw something register there. Doubt or dread, he wasn't sure.

"What's really out there?" he asked, voice low.

Mariana hesitated. "Something that could change everything we know about the solar system. And if the wrong people get it first, they could cause great harm to the system."

"It's not just me at risk. It's all of us. My entire crew. You know I won't follow an order that endangers them knowingly. Either arrest me or start talking."

Mariana lifted her hands in a gesture of restraint. "Captain Eckhart, I want to help. But there are things I don't know yet. Things even McConnell keeps hidden."

Before Jim could respond, BK's voice cracked through the comms. "Captain, we've got movement. Federation patrols. They're right on top of us. Transponders off, no response to hails. If it weren't for our spy drones, we'd never have seen them coming."

Jim spun to the console. Two sleek Federation ships were closing in fast. They were attempting to take them by surprise. They were detaining the crew of the Argo.

Mariana stepped forward. "They're not supposed to be here." Panic had crept into her voice. "McConnell must've changed the plan. He's going to force your compliance."

"Or put a gun to our heads," Grace said. "What's the play, Captain?"

Jim's mind raced. They were outnumbered, outgunned, and out of time. His eyes returned to the anomaly on the display. The glowing signals called to him like a last resort. "Liam," Jim said, turning cold. "Take a team. Remove the guards from the Argo. Put them in suits with ninety minutes of air and set an emergency beacon. We're not murderers, but it's too much of a security risk to keep them onboard."

"Consider it done," Liam replied, already heading for the door.

"Plot a course for the anomaly," Jim ordered. "If the Federation wants answers, we need to find them first. We need leverage."

He turned to Mariana. "You need to decide. Stay with us or go with your guards. If you choose to stay, you follow my command. No questions. No interference."

Mariana stood frozen. Her lips parted slightly, her mind clearly racing. "I don't want to be part of McConnell's plans. I've seen what he's capable of. He's dangerous. If it's all the same to you, I'd rather stay with your crew."

"Then follow my orders. If you don't, I'll lock you in your quarters. Are we clear?"

"Crystal clear, Captain."

Liam reported back. The guards had been dealt with. The thrusters came online. As the ship veered away from the patrol routes, Jim stood silent at the center of the bridge. The cost of obedience had always been high. But the cost of defiance would be even higher.

SO MANY SECRETS

The *Argo* cruised along cloaked in the shadows of the asteroid belt, its engines running quietly, using its side thrusters to maintain its course. On the bridge, Jim stood over the central console, reading the navigation readouts. Around him, the crew was locked in, though the strain of recent events was evident in their short tones and hurried movements.

"Lisa, what's our status?" Jim asked, glancing toward the navigator's station.

Lisa's fingers moved in a blur over her console. Her crispness cut through the air. "We're moving past a large asteroid field, Captain. Federation patrols are sweeping the area, but the asteroids' metallic compounds are masking our signal. We're heading in the right direction."

"Good work," Jim said. "BK, anything on comms?"

Seated at the communications station, BK shook his head. "No active transmissions, sir. Federation channels are silent, but we know they're scanning the area."

"Trust me, they're looking," Jim confirmed. "Grace, how are the engines holding up?"

"Stable, for now," Grace replied from the engineering console. "I'd recommend we not push them too hard, unless it's an emergency."

"Noted." Jim turned to Karl, who was monitoring the drone controls. "What about the scout drones?"

"All deployed," Karl replied. "They're lingering near the outer perimeter. No signs they've spotted us yet, but I'll keep scanning."

Jim surveyed the bridge. The weight of the Federation's looming presence hung over them all. He exhaled slowly as his mind raced through their options.

After four days of travel, the Argo had managed to avoid the patrols as it neared the gravitational anomaly. The bridge door slid open with a soft hiss, and Mariana stepped inside. She moved with quiet confidence, her green eyes scanning the room as if cataloging every detail. The Federation scientist's presence was met with mixed reactions. Lisa and BK barely glanced her way because they were so focused on their duties.

Mariana approached the central console, stopping a few feet from Jim. "You're hiding, Captain," she said, matter-of-fact.

Jim straightened and turned to face her. "We're trying not to get arrested."

"Semantics." Mariana wore an unamused look on her face. "The Federation doesn't like loose ends, Captain. You're painting a target on your back."

"Is that what you came here to tell me? Because if it is, you can save your breath."

"No. I volunteered to come aboard the Argo because the Federation is after me for what I know. If you want to keep your crew alive, you need to listen."

The bridge fell silent, their attention subtly drifting toward Mariana. Jim reeled back, stunned by the suddenness of the revelation. "Well, go on then. What is this really about?" he asked.

Mariana stepped closer to the console, tapping a few keys to bring up a diagram of their local region of the asteroid belt on the main screen. "The Federation's interest in this region isn't just about mining the organic compound. It's what they plan to use it for that's terrifying. They're experimenting with the compound to create an advanced FLS drive."

"Plutonium-core tech's been around for decades," Grace said skeptically.

"This next-generation FLS drive uses a thorium core combined with this organic compound."

She glanced at Grace, then back at Jim. "The Federation's been trying to make the drive self-sustaining, with unlimited range; capable of reaching speeds we've only theorized. It's the holy grail of propulsion. If they succeed, travel time from Mars to Jupiter drops from months to days. Once that happens, they'll control space travel across the solar system."

"You were part of this?" Jim asked.

"I was... involved." She paused, apparently reluctant to continue. "But I can't remember how it started. McConnell said I had an accident, that I lost my memory. They were taking me to Mars to see a specialist. Along the way, we made several stops where I was asked to assist with their research. Once I saw the risks they were taking and what they were trying to accomplish, I knew I didn't want any part of it. Listen, Captain, I believe what I know could stop them. Or at least slow them down."

Jim studied her without blinking, his face an impenetrable mask. "You're telling me this now because...?"

"Because the Federation won't stop until they've found me," Mariana said. "You're my one chance to stop the Federation. But if they catch us, they won't leave any witnesses behind."

"What have you gotten us into?" The captain's tone was sharp. "We didn't sign up for this."

"Captain, we've got movement," Lisa cut in. "Federation patrol ships moving to intercept. Two signatures, coming fast."

"Distance?"

"One hundred klicks and closing. They're scouting escape routes, but the asteroid composition is keeping them from getting a clean lock."

Jim turned to BK. "Get me a secure channel to the crew quarters. Lock everything down. Put the Argo on high alert."

"On it," BK said, already moving.

"Grace," Jim continued, "how much power can we push to the shields without compromising the engines?"

"Not much," Grace replied, scanning her readouts. "If we boost the shields, we'll have to cut propulsion. And if we cut propulsion…"

"They'll run us down when we make our move," Jim finished grimly. He turned to Lisa. "Plot us a course out of here that takes us closer to the anomaly."

"Understood, Captain," Lisa said.

As the crew scrambled to carry out Jim's orders, Mariana stepped closer, lowering her voice. "Captain, if they catch us, they'll destroy everything. Your ship, your crew, any reference to the compound."

Jim met her stare. "Then help us make sure they don't catch us. I'll hold you responsible if anything happens to my crew."

Mariana nodded, lips pressed thin. "For what it's worth, I'm sorry, Captain. I'll never be a Federation pawn again. I mean to stop them. At any cost."

"Good." Jim turned back to the console. "Because no one on the Argo is expendable. Not even dishonest Federation scientists. But I do agree with you on one thing: McConnell has to be stopped."

As the crew executed the escape plan, Federation patrols loomed closer, moving through the dark with surgical precision. "Let's see if this old girl still has any surprises up her sleeve." Jim gripped the console as the Argo slipped into the asteroid field.

The Argo moved in the shadows, floodlights casting shifting patterns across the surrounding rock. Its engines hummed at minimal power to avoid detection. The bridge was quiet with tense energy, each crew member focused. Captain Eckhart stood at the center. His eyes were glued to the viewscreen as he anticipated their next move.

"Status on the patrol ships?" Jim asked.

"They're running a smart pattern," Grace muttered, watching her engineering displays. "If we make a run for it, they'll spot us."

"Can we reroute additional power to thrusters?" Jim asked.

"Not with those stabilizers in their current state," Grace said. "We'd need at least an hour first. They'll be on top of us long before that."

"We need options." Jim glanced around the bridge. "BK, try to intercept their transmissions. Anything they're planning."

BK adjusted his headset. "They're coordinating something. Tough encryption, but... wait. One of their ships just changed course."

"Confirmed, Captain," said Lisa. "One's falling back to block our retreat. The other's holding steady, scanning forward."

"That evens the field," Jim said, exhaling. Let's take advantage.

The Argo's engines groaned as the ship adjusted course, slipping through a dense tangle of asteroids and debris. The viewscreen displayed a chaotic dance of space rocks, each moving unpredictably in the void.

"Steady as she goes," Lisa said. "Adjust bearing two degrees starboard. Bucky, you're on manual."

"Got it," Bucky replied, gripping the controls.

The bridge went silent. Tension thickened. Bucky's hands stayed firm as he maneuvered the ship through the chaos. Tight gaps, spiraling rocks, silent threats.

"Incoming. Port side!" Lisa shouted.

Bucky jerked the ship hard to starboard, dodging a massive asteroid that spun into their path. The Argo shuddered as gravity from the behemoth tugged at its hull, but she held.

"Nice save," Lisa said. "You're almost as good as me."

Bucky didn't answer. His eyes stayed locked on the screen, sweat running down his temple.

"Captain, we're nearing the edge of the field," Lisa reported. "Five klicks and we're clear."

"Where's the lead patrol?" Jim asked.

BK checked his display. "Maintaining heading. If we're lucky, we're about to slip right past."

"Let's pray we do," Grace muttered. "Or we're all going to find out who looks best in Federation prison attire."

"Hold on. Picking up the second ship. Telemetry shows they're probing the area," said BK.

Jim's head snapped around.

BK adjusted his headset. "Looks like they're trying to triangulate our position and squeeze us out."

"Damn it," Jim muttered. "Suggestions?"

Mariana, who had been standing silently near the back of the bridge, stepped forward. "I believe I know a way."

The crew's unease showed in sidelong glances.

"So," he asked, "what are you suggesting?"

Mariana turned toward the map on the screen. "If we can beat them to the gravitational anomaly, we can use it to outrun them. Most of it is unstable, but if we follow this trajectory, the gravitational forces will accelerate the Argo enough to slingshot us around the anomaly, and past the Federation's detection range. In theory."

Lisa frowned. "If you're wrong, we get sucked into the anomaly. If we miss our exit window, the cruisers will be waiting to tear us apart. Not exactly my idea of a good plan."

"Those Navy cruisers won't dare it. Their safety protocols lock them out. We can switch to manual and outmaneuver them."

"This will work. You have to trust me," Mariana pleaded. Her tone made it clear that she knew what no one else did.

Jim stared at her for a long moment, then nodded. "Lisa, plot the course. Bucky, prep the controls. Everyone else, hold tight."

As the Argo's propulsion systems powered up for the maneuver, Jim stood at the center of the command deck, eyes fixed on the viewscreen. "Time for the bridge crew to earn its paycheck. This is our one shot. Let's make it count."

The ship surged forward, asteroid clusters spinning around them in a chaotic blur. The anomaly loomed ahead—beyond the field's edge—a swirling vortex of energy that promised either escape or oblivion.

Mariana stood near the console, her green eyes fixed on the screen.

The Argo tore through space. Thrusters screamed as Bucky steered them through a narrow gap in the debris. The ship shook under the strain, its hull groaning. Mariana pointed at the screen. The anomaly grew larger with every second, a massive distortion rippling at its edges, light scattering in waves as gravity buckled the space around it.

"Trajectory plotted," Lisa said from her station. Her voice stayed even, a bead of sweat ran down her temple. "Three-second margin for error, Captain."

Jim's face hardened. "Bucky, you copy that?"

"Loud and clear," Bucky said. He gripped the controls tight, as every eye on the bridge bore down on him.

"Good. Keep us clean. Stay focused."

JT adjusted his seat at the copilot's console, scanning the secondary displays. "We're closing fast."

Bucky glanced at him but said nothing.

"The Federation cruisers spotted us," BK called out. "They're changing course to intercept. Weapons coming online. If we don't make this jump soon—"

"We'll make it," Jim said, cutting him off before doubt could spread. "Grace, how's the ship?"

"Engines are holding, but the stabilizers are running hot," she said. "If we push much harder, we risk a full shutdown."

"Just need a little time. Hold it together long enough to punch through."

Silence fell over the bridge, broken only by the hum of machinery and scattered beeps from the consoles.

"Anomaly ahead," Lisa said. "Ten klicks."

"Bucky," Jim said. "Stay on course. Don't fight the gravity's pull too much. It'll cause you to overcorrect."

"I've got it, Cap. Easy peasy," Bucky said, though his white-knuckled grip told another story.

Mariana stood near the back. Her eyes darted between the crew and the vortex ahead. A crease had formed between her brows. "Tell me you've done something like this before, Captain?"

Jim turned to her. "Honestly? I don't think anyone has."

"Somebody call Guinness," Bucky joked.

Mariana kept her eyes on the anomaly. "You'll need to rotate the ship as we enter. The pull will shift our path. If you don't compensate, we'll miss the exit."

Bucky squinted at the screen. "That's impossible to calculate in real time. How do you know that?"

"Because I used to study anomalies for the Federation. It's physics and math."

Lisa glanced at Jim. "She's right. Based on the data, we've got a fifty-fifty shot. Those are the best odds we're going to get."

Jim studied Mariana, then turned to his team. "Lisa, make the adjustment. Bucky, keep us on this vector."

"Yes, sir," Bucky said. The tension in his voice was undeniable.

The anomaly loomed large on the viewscreen now, its edges flaring with unpredictable energy bursts barely visible to the naked eye. The ship's artificial gravity wavered as the Argo approached, the distortion playing havoc with its systems. The crew felt the G-forces surge and fade as internal controls faltered.

The engines pushed harder, approaching their limits as they drove toward the anomaly before the Federation ships could lock on and open fire.

"Five klicks," Lisa said. "Four... three... two..."

"Hold steady," Bucky muttered, his eyes locked on the monitors.

The ship lurched as it crossed the anomaly's gravitational threshold. The pull yanked it off course. Bucky gritted his teeth, fighting to keep the nose forward as alarms screamed.

Unseen forces slammed into the hull and threw the Argo into a velocity it wasn't built to handle.

"Adjust rotation!" Lisa shouted. "Bearing 16.3 degrees!"

"Got it!" Bucky barked, wrenching the ship into the correction. The hull groaned under the strain as they skirted along the anomaly's perimeter. Engine readings redlined just to keep pace.

"We're through the worst of it," Grace called out. "Just a little more!"

"Trajectory correcting in three... two... one," Lisa said. She let out a breath. "We're clear. Federation ships aren't following, Jim. They didn't feel like risking their pensions attempting Bucky's slingshot ride around the anomaly."

The distortion faded behind them. The clear vacuum opened ahead. System after system stabilized. One by one, the alarms went silent.

Cheers erupted on the bridge. The crew had pulled off the impossible: escaped two superior Federation cruisers.

Even Jim allowed a nod.

"Nice flying, Bucky," he said, clapping the younger man's back. "Buck Rogers, eat your heart out."

Bucky exhaled hard. His hands trembled as he let go of the controls. "Thanks. Reminded me of that time you almost crashed us into Ruby's."

"Captain," BK cut in and sliced through the celebration. "Incoming transmission. Federation frequency."

"Let's hear it."

Static crackled, then McConnell's voice filled the bridge. It was cold and precise. "Captain Eckhart. Congratulations on your escape, but don't think for a second this is over. We'll find you, no matter where you run."

Jim ditched the formalities. "Hey. How's your jaw, Benjamin? Looking for a rematch?"

McConnell didn't reply. He seemed to have been caught off guard.

"Let's skip the pretense. Tell us what you want," said Jim.

"What I want," McConnell replied, clearly annoyed, "is the criminal aboard your vessel. As a Federation officer, Dr. Kade stands accused of serious crimes. You've made a grave mistake harboring her. I warned you what would happen if you disobeyed orders."

Jim turned toward Mariana, who stood still as stone. "She's not property. And I don't answer to you. I answer to my crew."

McConnell chuckled, humorless. "The Federation doesn't take kindly to thieves. Or traitors."

The transmission cut short.

"They're not going to stop," Grace muttered.

"No, they're not," Jim agreed. He faced Mariana. His expression was serious now. "You'd better hope you really are that valuable to the Federation."

She met his gaze, calm and unwavering. "I am. You may not see it yet, Captain, but the whole human race is counting on us."

The Argo moved unimpeded through a long stretch of open space, settling in at cruising speed. Stars stretched endlessly before them as they slipped past scattered rock clusters. The crew busied themselves with repairs and maintenance across the ship, but the weight of McConnell's words stayed in Jim's mind.

On the observation deck, Jim stood alone, staring into the void. He had gambled everything to protect Mariana, and the stakes were only rising. If he'd known how high, he wondered, would he have made the same choice to protect Mariana?

The door slid open. Mariana stepped in, hesitating before speaking. "I can't blame you for not trusting me, Captain."

Jim didn't turn. "Why should I? You lied to us, Mariana. You used us."

"I'm sorry," she said, voice low. "But I had to escape McConnell. It was the only way. If you want your crew to survive, you'll have to trust me."

He stayed silent, then slowly turned to face her. "Then start talking. The truth. No more riddles." His voice was cold.

The engines thrummed steadily as the ship sailed through emptier regions of the belt. The exterior hull bore fresh scars from their slingshot escape, but somehow, she held together. Inside, the fear that had gripped the crew now burbled beneath the surface.

In the briefing room, senior crew members gathered around the central holographic display. Jim stood at the head of the table, arms crossed, face shadowed by the dim glow of the map. Grace, Bucky, Raegan, JT, Karl, Lisa, and Liam occupied the other posts. Their expressions ranged from wary to undecided. Mariana stood at the far end, her face unreadable.

"We managed to escape McConnell and the Federation," Jim began. "But we're not out of danger. The Federation knows we have Mariana. They won't stop coming."

"Then why not give her up?" Grace asked. "Why are we risking everything for someone we don't even know?"

No one spoke. All eyes turned to Mariana.

She straightened. "I understand your frustration, but I didn't ask for this either. The Federation took me and used me to advance their experiments. I planned my escape when I saw how far they were willing to go, how they treated people."

"What exactly are they doing?" Bucky asked.

Mariana stepped forward. "The Federation's pushing for a more powerful engine, experimenting with completely new power core designs.

"We've heard this part," Grace said. "What's new?"

"What's new," Mariana said, "is the organic compound in this region of the asteroid belt. It's the key. They're using it to en-hance FLS tech, but also to weaponize it. Their tests combine the compound with prototype cores to create something devastating."

The room fell quiet.

"You're saying they're not just turning it into a better engine... but also a weapon?" Raegan asked.

Mariana nodded. "It's unstable and dangerous. I was on the research team for a brief while. But when I received an anonymous message saying I had to escape the Ferrell, I made my move."

"Why didn't you tell us this sooner?" asked Jim.

"Would you have believed me?" she snapped. "Or turned me in at the first chance?"

"She's got a point," Bucky muttered. "It's not exactly outside the Federation's playbook."

Grace folded her arms. "How convenient. She gives us just enough to stay useful, but not enough to get the full picture."

"You think I want to be here? You think I chose this?" Mariana asked, her voice cracking.

"Enough," Jim said. "She's here. That makes her our problem. We can't ignore what she's told us."

"So what do we do with it?" Lisa asked. "Even if it's true, we can't take on the Federation. We're a mining crew, not a rebellion."

Jim sighed and rubbed his temples. "We're not fighting any-one. Not yet. Right now, we focus on what we can control. Grace, prioritize the stabilizers. Lisa, plot a course out of the belt, toward Mars. We'll replenish the core and figure out our next move from there."

"And Mariana?" BK asked.

Jim looked at her. "She stays under watch. Raegan, have her assist you in the med bay."

Raegan gave a tight nod. "Understood."

As the meeting broke up, the crew filed out of the room, burdened with the magnitude of their situation. Mariana stood near the holographic display, shoulders stiff. Jim remained behind, his eyes fixed on the map of the asteroid belt.

"I wanted to let you know I appreciate you putting your trust in me," Mariana said, trying to start a conversation.

Jim turned, guarded. "It's not trust. It's a lack of options."

Mariana gave a weak smile. "I suppose that's better than nothing."

"That's all you're getting for now," Jim said. "If you want more, you'll have to earn it. Go help Dr. Inoue in the med bay."

Mariana shrugged, face flat. "Fair enough."

In the mess hall, Grace sat with Liam, Diane, and Bucky. She noticed that Diane and Bucky were sitting closer than what would be considered casual. They were trying to keep their relationship discreet, but they were failing. Anyone could see they were in love. On the Argo, where most of the crew slept in shared quarters, privacy was at a premium.

"She's going to get us all killed," Grace muttered, poking at her food.

Bucky shrugged. "Maybe. But what choice do we have? The Federation's not exactly leaving us with options now that she's dragged us into this."

"It's not just about Mariana," Liam said. "It's about what she represents. If she's telling the truth, this is bigger than all of us."

Diane shook her head. "I just hope she's worth it. Otherwise, we threw our lives away for nothing."

✺✺✺✺

On the bridge, Lisa monitored the scanners. The asteroid belt stretched endlessly ahead, a shifting maze of rock and void.

"Captain," she said. "We're picking up a new signal."

Jim straightened. "Federation?"

Lisa frowned. "Negative. It's coming from up ahead, near some heavy-duty asteroids."

"Put it on screen."

The display flickered, revealing a faint, pulsing signal. It wasn't Federation. It wasn't anything they'd seen before.

"Whatever it is," Lisa said, "I'm betting it's not friendly."

"BK, have the crew on lockdown in case of detection. Let's be ready." Jim's tone had sharpened.

The bridge glowed with soft instrument light as the crew worked in silence. A low hum filled the comms. The strange signal appeared to be transmitting from nearby.

"No match in the comms database," BK said, fingers flying across the console. "Encryption's not standard Federation, Martian, or Earth tech."

Jim stood at the center of the bridge, arms crossed. "Could it be from one of the rogue colonies or spaceports?"

Lisa shook her head. "Doubt it. Most colonies don't transmit this far out, and if they did, they'd be using standard frequencies to attract trade ships, not this cryptic signal."

"Then what the heck is it?" Grace asked from her engineering console. "And why's it all the way out here?"

"It's a deterrent," Mariana said softly.

Grace glanced at her. "What do you mean?"

Mariana didn't answer. Her eyes were locked on the screen.

"You're sure about that?" Jim asked.

Mariana nodded. "The Federation uses signals like this as a warning to keep ships away from top-secret sites. Most captains don't want trouble, so they turn around."

"So, we're supposed to barrel forward even though they don't want us to?" Grace said.

Jim added, "There could be Federation ships patrolling. Or raiders. The smart move is to regroup somewhere else."

"That's true," Mariana said, "but this could be our only shot at figuring out what they're planning. We may not get another chance."

Jim stared at the pulsing signal on the central display. The crew watched him, waiting.

"We'll move closer," he said. "Slowly. If Mariana's right, we need answers."

He turned to Lisa. "Adjust course. Take us toward the source. Stealth mode. I don't want us pinging anyone's radar."

"Yes, Captain."

"BK, monitor for any chatter that might tell us what's out there."

"On it."

"Drones?" Karl asked.

Jim nodded. "Deploy one for recon. Let's see what we're walking into."

Minutes later, Karl broke the silence. "Drone's approaching the signal's source. We should have visuals in thirty seconds."

"On screen," Jim said.

The main viewscreen lit up, then displayed a live feed from the drone's camera. At first, there was nothing but the dark expanse of space, but then it was punctuated by a large asteroid. As the drone moved closer to the asteroid, a structure began to take shape on its surface, a massive facility nestled into the shadows, its towers bristling with antennae and weapons emplacements.

"Is that..." Grace started, leaning forward in her seat. "A Federation black site?"

"Looks like it," Bucky said. "What's it doing all the way out here?"

"It's not just a black site," Mariana said. "It's a top-secret Federation research facility. One of the most advanced facilities in the entire Federation."

"How do you know?" Lisa asked.

"Because I worked there. Briefly."

The bridge fell silent.

"What kind of research is the Federation doing in the asteroid belt?" asked Jim.

Mariana's brow furrowed. "Advanced applications of the organic compound's effects on the next-gen FLS drive. And weapons development."

"Now they want you back because you know too much," Jim said, his voice low.

"Yes," Mariana admitted. "If they've reactivated this facility, it means they're close to a breakthrough. That puts everyone in the belt, Earth, and Mars at risk." If they scale this technology, civilians will pay the price."

"So, what the heck are we supposed to do about it, Jim?" Grace asked. "We're not exactly equipped to take down a Federation facility."

"No," Jim agreed. "But we can expose it. Get the evidence to someone who can do something about it."

"How on Mars do you plan on doing that without getting us captured?" Grace asked.

Jim's thoughts drifted to JT. The reality of what could happen to his son if they were caught here overwhelmed him. "Maybe you're right, Grace."

Mariana hesitated, then stepped forward. "Are you really going to throw away our best shot at uncovering the truth about the Federation's plans? We could save countless lives, Captain."

Jim raised a hand. "We need to choose the better part of valor here. The Argo isn't up for another round against Federation heavy cruisers. My decision is final. We head back to Mars for repairs. We'll come up with a solid plan once we're there."

"Breaking into a heavily armed Federation facility may seem crazy, but it's worth the risk. We can stop this here and now," Mariana replied.

"I've been taking risks since the day I started mining," Jim said. "Only this one's different."

Mariana tilted her head. "It's different because now you're risking more than just your ship. You're risking your crew. Your son. We could lose everything if we walk away now."

Jim stood up, eyes hard. "Don't think I don't know what's at stake. If we don't leave soon, we're as good as dead. Or worse, Federation prisoners. I won't let that happen."

Mariana shook her head. "You're making a mistake, Captain."

04

CHAPTER

CATCH ME IF YOU CAN

Jim stood at the center of the bridge, reviewing the data displayed on the central console's holographic map of the asteroid belt. The translucent image flickered, casting shifting patterns of light across the bridge. Outside the ship, a swirling expanse of jagged-peaked asteroids loomed in the distance, their slow drift deceptively serene in the cold vacuum of space.

He saw Mariana hovering just out of sight, fuming over his decision to shut down the Argo's brief stint in espionage. Her anger was still evident in her clipped responses, but Jim knew Grace was right. For all of Mariana's bluster, Jim knew he'd made the right decision.

They had barely escaped detection from a Federation science vessel that passed within half a klick of their position near the black site. Bucky's quick thinking from the pilot console had saved them. Karl had deployed the harpoons into a nearby asteroid while Bucky threw the Argo into a dive and punched the engines. The momentum spun the ship at a hard angle before Karl released the anchors.

The crew around Jim wore the strain of the last few days. Grace leaned against the edge of the engineering console, hands locked behind her head. Lisa, seated at navigation, absently twisted a stylus in her fingers. Bucky stood near JT, his reassuring presence the quiet pulse of the Argo. In the corner, Diane adjusted the sleeve of her lab coat while Karl tapped impatiently at a small display, scrolling through drone diagnostics.

"Now that we're out of the Federation's reach, we need full diagnostics on the Argo's damaged systems. Work while we can," Jim said, then turned to Grace first. "Grace, keep us under the redline."

"Sure thing," she said. "Don't call me unless it's an actual emergency."

"Appreciated," Jim said dryly. "Bucky, pull a stabilizer triage. Get the crew out of their bunks and have them start a maintenance round."

Jim turned to Karl. "Deploy a couple of drones to inspect the hull. Patch up the weak spots and seal any breaches. Prioritize anything that could depressurize critical areas."

Then he turned to Liam. "Monitor comms and sensors with BK. If there's even a whisper of Federation activity nearby, I want to know before they spot us first."

"Yes, Captain," Liam said crisply.

Finally, Jim turned to JT, who instinctively straightened under his father's gaze. "Assist Bucky with the stabilizers. Learn from him. Follow his lead."

He looked into Jim's eyes and nodded. "Yes, sir."

Jim stayed behind, watching them go. His focus returned to the holographic map showing the Argo's trajectory as it wove precariously through the asteroid belt. The expanse in front of them stretched endlessly, a labyrinth of potential hiding places that offered refuge and peril at the same time.

The bridge felt cavernous in their absence. The stillness amplified the unobtrusive sounds of the life support systems and the subtle creak of the ship's hull under its own strain. Jim sank into a chair, his elbows resting on the table as he ran a hand over his face. His mind turned over Mariana's cryptic warnings and the Federation's relentless pursuit. If what she'd said about their experiments was true, the stakes were bigger than he could have possibly imagined. True or not, he had a crew to protect.

"Captain," Lisa's voice crackled through the comms. "Course adjustments are ready. We're clear of immediate impact hazards, but the belt can throw the unexpected at any time in this region."

Jim straightened, the stress coiling in his chest. "Understood. Keep me updated."

He tapped the comms panel, opening a line to Grace. "How are the system diagnostics coming along?"

"Painfully slow," Grace replied, clipped as ever. "But unless you want me to cut corners and risk blowing out the power core's containment unit, you'll have to wait for us to finish up the repairs before pushing the engines any harder."

"Take whatever time you need," Jim said. "Just keep me updated."

"Don't I always?" Grace shot back. The line went dead.

⬛⬛⬛⬛⬛

Jim leaned back, letting the ambient noise of the bridge settle around him for a brief moment, when a loud beep from the comms console drew his attention. He frowned, examining the display. A new signal had appeared. It was weak, intermittent, and pulsing in irregular intervals.

"BK, who's transmitting messages all the way out here?" Jim asked.

BK scanned his console, his brow furrowing. "Unknown signal source. Not Federation or raider standard. Destination appears to be Mars."

"What is it then?"

"Just because it doesn't match any standard Federation frequencies doesn't mean it's not them. Maybe an emergency channel, some kind of encrypted SOS."

Jim stared at the readout for a moment, his gut twisting. Another question, another unknown. Given their current situation, everything had to be considered dangerous.

"Let's keep it between us for now. No need to spook anyone until we know what we're dealing with."

"Yes, Captain."

In the lower deck maintenance bay, the clatter of tools and the murmur of voices filled the air as the repair crew set to work. The room was a tangle of pipes, conduits, and machinery, every surface smudged with grease and the wear of hard labor. The damaged stabilizer loomed in the center of the bay, its bulky housings humming loudly as the test equipment ran through a diagnostic routine.

JT stood near the edge of the platform, shifting awkwardly as Bucky barked orders to the small team bustling around him. A seasoned hand in chaos, Bucky exuded confidence, barking orders that cut through the din like a drill sergeant terrorizing new recruits.

"Get those mounts secured on stabilizer two!" Bucky shouted, pointing toward a young deckhand who looked a bit too relaxed. "Don't rush just to hit the mess hall. Use the torque wrench and confirm spec. We don't want those mounts failing when the captain starts dodging asteroids again."

The deckhand jumped to comply, and then Bucky turned his attention to JT. "You. Over here."

JT swallowed hard and stepped forward, his boots clanging on the metal grating. "Yeah?"

"Yeah, what?" Bucky said, arching a brow. "It's 'Yes, Commander Buchanan.' If you want respect on this ship, you have to earn it like everyone else."

JT flushed, but he nodded. "Yes, Commander Buchanan."

"Better." Bucky handed him a datapad loaded with technical schematics of the stabilizers. "Start here. These diagnostics aren't going to run themselves. You know how to interpret these readouts, right?"

JT took the pad, trying to keep his irritation from showing. "Of course."

"Good. Then show me," Bucky said, tilting his head toward the schematics, daring him to prove it.

JT crouched by the stabilizer, the datapad balanced on his knee as he studied the test results. The numbers scrolled in precise columns. Wear levels, power draw, alignment ratios. He frowned as he tilted his head and cross-checked one of the readings with the schematic.

"This power distribution reading looks wrong," JT said, pointing to a line that dipped erratically. "It's pulling too much power from the secondary core."

Bucky leaned in and gave a nod. "You're not wrong. That's been messing with the inertial dampeners. What's the fix?"

"Recalibrate the coupling manifold?"

"Exactly. Good. Now find the right parts and go fix it."

JT blinked. "You want me to do it?"

"Why not? You spotted the problem. Let's see if you can handle the solution."

JT stood slowly, glancing around the bay. When no one came to help, he squared his shoulders and moved to the manifold. He opened the access panel and crouched beside it, revealing a snarl of wires and circuits.

As JT worked, Karl's voice came over the intercom. "Hey, Bucky. Got a visual from the drone near engine three. You're going to want to see this."

Bucky tapped his comm. "What's the problem?"

"Not so much a problem as... something strange. Hull's fine, but the drone found a device mounted on the hull. Data-pad-sized. Signals-encrypted. We definitely didn't leave port with that. Could be a tracker," Bucky muttered. "Jim needs to know."

JT looked up. "A tracker? From the Federation?"

"Probably. That would explain how they've been picking up our trail." Karl, marked the location and programmed the drone to retrieve it.

"On it. Want me to ping Grace to help analyze it?"

"Are you crazy? We don't need Engineering freaking out. Just get it inside. I want to see who made it."

He turned back to JT, voice lower. "Keep going. You're doing fine."

JT had just finished recalibrating the manifold when Diane walked in, her white lab coat looking out of place among the grease-stained uniforms. She wrinkled her nose at the smell and crossed her arms.

"Don't tell me you're dragging JT into this mess," she said, half-teasing.

"He's got to learn some time," Bucky said. "And he's not half bad once you get past the griping."

"I don't gripe," JT said, glaring.

"Oh, you absolutely do gripe," Bucky said. "But at least you're useful while doing it."

Diane laughed. "Let me know when he's a proper grease monkey. I need to go over the latest mineral scans with you." She winked and left.

Bucky watched her go, eyes lingering a moment too long.

JT caught the look. "How are things with Diane?"

"Things are fine, JT," Bucky muttered, still looking toward the door. "Let's get back to work."

They turned their attention back to the stabilizer. Bucky gave it a quick once-over and sighed. "Looks like it's going to be one of those days."

JT set his jaw. "That's life on a mining ship for you."

Bucky clapped him on the shoulder. "You're a quick learner, kid."

Word of the discovered tracker spread fast. The crew buzzed with theories as tension grew. On the bridge, Lisa Cross sat at the navigation console, her eyes locked on the viewscreen.

"Course adjustments programmed. Holding current velocity," she said. "No immediate threats, but one miscalculation, and we're space roadkill."

Jim stood at the command console, eyes on the holographic map. "Good. Keep an eye out for stray asteroids. Karl, any update on the tracker?"

Karl checked in from the drone lab. "Drones are retrieving it now. It should be back inside the lab in five. No idea if it's still transmitting, but I'll confirm once I've got it on the bench."

"Make it quick," Jim said. "We need to know if the Federation's catching up to us."

Down in the maintenance bay, Karl stood over a sleek examination table, the retrieved tracker lying in the center. Its metallic surface gleamed under the harsh lights, a blue glow pulsing from its edges.

"Looks pretty advanced," Bucky said, hovering over Karl's shoulder. "Federation tech?"

Karl glanced up. "It wasn't just mounted to the hull. It tapped into a conduit that gave it access to the Argo's internal systems. It's a harmonics leech. Tracks our FLS signature, comms, telemetry, and transmits back to the Ferrell.

"Comforting," JT shot back.

As Karl unplugged the power source, a distressed whining sound came from the device, followed by a soft click. The glowing edges dimmed, and the room fell silent as it deactivated.

"Okay," Karl said, stepping back and wiping his hands on a rag. "These transmission components confirm it's a Federation tracker. Whoever planted this on the hull of the Argo knew exactly what they were doing."

* * * * *

The comms crackled, and Jim's voice filled the bay. "Karl, what's the verdict?"

"It's a Federation tracker, Captain," Karl replied. "Sophisticated, but I was able to deactivate it. It was probably broadcasting accurately until I turned it off. The anomaly might have caused them to lose track of us for a while, but I'm sure they're close by now."

"Can it be reactivated?" Jim asked.

"Yes, I can reset it," Karl said. "I'd bet good money the Federation will pick it up right away. They'll be on us soon either way."

"Then we don't have much time," Jim said. "Get back to your stations. We're picking up the pace as soon as the ship's ready."

"Yes, sir," Karl replied before cutting the line.

Bucky turned to JT. "Looks like your dad's ready to make a move. You good to go?"

JT nodded. "Yeah. I'm ready."

"Good. Because things are about to get a whole lot messier."

Back on the bridge, Jim relayed the latest updates to the senior crew. Grace's face showed her frustration, her hands planted on her hips as she stared at the holographic display.

"So, the power core is stable again. Engines are holding for now," Grace said. "No time to properly repair the stabilizers or the dampeners until we dock. My team is doing what they can to get the engines near adequate levels."

"It's not ideal," Jim admitted. "Even so, we don't have a choice."

"Whose fault is that?" Grace snapped at Mariana, who stood silently near the back of the room.

Mariana didn't flinch, and she met Grace's glare. "If the Federation catches us, your damaged stabilizers will be the least of our worries."

"Convenient answer," Grace retorted. "We're risking everything for someone we barely know."

Jim gave a wave of his hand. "That's enough. She's a member of the crew now. We don't have to agree, but we have to work together. Let's focus on getting out of the asteroid belt in one piece."

Grace swallowed her retort and turned to her console. "Fine."

The ship shuddered slightly as the engines ramped up. Vibrations rippled through the deck plates.

"Captain, scanners have detected Federation patrol ships approaching our location. They must have locked on to us," Lisa said.

Jim's attention snapped to the display. A bright red blip cut a path through the asteroid field, heading straight for the Argo.

"They're moving faster than they should in this terrain," Lisa said. "They must have upgraded Federation shields."

"Of course they do," Jim replied. "Lisa, plot the best course out of here. Karl, prep the drones for decoys and flares. BK, give a ship-wide announcement. All crew brace for evasive maneuvers. Lockdown in thirty seconds."

The bridge erupted into controlled chaos as the crew scrambled into action. JT arrived moments later, his face set with determination as he took his place alongside Bucky.

Jim's voice rang out above the noise, loud and clear. "This is it. Let's show the Federation what the Argo can do."

The ship roared to life. Thrusters flared as Lisa adjusted their heading through the asteroid belt. Every station came alive, the crew working in rhythm like a well-oiled machine.

"Course is set," Lisa called. "We've got a clear path for now, but the asteroid field is far denser in the region ahead."

"Do what you have to," Jim replied. "Our best bet is to try and outmaneuver them through the field."

On the display, the Federation cruiser closed the gap moving with unsettling precision, threading through the field with more ease than any ship that size had a right to.

⬛⬛⬛⬛⬛

Down in the lower decks of Engineering, Grace barked orders to her team, her frustration evident in every clipped word. "Get me a status update on the stabilizers. If we lose one mid-turn, we'll crash into an asteroid."

A frantic junior engineer scrambled to check the readings, his face pale. "Stabilizers holding at eighty percent, but the strain's increasing as the ship accelerates!"

Grace cursed and hit the comms button. "Karl, how are those drones coming?"

From his lab near the cargo bay, Karl said, "Decoys are prepped. Deploying now."

"Karl, new plan," Jim said. "Launch all decoys but one. Clone the tracker's handshake and mount it on the last drone. Hold that one for a special delivery I'm sure McConnell won't like."

Outside the ship, two decoy drones departed from the cargo bay and veered off in opposite directions. Their signal arrays mimicked the ship's signatures. On the scanner, the drones lit up as identical green blips, creating the illusion of multiple Argos.

"They've taken the bait," Karl reported. "Patrol is splitting off to investigate the drones."

"Good work," Jim said. "That buys us time. Lisa, adjust our course and pick up speed."

Lisa's hands worked the navigation controls. "Aye, Captain. Pushing the engines like this won't give us much margin for error."

"She'll hold together," Jim said. His false bravado didn't quite mask the weight of the risk.

※※※※※

In the lower deck maintenance bay, JT worked alongside Bucky, securing loose equipment and reinforcing critical systems. Both men were tethered to the floor and walls for stability. The ship's sudden lurches and vibrations kept them on edge.

"Think this'll hold?" JT asked. He had been using a blowtorch and welding rod, reinforcing a series of fractures on the damaged stabilizer's mounting support.

"It should hold just fine. Nice beads, especially with the shaking," Bucky replied.

JT inspected his handiwork. He was learning more every day. He wasn't the same hesitant kid he'd been even a few weeks ago. There was a determination in his movements now, a growing confidence that hadn't gone unnoticed by the crew.

Grace activated the comms. "Bucky, I need a stabilizer status update now. We're accelerating hard, and I don't trust these readouts."

"We're on it," Bucky replied. He turned to JT. "You've been paying attention, right? Walk me through it."

JT hesitated, then nodded. "We need to recalibrate the alignment rods to reduce the load. Replace any that have fractured. I'll check the readings while you handle the adjustments."

Bucky gave JT a slight nod of approval. "Not bad, kid. Let's move."

On the bridge, Lisa called out updates in a curt voice. "The patrol ship's back on our trail. They're gaining speed. Guess the decoys didn't fool them for long."

"Damn it," Jim cursed. "Options?"

"Not many," Lisa admitted. "We're boxed in on both sides by the asteroid field. One of the ships is the F.S.S. Ferrell. McConnell's ship is with them."

"We have to make a move before they catch up to us," Jim said. "Lisa, change course. We're close to an exit vector. Let's lose them in the asteroids and then we set a course out of the belt."

As the crew scrambled to counter the threat bearing down on them, Mariana sat at the back of the bridge, drawing wary glances. She whispered to Jim, her tone tense.

"Their ships will tear us apart, Captain."

"That doesn't mean we give up. There's always another way," Jim replied. "I've already got this figured out. We give them the slip, then make our way back to Mars."

Mariana studied him, then countered, "Hard to see how, Captain."

The thrusters roared again as the ship surged forward, weaving past asteroids at terrifying speeds with a precision born of necessity. Behind them, the Federation ship struggled to match the smaller vessel's course changes, but the pursuit was far from over.

The Argo raced through the final stretch of the asteroid field, approaching their exit vector. Its engines strained as Lisa continually updated the trajectory through the dense maze. On the bridge, anxiety hung thick in the air. Every crew member was locked in their role. Jim stood at the center, eyes darting between the holographic display and the viewscreen.

"They're gaining on us, Captain. The Federation ship is almost in weapons range. We won't hold this lead for long," Lisa said. "Here comes our cover. A huge cluster of boulder-sized rocks, all moving erratically. Once we enter the field, we can make their size a disadvantage."

"Perfect," Jim said. "If we time this right, we can throw them off our trail."

"Yeah, and we're dead if we make one wrong move," Lisa said.

"All right. Take us in."

The Argo plunged into the maze of asteroids, the ship shuddering with every minor impact that struck the hull, each sounding like a hammer strike.

"Stabilizers holding at seventy percent," Grace reported from Engineering.

"Okay, time to make our move," Jim replied. "Karl, are you ready to deploy the tracker drone?"

"Ready," Karl said. "The asteroids will give us the interference we need to launch, ready to reactivate."

"Understood," Jim said. "Not reactivating. Replicating. Karl, launch the decoy drone. Lisa, give us a clean corridor."

On Jim's mark, Karl launched the decoy package, the drone ruse pulsing like a false heartbeat among the asteroid echoes.

A sudden jolt threw everyone forward in their seats.

JT, stationed at a secondary console, gripped the edges to steady himself. "What was that?"

"Impact on the port side," Karl replied. "Shields are still holding, but we can't take another hit like that. Hull integrity is almost critical."

"Lisa, keep us moving," Jim said. "Steady as she goes."

As the tracker drone twisted through the chaos, the Argo shifted its course under the cover of a series of asteroids.

On the bridge of the Federation cruiser F.S.S. Ferrell, Mc-
Connell monitored the pursuit.

The comms officer turned. "Sir, we've picked up the tracker
again. Altering the Ferrell's course to match its trajectory.
We'll overtake the Argo in fifteen minutes."

McConnell's fist slammed into the captain's chair with excitement. "Finally, we've got them now. Hunt down the Argo
and launch the harpoons when we're in range." He stood to
leave the bridge, then added, "Prepare a boarding party."

JT studied the asteroid patterns ahead. "Captain. If we shift
course by five degrees starboard, we can take a shortcut
through this vector. It'll lessen the stress on our stabilizers
too."

Jim glanced at him, then at the display. "Lisa, what do you
think? Can we lose McConnell through here?"

Lisa scanned the data JT had pulled up. "He's right. It's tight,
but it'll take some of the strain off the stabilizers."

"Do it," Jim said.

Lisa adjusted their course, and the Argo shifted smoothly.
The impacts lessened as the ship entered a clearer path. JT
exhaled, and relief flooded across his face.

"Good call," Bucky said from his station, giving JT a rare nod of approval in front of the crew.

JT couldn't hide his joy, though he quickly turned back to his console to avoid showing it.

⸻

The Federation ship fell farther behind as they chased the drone deeper into the belt. Onboard, a high-ranking officer now in command issued orders with cold precision.

"Deploy seeker drones," the officer said. "Force them out of the asteroid field."

⸻

Karl's console lit up with a warning. "Captain, they've launched drones. Three signatures closing hard."

Jim chuckled. "They're going to be pissed off when they find out they've just captured Karl's drone and their own tracker."

"Wish I could see their faces when they read the note I left," Karl replied. "It says, 'Return to Sender.'"

Jim groaned. "Grace, can we generate any extra power for the engines? I'll take whatever you can give me."

"Not without frying half the power grid," Grace snapped. "You want me to pull miracles out of thin air?"

"Just one. And make it fast."

Grace let out a string of curses but got to work. She rerouted power from internal systems to the engines. "I can give you thirty seconds max. After that, we're on borrowed time."

The Argo surged forward, the engines pushed to their limits. The crew braced as the ship weaved through dozens of small asteroids.

"Ten seconds!" Grace called out.

Jim's grip on the console tightened. "Lisa, prepare for evasive maneuvers."

"Five seconds!"

"Now, Lisa!"

Lisa executed a sharp turn, guiding the Argo through a narrow gap between the asteroids. The ship cleared the inner edge of the belt and shot into open space. Behind them, a wave of swirling debris closed off the path they had taken.

"We've lost them!" Lisa called out, triumphant.

The crew erupted into cheers, but Jim stayed steady and collected.

"Good work, everyone. Grace, ease the engines back to safer levels. BK, monitor the comms for any Federation chatter. Let's make sure it was a clean escape."

As the Argo moved into open space, the bridge fell quiet. The crew exchanged glances, the weight of their narrow escape beginning to settle.

Jim turned to JT, his voice softer. "That call you made... good thinking."

JT blinked, caught off guard by the praise. "Thanks, Captain."

Jim faced the display again. "We need to put distance between us and that cruiser fast. Lisa, plot a course to Mars. We'll keep a low profile until we dock in the Southern Sector. We can refuel, repair, and regroup there."

BK looked hesitant. "Captain, about that signal we picked up earlier... if it was the Federation, Mars might not be safe for us."

"We'll deal with that when we get there. For now, we need a safe harbor."

The crew turned back to their stations. The adrenaline faded, leaving only exhaustion.

Jim stayed at the central console, eyes on the stars ahead.

Behind him, Mariana stepped forward. "You're making a lot of sacrifices for me. Thank you, Captain."

Jim didn't turn. "It's not just for you. It's for all of us. The Federation doesn't get to decide who lives and who doesn't. Not on my ship."

Mariana sank lower, already having pulled the packet header off BK's system. "That 'unknown' signal to Mars...That's not just a Federation SOS. It was coming from deep space. It shouldn't be here."

"Let's come back to it when we reach Mars, but let's make sure we don't die first."

Mariana left the bridge without another word.

Jim let out a slow breath. The weight of command settled over him like an old, worn-out coat.

The Argo sailed on. The hull was battered, barely space-worthy. Mars loomed ahead, growing closer by the week. Whatever waited there remained a mystery.

05

GET YOUR ASS TO MARS

The *Argo* had emerged from the asteroid belt a victorious but battered survivor, its hull scorched and streaked with the scars of its harrowing escape. The lights of Mars's protective New-Age polymer-composite domes glimmered ahead, the planet a red beacon against the vast black expanse of space.

On the bridge, the crew sat in silence, burdened by what they had endured. The long journey back to Mars had given them time for their new reality to sink in.

"Lisa, how's our approach?" Jim asked.

"Landing trajectory set. Mars Control cleared us. Can't believe Gus's fake creds worked. Apparently, we're the 'ScarJo' now. Crew painted over the hull already. They're assigning us to Sector 18."

"Good," Jim said. He turned to Grace. "Status?"

Grace didn't look up from her station. "Engines holding; stabilizers at fifty-five percent. We're limping, Captain. One more evasive maneuver will break her apart."

"I knew she would hold together," Jim said triumphantly.

"Sure you did," Grace said, her fingers a blur across her console.

Jim sat at the command console, his gaze fixed on the planet ahead. The escape had shaken him more than he let on. The Federation was hunting them with relentless determination. Why was Mariana so important? A scientist with vague knowledge of their projects didn't explain this. The stakes had grown larger than the Argo, and that truth left him uneasy.

"Captain," Lisa said. "We're five minutes out from docking."

"Understood." He turned to Bucky. "Once we're docked, oversee the offloading of the damaged cargo. Coordinate with the lower deck crew and set a security perimeter."

Bucky nodded. "You got it, Captain."

Jim's attention turned to JT, who had been quiet since leaving the belt. "James, help with the rig. Then assist Karl with those drone repairs."

JT gave no signs of disappointment as he replied, "Yes, sir." He went to work without a second hesitation.

Bucky shot JT a look that was half encouragement and half warning, but JT gave him a reassuring nod. He knew this was just part of the job.

The Argo descended into the Martian atmosphere with a series of shudders, the engines groaning under the strain. Lisa guided the ship through the hangar doors at Sector 18 with expert precision. Docking clamps locked into place with a hiss.

"Docking complete," Lisa announced. "Welcome to Mars."

"Good work," Jim said. He straightened and addressed the crew. "We've got at least a week of repairs, resupply, and rearming. No unnecessary risks. We stay together and avoid drawing attention."

The crew filed out with weary steps, their boots echoing in the corridor. Jim remained on the bridge, staring through the viewscreen as workers in blue uniforms swarmed the Argo, attaching cooling lines to the power core containment unit and running diagnostics.

Bucky stayed behind, arms crossed. "I need to talk to you about JT. Why keep holding him back, Jim?"

Jim's eyes stayed on the workers below, as if the answer lay with them. "He's not ready to be a miner, much less a rebel. The Federation's hunting us. This is too dangerous for a kid."

"He's not ready because you won't let him be," Bucky said flatly. "You've got him stuck with menial work while he's trying to prove himself. You're sending him the wrong message."

Jim rubbed the back of his neck. "You saw what happened. The Federation nearly tore us apart. My job is to protect this crew. If that means keeping James out of the line of fire, then so be it."

"He's in their crosshairs just like the rest of us," Bucky countered. "He's got talent and instincts already. He'll never be ready if you don't give him the chance. Think about the stunts we pulled at eighteen after your father went AWOL."

Jim didn't answer for a time. At last, he straightened. "Just make sure his recklessness doesn't get himself or someone else hurt."

Bucky smirked. "The kid's got a mind of his own. They grow up whether you're ready for them to or not."

"Don't remind me," came the captain's reply.

As Jim left the bridge, he tapped his comm. "Liam, meet me in the ready room. We need to talk about that encrypted signal we detected that was headed for Mars."

"On my way," Liam replied.

The ready room was dim, the hum of the systems an indistinguishable backdrop. Jim sat at the central console, pulling up the signal's data on a holographic display. Liam entered, looking exhausted.

"What do we know?" Jim asked.

Liam crossed his arms, studying the display. "It's not Federation standard, but it has their fingerprints all over it. I'd bet my last credit it's tied to an operation across the belt."

Jim frowned, leaning back in his chair. "Do we have a signal location?"

"Roughly," Liam said. "Lucky for us, there's a Federation relay hub here in the Southern Sector. We can use it to find the signal's destination, but this isn't a place you want to be wandering around after dark."

Jim stood slowly. "We're not here to stir up trouble, but if that signal ties to Mariana or the Federation's plans, we need to know what it says."

"That's a risk," Liam said. "The kind that could get us killed."

"When did that ever stop us. Besides, this one is worth taking. I'll get my coat."

As the crew settled into their duties, JT loitered near the cargo bay, overwhelmed with the damage done to the ship. He glanced at the rigs and drones, knowing he would spend the next few days buried in grunt work while the others tackled bigger challenges.

From across the bay, Bucky caught his eye, giving him a look that mixed reassurance with challenge. JT sighed and went to work, unaware that the decisions made in the ready room above would soon drag them all into far more danger.

The Martian docks were a cacophony of activity. Workers in jumpsuits hauled crates and inspected the hull. The dry, recycled air carried the tang of oil and dust, a reminder of Mars's industrial underbelly.

JT wrestled a bulky stabilizer component into place. His muscles ached from the repetitive labor, but the sting of being sidelined by his father gnawed at him more than the physical strain.

"Careful with that," Bucky said. "Last thing we need is you smashing the mounting brackets."

"I've got it," JT scowled.

"Sure, you do," Bucky said lightly. "If you put half as much energy into lifting as you do sulking, we'd be done already."

"You think I'm sulking?" JT asked, adjusting his grip.

"Kid, you're a storm cloud. What's eating at you?"

JT hesitated, then muttered, "It's him. Dad. He thinks I can't handle it, but you know I can, Bucky."

Bucky leaned against the wall. "Listen, this isn't about you alone. It's about the crew's survival. Your father cares about nothing but keeping you safe."

"By treating me like a deckhand?" JT shot back. "How do I prove myself if he won't let me do anything that matters?"

"Proving yourself isn't about flashy moves. It's about showing up, doing the work, and earning trust. Keep your head down and do what's asked, and they'll see what you're made of, just like I do."

JT frowned but didn't argue. He returned to the rigs, his thoughts impossible to corral.

Meanwhile, in the dim corridors of the Southern Sector, Jim and Liam moved with purpose, their boots echoing on the metallic walkways. The air was cooler here and carried a faint trace of ozone.

"This is the place," Liam said, gesturing to a nondescript door. "Signal's strongest here."

Jim scanned the back alley of the facility as he absently put his hand inside his trench coat. Too quiet for a district usually buzzing with black-market trade. His hand went to the grip of his sidearm. "Stay ready."

Liam nodded and pulled a small scanner from his belt. The device beeped, its display filling with data. "Electromagnetic shielding. Whoever's behind this door doesn't want visitors."

Jim tapped his comm. "Mariana, we're at the relay hub. Can you patch in and tell us what we're dealing with here?"

Mariana's voice came back, pensive and efficient. "Give me a moment." Keys clacked in the background. "Got it. Federation tech, but heavily modified. This hub collects data and forwards it to a central site deeper in the sector."

"That must be the central comm station transmitting deep-space signals," Jim said. "Can you hack it?"

"Not without direct access to the main console. Get inside. Hopefully we can find the central station's location from there."

Jim exchanged a look with Liam. "Let's get this door open."

Liam produced a small cutting tool from his belt and set to work on the door's access panel. Sparks flew as he sliced through the locking mechanism, the constant hum of the colony's environmental systems the only backdrop. After several tense minutes, the door slid open with a soft hiss.

Inside, the walls were lined with monitors and workstations. At the center stood a computer hub bristling with cables, its glow casting an eerie blue light across the room.

"Federation, all right," Liam muttered, stepping inside. "No way this setup's here by accident."

Jim approached the console and slid a memory device into a port. Lines of code scrolled across the screens, gibberish to an untrained eye. He tapped his comm. "Mariana, are you in the system yet?"

"I'm already in," she answered. The monitors flickered, the stream of code hesitating before resuming. "This is... not standard."

"Define 'not standard.'"

"Encrypted files, plenty of them," Mariana replied. "This hub collects information from the Southern Sector: ship manifests, mineral shipments, personnel files. It's a satellite node for tracking local activity."

Jim's brow furrowed. "So, they've been spying on the entire sector."

"I'd wager it's not just here. There's probably one of these in every colony sector, monitoring independent operations across the belt. This isn't only about the Argo. It's about system-wide surveillance."

Before Jim could respond, footsteps echoed down the adjoining corridor.

Liam froze, hand tightening on his weapon. "We've got company."

Jim raised a hand for silence, his own sidearm sliding free from inside his trench coat. The footsteps quickened, voices carrying toward them. His comm crackled again with Mariana's voice.

"Captain, I'm detecting an outbound transmission. Whatever they're sending, it's happening now."

"Can you track its destination?" Jim asked.

"Got it," she replied.

"We're out of time." Jim yanked the memory device out. "Get ready."

The shadows of approaching figures stretched across the corridor walls. Jim and Liam bolted for the exit, sprinting through the open door as the sound of boots closed in. "They're right behind us," Jim barked.

"Run!"

They pushed into the Southern Sector's busy streets, Jim's coat billowing behind him. They vanished into the crowd of shoppers clustered around makeshift stalls in all directions. Whatever lay ahead, Mars was far from the safe harbor they had hoped for.

※※※※※

The colony's Southern Sector pulsed with life. Dealers barked from stalls packed with counterfeit electronics, bootleg liquor, and ration packs of questionable ingredients. The air reeked of ozone, fried food, and rust.

Bucky and JT moved through the press of bodies, a heavy crate of stabilizer parts balanced between them. The younger man grimaced, his nostrils flaring. "This place smells like burnt socks."

Bucky pointed toward a greasy stand where an old man fried slabs of meat. "Jed's Famous Fried Protein. Don't knock it until you've tried it."

"I'll pass, thanks," JT muttered.

"Suit yourself. Don't come whining when you're starving later." Bucky laughed as Gus's mechanic shop came into view.

The shop's garage was a wreck of parts and tools, half-gutted drones spread across the benches, wires and engine housing components littering the floor. Behind the counter stood Gus, wiry and oil-stained, his hairline nearly gone.

"Commander Buchanan," Gus greeted with a wide grin, waving them over. "Back again for another one of my friends and family specials?"

Bucky chuckled. "You know me. Can't resist your brand of mechanical robbery."

Gus cackled, wiping his hands on a rag. "So what's the damage this time?"

"We need stabilizer repairs, new seals on the containment unit, hull panels, these drone parts here, and a core overhaul," Bucky said. "And before you ask—yes, we're paying in credits, and no, we don't want Federation mods."

"Smart," Gus said with a shrug. "Mods give you easy clearance, but they're easy to trace. The Federation can sniff them out from half a system away."

JT dropped the crate onto the counter with a grunt. "Why does everything here feel like a scam?"

"Because it is," Gus said brightly. "Welcome to Mars."

As Gus tallied the repair costs, JT wandered to the back of the shop, his curiosity snagged by a row of old navigation systems stacked crooked on a shelf. Bucky leaned against the counter, watching Gus work.

"So, what's the Bucky Special?" Bucky asked, his tone casual.

Gus glanced up. "You know the deal, Buchanan. Credits cover the parts and labor. Keeping it off the Feds' radar, that costs a favor."

Bucky sighed and rubbed the back of his neck. "Figures. What do you need?"

"There's a shipment I've been trying to move through the southern sector," Gus said. "Federation patrols are thick as fleas, and I need someone with a lighter touch than mine to sneak it past inspections."

Bucky frowned. "You want us to smuggle something again?"

"Call it a favor for an old friend," Gus shrugged. "You do this for me, and I'll cut the repairs to cost. Otherwise you're short."

Bucky hesitated. "I'll have to clear it with the captain."

"Don't take too long," Gus warned. "The Federation's edgy these days."

JT returned to the counter, holding a small electronic device in his hands. "What's this?" he asked, turning it over.

"That?" Gus said, glancing at the mobile phone. "Relic. Used to be top-shelf tech when Pluto still counted as a planet."

"I think it's kind of cool. Can I have it?" JT asked.

"Tell you what," Gus said. "Get your old man to agree to my favor, and it's yours."

JT looked at Bucky, puzzled. "What favor?"

"Nothing you need to worry about," Bucky cut in. "Put it back before it shocks you."

JT rolled his eyes but set the device on the shelf. "Feels like you old guys are always sticking together."

"That's because we are," Bucky said. "Keeps you sharp."

On the walk back to the ship, JT couldn't shake his frustration. The mix of grunt work and being kept in the dark gnawed at him.

"You're being unsociable," Bucky said, glancing sideways.

"Sorry, just tired."

Bucky stopped and set a hand on his shoulder. "Listen, I know it feels like you're shut out, but there's a reason. Your dad's got a lot on his mind and keeping you safe is what he worries about most."

"I don't need coddling. I'm part of this crew, same as everyone."

"In time you'll earn your place, same as everyone," Bucky replied. "For now, take the wins where you can. Like not having to choke down Jed's Fried Protein."

JT cracked a reluctant smile. "Guess that's something."

"Damn right." Bucky clapped him on the back. "Now come on. We've got a ship to fix."

When they reached the Argo, Bucky's comm buzzed. "Commander, this is the captain. We need to talk."

Bucky's expression shifted. "On my way."

JT watched him go, his thoughts twisting. Something on Mars was brewing, and his dad was keeping it from him.

The captain's ready room was quiet, the low hum of systems a dull counterpoint to the chaos outside. Jim sat at the central console, elbows braced on the table as he reviewed the coded transmission Liam had lifted from the relay hub. His jaw was set as if sheer will might force the puzzle into place.

The door hissed open, and Bucky stepped in, his usual easy calm replaced by rare gravity. "You wanted to see me?"

Jim gestured to a chair. "What's the status on repairs?"

"Gus is on it," Bucky said, then paused. "For a favor."

Jim's brow creased. "What favor?"

Bucky leaned back. "He wants us to pick up his cargo, then deliver it to his contact before we leave. Says it's the only way he'll cut us a deal and keep it quiet."

Jim dragged a hand through his hair. "Damn it. I thought Mars might give us a break."

"That's on you for being an optimist," Bucky said, dry as dust.

Jim's lips twitched, but the humor faded quickly. "What's your take? Worth the risk?"

Bucky shrugged. "After that last job, we're short. Without accepting his offer, we're stuck on Mars. It's the only way I see us finishing the repairs. Even so, we still have to figure out how we get the hangar doors open to depart."

Jim drummed his fingers against the console, silent a moment. "Get him moving. Keep his focus on the work. If Gus tries to pull anything slick, I want to know before it happens."

"You got it," Bucky said, rising.

Jim's voice softened. "And Buck... thanks. For everything."

Bucky paused at the door, then nodded. "Anytime, Captain."

After Bucky left, Jim tapped his comm. "Mariana, any updates on that location?"

"I've confirmed the transmission's destination," Mariana replied. "This hub connects to a Federation communications tower deep in the Southern Sector. That tower is powerful enough to send and receive transmissions from deep space well past the asteroid belt. Whoever is receiving this data knows everything about Martian mining operations, including ours."

"Anything we can use?" Jim asked.

"Not that I see," Mariana answered. "If we can get inside the central tower, I might be able to hack into their systems and learn more about their plans."

Jim frowned. "That's a big risk, if the Federation catches us."

"They won't. Not if we're careful. I know how their systems work. I can get us in and out before they detect us."

Jim looked up, staring at the ceiling. "Careful hasn't been our strong suit lately."

Down in the cargo bay, JT was elbow-deep in a stabilizer housing, his hands slick with grease. He muttered to himself as he fought with a stubborn bolt. Footsteps echoed behind him, and he glanced up.

"You look like you're having fun," Raegan said, leaning against a crate.

"Loads," JT said sarcastically. He wiped his forehead, leaving a smear of grease. "What's going on?"

"Just checking in," Raegan said with a shrug. "Figured someone ought to make sure you haven't hurled a wrench through a bulkhead yet."

"Not yet, but don't tempt me."

Raegan tilted her head, studying him. "You're allowed to be frustrated. None of this is what anyone would call normal."

JT sighed, resting against the stabilizer. "It's not just the work. It's Mom being gone. I used to rely on her."

"You can rely on us, James. We're your family now." Raegan said gently. "The crew has your back, including me."

JT finally smiled. "Yeah. Thanks, Rae Rae. That means a lot."

"Of course, JT. Anytime you need to talk, I'm here for you." Raegan said. "You're not alone."

A couple of days later, with Gus overseeing repairs, Jim called a meeting with Grace, BK, Liam, and Lisa on the bridge. Every face was tight.

"We've got two problems," Jim began. "First, finishing repairs without drawing attention. Second, Mariana uncovered information that could show us what the Federation is planning. But it means accessing a Federation tower here in the Southern Sector."

Grace crossed her arms. "So, we sneak into a Federation-controlled facility? Great. That's a fine way to keep a low profile."

"Do we even know what we're looking for?" Lisa asked.

"We'll know it when we see it," Jim admitted. "If Mariana's right, this information could explain why they're hunting her."

Liam frowned. "Feels like a bad idea from the get-go."

"It definitely is. But we're out of safe options." He turned to Grace. "Can you take a break from repairs?"

"They're coming along," Grace answered. "I can take a break."

Jim nodded. "All right. Lisa, keep a close eye on Gus and make sure he finishes the job. Liam, you're with me on security. I'll lead the team into the station."

"What about Mariana?" Liam asked.

Jim sighed. "She's coming with us. She's the only one who can access their systems. Mariana?"

"Yes, Captain," she said.

"Do you still have your Federation officer's uniform?"

Mariana blinked. "Yes, in my locker."

"Go try it on, see if it still fits, but put this shirt on underneath it."

Her eyes narrowed as she accepted the T-shirt from Jim. "Walking through the docks in a Federation uniform is suicide. People will report us, or worse, the real guards will stop us."

Jim fixed her with a hard look. "This is where you trust me, the way I trusted you. That's how you show the crew you're one of us. Go put it on."

Liam muttered, shaking his head. "Oh no. Not this again. Last time we tried something like this, I got shot and you had to carry me out of Ruby's with me firing my blaster over your shoulder."

"Exactly. See how much fun this is going to be? It's time. Grab the trench coats and let's suit up."

As the meeting ended, Jim stood on the bridge, staring out at the Martian skyline. The colony lights cast long, dark shadows across the glass.

"Captain," Lisa said quietly, stepping up beside him. "You think the risk is worth it?"

Jim didn't look at her. "I do. But even if I didn't, it's the only move we've got."

"I'll make sure the Argo is ready for departure as soon as possible."

"You're the best, Lisa. What would I do without you?"

Lisa arched a brow. "Perish the thought, but you'd probably be rotting in a Federation penal colony by now."

Jim chuckled, though his mind was already elsewhere.

The Argo's lights flickered as the crew scattered to their tasks. The constant rumbling of machinery filled the air, broken by the clang of tools. Every crew member moved with purpose, weighed down by the uncertainty of what lay ahead.

In the cargo bay, Jim stood with Liam, Grace, and Mariana. The infiltration plans looked simple on the schematic, but he knew the risks. With Bucky buried in repairs and Lisa watching Gus, Jim was leaving the ship in capable hands. That didn't ease the pressure sitting in his chest.

"Let's go over this one more time," Jim said. He pointed to the glowing schematic on his handheld. "Liam, you, and I handle entry and cover the exits. Grace, you'll cover Mariana's back while we're inside. Mariana, you log in and collect the data, then we're out. Questions?"

Mariana raised her hand slightly. "What if Federation security shows up mid-download?"

Jim shrugged. "Then we improvise."

"Brilliant strategy," Grace muttered.

The team slipped through the Southern Sector's maze of corridors, their footsteps muffled by the colony's background buzz. The comms tower loomed ahead, a squat high-rise wedged between a drone repair shop and a gutted storage facility. Transmission satellites bristled across the roof. Each of them wore long leather trench coats, open at the neck, boots polished black.

"All right," Jim said. "Time to ditch the coats."

"Every time we come to Mars, you make us wear these," Liam complained. "It's seventy-eight degrees inside the dome. We look ridiculous."

"Think of the wanted posters. Besides, we have to hide our cover 'til we're close," Jim said.

"We look like Matrix extras, Jim. And that's not a compliment."

Mariana stared at them, astonished that they were arguing at a time like this.

When they stepped back into the street, the trench coats were gone, Federation uniforms visible beneath. Mariana's science officer insignia gleamed on her lapel.

"Security's light," Liam murmured. Two guards stood at the entrance. "Almost like they don't want to spook the locals."

"Mariana, you're in charge," Jim said. "Lead the way. They'll be too busy staring at your rank to notice we're wearing outdated uniforms."

As they approached, the guards snapped to attention, caught off guard by the unannounced arrival. Mariana's disapproving glare made them shrink; her beauty edged with something almost frightening.

She stepped to the access panel, fingers tapping firmly on the pad. After a tense moment, the lock clicked and the door slid open. The team slipped inside. Liam caught one guard studying his suit too closely. The man's eyes widened. Liam and Jim drew their weapons first.

"Easy, partner," Jim whispered. "Drop the weapons and step inside."

The dim room beyond was cold and silent. Inside, three technicians froze mid-task. Jim bound them while Liam and Grace covered the group.

Mariana was already at the central console. "This is it," she said. "Give me five minutes."

"You've got two," Jim answered, scanning the shadows.

Liam posted by the entrance, weapon ready. Grace leaned in to watch Mariana's progress, muttering as her eyes scrolled across the screens.

"This system's a mess. Over-engineered, Software is glitchy. Typical Federation garbage."

The sound of rapid footsteps echoed from the corridor that led deeper into the facility.

Liam drew his sidearm. "We've got company."

Jim snapped to Mariana. "How much longer?"

"Almost there," she said, giving the console a kick. "Just give me a minute."

The far door burst open, and a squad of security officers stormed in, weapons raised. Jim and Liam fired instantly, their shots forcing the intruders into cover.

"Grace, help Mariana!" Jim barked. "Liam, cover them!"

The room erupted, trails of plasma fire bouncing from the steel walls. Jim and Liam pinned the squad in the corridor, firing in rapid succession. Grace crouched beside Mariana while splitting her focus between the console and the firefight, squeezing off bursts whenever she could.

"Hurry!" Grace shouted.

"Almost!" Mariana's voice was tight. Then a filename appeared on the screen: For Mariana. Her eyes widened. Who could have left that for her here?

The console beeped. Mariana ripped her memory stick from the port before anyone else saw the message. They didn't need to know, not until she knew what was inside. "Got it!"

Her pulse hammered. If she told them, would they believe she didn't know who left her the message.

Liam glanced at the scrolling data before they fled. "If they're mapping Mars this tightly, they're doing it everywhere."

Jim's heart sank. "Which means every station, every colony. Nobody's outside their net. "Time to move!" Jim ordered. "Liam, cover our exit!"

They spilled into the exit path, Liam's fire keeping the guards pinned. The team tossed their spent mags aside, reloading as they sprinted through the streets.

"I love it when a plan comes together," Jim said between breaths.

"Just like Ruby's," Grace zinged.

"Hardy har har," Liam added sourly.

In the far shadows of the street, they tore off their Federation uniforms, revealing plain clothes beneath. Tourists now, swallowed by the crowd. Jim smirked at Mariana's T-shirt: "My parents went to Mars and all I got was this lousy shirt."

They dumped their weapons in the nearest trash bin to complete the look. He scanned the crowd. "Split up. Mariana and I will head back to the Argo. Grace, you and Liam draw the heat. Lose them first and regroup."

Liam nodded. "Got it. Good luck, Jim."

"You too." Jim clapped his shoulder.

As Jim and Mariana threaded through quieter streets, sirens fading, he shot her a sidelong glance. "Looks like you pulled something valuable from their systems. Good job."

Mariana raised a brow. "That's your idea of a thank you?"

"It's as close as you'll get," Jim said, amusement dancing in his eyes.

Her lips twitched, but she stayed silent, eyes on the device in her hand. Whatever was inside it might reveal everything about the Federation's plans, or nothing at all.

The Argo's silhouette loomed ahead. Jim tapped his comm.

Bucky's voice came back, stripped of his usual bravado. "Captain, we've got trouble."

Jim exhaled. "What now?"

"The crew's asking when the Argo's leaving. They're spooked about the repairs and the attention we're getting from the Federation," Bucky said. "We need to get ahead of this."

UNDERWORLD OF THE
RED PLANET

The mess hall's fluorescent lights buzzed intermittently casting an uneven glow over the assembled crew. The long metal table, scuffed and dented from years of use, stretched between them like a silent barrier. Jim stood at the head of the table, scanning the faces around him. His crew, his family in all but name.

"We'll be on Mars at least several more days," Jim said, his voice reluctant. "The Argo's repairs need more time. If we push her now, we won't reach the belt, let alone make the return."

The reaction was immediate. Murmurs rippled through the group, ranging from concerned whispers to low gasps.

Grace sat back in her chair, crossing her arms over her chest. She was concerned by Jim's answer, her dark eyes scrutinizing him. "So, what do we do?" she asked. "We have to find a way to pay for the repairs?"

Jim nodded in agreement. "Yes. Gus has offered to finish the repairs at cost, but there's a catch."

"There's always a catch with Gus. What's he want?"

"He needs us to do a delivery job."

The room fell into stunned silence. BK raised his eyebrows. Seated at the far end of the table, Raegan stopped fidgeting with her med scanner to observe the interaction between Jim and the others.

"You mean smuggling?" Liam asked. "What are we supposed to be moving?"

"High-value cargo," Jim replied. "The contents don't matter. Gus says it's the only way he'll finish the repairs since we don't have enough credits to cover the costs. Whatever it is, it can't possibly make us a bigger target than we already are. The trick, obviously, is avoiding any Federation patrols while we're in possession of his cargo."

"Captain, that's not just risky. It's a death sentence if Gus is playing us."

Jim's frustration was evident. "I'm not thrilled about it either, but we don't have another option. Without this job, the Argo won't be spaceworthy, and our luck avoiding patrols won't last forever. If anyone has a better idea, let's hear it."

The room remained silent. Lisa exchanged a worried glance with Raegan, while Karl muttered something inaudible, his usual stoicism faltering.

"Look," Bucky said. "It's not like this is the first time we've been in the smuggling game. We'll be in and out before the Feds even know we were there."

"Okay, but what if they do?" Grace snapped. "What then, Bucky? We're not just talking about a slap on the wrist. We're already one step away from being fugitives."

"Like you said, we're already on their radar. And they'll be too busy investigating who broke into their facility to worry about smugglers for a while."

JT, seated near the middle of the table, shifted uncomfortably, but he didn't speak. His focus was on the conversation. When Jim's gaze finally landed on him, his father's eyes seemed impenetrable.

"Liam, Bucky, and James will be the shuttle team for the cargo pickup."

"You're letting me go?" JT asked, louder than he intended.

"You've been asking for a chance to prove yourself," Jim said. "Here it is."

The room erupted in overlapping arguments. Lisa started to say something, but Grace cut her off with a sharp gesture.

"Captain, this is reckless. JT has no business being part of a mission like this. He could put us all in danger."

"I hear you, Grace, but protecting James won't keep him safe anymore," said Jim, scowling.

Her face flushed with heat. "You're putting him in danger, Jim."

Jim stepped away from the chair and leaned forward, planting his hands on the table. "The Federation is after him just like the rest of us. He has to learn how to fend for himself sooner rather than later. This is about survival. You think I like this? That I want him to risk his life for this cause? Or any of you? We're doing this because the alternative is unthinkable. It's time he gets his feet put to the fire like everyone else. End of story."

Grace didn't budge, but she gave him room to continue.

"Here's how this is going to work," Jim said. "Bucky, you'll lead the mission. Liam and James will go with you. Grace and I will stay here to make sure Gus doesn't disappear before he finishes the repairs."

"And Mariana?" Raegan asked.

Jim glanced toward Mariana, who had been sitting quietly at the edge of the group. Without blinking, she waited for Jim's answer.

"She stays on the Argo," Jim said. "Mariana's skill set is best suited for assisting Raegan in the med bay."

"Understood." Mariana's tone was neutral. She didn't offer more, and no one pressed her.

"Jim," Bucky said, sounding earnest, "if we're doing this, I need to know you're okay with the risks. All of them."

Jim pivoted toward Bucky, his intensity unwavering. "I wouldn't let him go if I wasn't. He can handle himself."

As the crew dispersed, their footsteps echoing through the mess hall, Jim stayed behind. He watched them leave one by one, their weariness plain in every movement. JT was the last to go, pausing at the door.

"Thank you for letting me go, Dad. Do you really think I'm ready for this?" JT asked. He sounded unsure.

Jim's eyes softened. "You're never truly ready James. The trick is to convince yourself you've done it before. Then your mind knows it's possible. Trust your instincts and listen to Bucky."

JT's joy was obvious as he turned and left. When the door hissed shut behind him, Jim let out a long breath and ran a hand across his face. The vibration of the ship's systems filled the silence. The clock was ticking, and there was still a long way to go.

The cargo bay was a flurry of activity. Crew moved with practiced efficiency under the fear of detection. The clatter of tools and the whine of diagnostic gear created a discordant symphony, broken by static bursts from comms.

JT stood near the shuttle, its matte-black hull gleaming under the harsh lights. He watched as Bucky inspected the vessel, running his hands along the seams of the exterior plating.

"Don't worry. She'll hold together," Bucky muttered, half to himself. "She's tough as nails, and with the mods your dad and I have done, she's far superior to my old shuttle, the Scarlett."

"She's one of a kind," JT said, his hand running along the hull.

"We're almost ready, kid." Bucky jerked his head toward the open hatch. "Get inside and check the cargo hold. Time for final prep before we fly."

JT climbed aboard. The shuttle's bridge was cramped, the seats worn, the controls set to Bucky's liking. He moved aft where a stack of crates sat strapped in place. As he tightened the bindings, footsteps clanged on the metal ramp.

"Almost time. You nervous yet?" Liam asked, stepping inside, his presence filling the space.

JT shrugged. He kept his eyes on the straps. "Not really, should I be?"

Liam leaned on the frame, arms crossed. "Depends. We've been in tight spots before, but this isn't asteroid mining, kid. These people play for keeps."

"Like we don't?" JT sounded surprisingly confident.

Liam studied him for a moment. "Good. Just remember. Stick to the plan, and if something goes wrong, don't try to be Achilles."

JT smirked faintly. "What if Achilles had a trench coat?"

Liam groaned. "Kid, don't start with the coat."

"Yes, Chief," JT said, finishing with the straps and turning to face him. "Anything else?"

Liam grinned. "Yeah. Don't touch the controls unless Bucky says so."

Bucky paced around the shuttle, his mind running through the plan for the tenth time. He'd worked plenty of dangerous jobs, but this one felt different. The stakes were no longer personal. Failure meant all of them went down.

"Everything good to go?" Jim's voice pulled Bucky from his thoughts. He approached with his usual calm intensity, hands in his coat pockets.

"Good as it's gonna get," Bucky replied. "Shuttle's prepped, cargo's secured, and Liam's making sure the kid doesn't hyperventilate."

Jim gave a forced smile. "He'll be fine. He's got you watching his back."

"You know, I don't say it enough, but I've got your back too, Jim. Always have; always will."

"I'll never stop being grateful for that, brother," Jim said. His voice was sincere. "Don't forget, I've got yours too."

As Bucky moved to double-check the shuttle's systems, Diane appeared at the edge of the bay. Her lab coat had been replaced with cargo pants and a jacket. Her dark hair was tied back, and her sharp eyes softened when they met his.

"You're really doing this?" she asked, distress in her face.

"We don't have much of a choice," Bucky replied, still inspecting the shuttle. "Until we pay Gus for repairs, we're grounded. Without them, we're dead in the water. Or space."

Bucky ran his fingers through her hair. "It's who we need to be right now. For the crew. For Jim."

"And for JT?" Her voice sounded almost motherly.

"Yeah. He's a good kid. Just needs guidance. When his mother died, his world flipped upside down. And Jim..." Bucky paused. "Being a father like this is new for him. Belt mining didn't leave much time for Little League. JT's still working through that, but it'll take time."

Diane rested a hand on his arm. "Be careful out there. For us."

Bucky looked into her eyes. His bravado was tempered by real affection. "Of course, you know me."

"That's exactly why I'm worried," Diane said, grinning.

Bucky straightened, slipping into an impression. "I'll be back. I promise." He leaned in, kissed her softly, then gave her a playful peck on the nose.

Diane shook her head. "You don't take anything seriously, you know that."

She stepped back as Bucky climbed aboard. The ramp closed with a hiss of hydraulics that signaled departure.

She couldn't shake the sense of unease that settled in her stomach.

Inside the shuttle, the atmosphere was taut. Bucky took the pilot's seat. His hands moved with practiced ease over the outdated controls. Liam settled into the copilot's chair, and JT was strapped in at the rear.

"Last chance to back out," Bucky said, half-joking as he glanced at the others.

"Not a chance, Commander." JT's tone more resolute than before.

Bucky grinned. "Good. Let's finish the job so Gus will finish the repairs."

The shuttle's engines rumbled to life. Vibrations coursed through the cargo bay as it lifted off. Through the viewports, the sprawling Martian docks stretched below, a labyrinth of neon and shadows. Each man understood the risks. The stakes were high, and failure wasn't an option.

Bucky settled the shuttle into its path, slipping out of the southern docks. JT craned his neck, marveling at the neon signs sputtering across the protective domes. Seedy advertisements flickered endlessly above the Southern Sector that cast jagged reflections on cargo stacks. The black market pulsed outside. Its unspoken rules were at the front of everyone's minds.

Bucky scanned both the navigation console and the viewport. His calm exterior hid the fear coursing through him.

Beside him, Chief Security Officer Power kept watch, his hand going to his holstered weapon. JT shifted in his seat. Everyone could sense the nervous energy.

"Keep your eyes sharp," Bucky said, even and firm. "This place doesn't forgive mistakes."

"Yes, sir," JT replied, gripping the seat.

The shuttle dropped into a narrow alley, and its landing gear extended with a hiss. The walls pressed close. Shadows stretched long into the dark. Bucky eased the ship into place, the pulse of the engines fading as he powered them down.

"This is it," Bucky said, standing as he checked his sidearm. "Liam, you're with me. JT, stay with the shuttle. Keep her systems primed in case we need to lift off in a hurry."

"Understood, Commander," JT said.

Buchanan and Liam exited, their movements fluid and precise. The ramp sealed behind them, and JT was left alone with the security feeds, watching the shadows and bracing for trouble.

They threaded through the alley of stacked crates. Their steps were nearly silent on the metal deck. At the drop point Gus had given them, a wiry man in a tattered jacket waited. His eyes darted like an insect's.

"You're late," the man rasped.

"Traffic," Bucky replied. "Let's keep this quick."

The man pointed at four crates stamped with Federation markings. "That's your load. Don't ask, don't open. They'll know when you deliver."

"We weren't planning to," Liam said, running a scanner across the cargo. The device chirped in sequence.

"Readings are clean. No radiation leaks," Liam reported.

"Good," Bucky said. "Move them."

They hauled the crates toward the shuttle with practiced efficiency. Behind them, their contact twitched nervously while scanning the alley.

"You'd better hurry," he snapped. "This place isn't as safe as it looks."

Bucky and Liam returned for the last two crates. As they bent to lift them, Bucky froze.

The sound of boots clanged against the metal. Bucky stiffened, his hand on his sidearm.

"Liam," he said. His voice was a warning.

Liam swept the shadows. Figures stepped into the neon light one by one, Federation insignias glinting on their uniforms.

"Hands up!" an officer barked, pistol raised. "Step away from the cargo."

Bucky's mind snapped into overdrive. He dropped the crate and drew his weapon in a single motion. He fired a shot that ricocheted off a barrel, causing the group to take cover.

"Move!" he barked.

They lunged for the crates and bolted down the alley, boots pounding against steel. Bucky dropped his load and drew his weapon and fired, pinning the patrol behind their cover.

*****

Inside the shuttle, JT froze at the crackle of gunfire. He forced himself into motion, hands steady as he keyed the controls.

"Commander, what's happening?" JT shouted over comms.

"We're coming in hot!" Bucky barked. "Prep for takeoff!"

The thrusters roared to life, and the hull rattled as JT ran preflight. He caught sight of Liam hauling a crate up the ramp.

"Where's the Commander?" JT asked.

"Right behind me!" Liam snapped, firing back down the alley.

Bucky burst aboard with the last crate and slammed the panel, sealing the hatch. "Get us out of here, JT! Now!"

As the shuttle lifted off, plasma blasts hammered the shuttle, the alley seeming to collapse inward. The Federation patrol appeared. Two drones zipped into view, with their red sensors locked onto the fleeing vessel.

"We've got company!" Liam shouted from the rear turret.

"Hold them off, Chief!" Bucky barked as he slid into the copilot's seat beside JT. "JT, head for the transport tunnels. They won't follow us inside."

At the last fork, Bucky spotted a collapsing support strut on the nav feed. JT hadn't seen it yet. He jerked the yoke just in time, scraping through with centimeters to spare. The shuttle rattled, but it held.

JT steadied his hands on the controls and guided the shuttle toward the dark, gaping entrance. The drones closed in, their plasma cannons charging.

"Fire, Liam!" Bucky commanded.

Liam answered with a torrent from the turret. The first drone exploded in a fiery bloom. The second evaded the blasts and pressed forward.

"Brace yourselves!" JT shouted as the shuttle plunged into the tunnel.

The walls blurred past. The narrow space left no margin for error. The surviving drone hesitated. Its logic was unable to account for the shuttle's escape.

Inside, the crew exhaled in unison. Liam slumped back, his chest heaving. Bucky glanced at JT, whose pale face gleamed with sweat.

"Not bad, kid," Bucky said at last. "Just don't let it go to your head."

"Yes, Commander," JT replied, steadier now.

The shuttle corrected its course and broke free of the tunnel. The red glow of the southern docks grew ahead. They had survived another close call together, and for the first time JT felt like he had contributed.

The shuttle touched down in the Argo's bay. Its engines wound down with a tired sigh. Buchanan strode off the ramp first, his steps deliberate. Liam followed. His arms were taut around the crate he carried. JT came last. He was pale but resolute; his hands trembled as he tried to force composure.

"Unload the cargo," Bucky ordered. "Secure it in Bay Three. JT, assist Liam."

"Yes, sir," JT said, hurrying to comply.

The bay filled with the thud of crates, the clang of tools, the drone of voices. Mariana entered. Her eyes were sharp, and her walk was direct. She closed on Bucky. Her anger was visible in her eyes.

"The Federation will scour every corner of the Southern Sector for fugitives now," she said.

Bucky faced her. "We'll handle it when the time comes. Right now, we finish repairs."

"When they sweep the docks, we'll be exposed."

"That's why we leave the second the Argo is ready."

Mariana's expression stayed guarded. "You trust him too much. He might not keep his word."

"I always trust too much. Call it charm," said Bucky, amused.

With the last crate secured, JT helped Liam with the inventory. The older man worked with quick precision, every motion deliberate. JT tried to match him, but nearly dropped a scanner.

"Easy," Liam said, catching it. "You don't have to prove anything right now."

JT replied lightheartedly. "You're not learning if you're not making mistakes. Sir."

"Oh no, not another one." Chief Power laughed, "Next thing you'll be asking for your own trench coat."

Later, in the quiet of the Argo's observation deck, Bucky and Diane sat side by side. His arm circled her shoulder while their voices stayed low. The vast expanse of Mars stretched out before them. The dusty surface glowed faintly under the distant stars.

"You didn't tell me this mission would be so dangerous. The Federation already has patrols sweeping for whoever broke into their facility," Diane said. Her voice was caught between worry and frustration.

"What we do is always dangerous." Bucky leaned back in his chair. "You knew that when you came aboard."

"But this feels different. We want to start a family, and I don't understand why you aren't thinking about how this affects our future. I'm pregnant, Bucky. Everything is different now."

Bucky turned, his voice softening. He took her hand and placed it on her belly, where the faintest curve had just begun to show. "I'll always take care of you and our baby. I love you more than anything. That's the reason I'm doing this, so our son can grow up free of the Federation. This isn't just about us. It's about the crew too. They're family, Diane. I'll do whatever it takes to keep them safe."

Diane sighed, and her eyes drifted to the red horizon. "Just promise me you'll be careful."

"Always. Careful is my middle name."

Diane gave a pleasant smile and said, "It's actually Peyton."

As the Argo settled into an uneasy calm after the mission, each crew member reflected in their own way. Jim stood alone on the bridge, watching the Martian sky. He squared his shoulders, his resolve hardening.

Below deck, JT sat in the crew quarters, his thoughts racing. He replayed every moment of the mission. He carefully measured each choice, each order. Pride and doubt mingled in his mind. Had he done enough? Was he ready for what came next?

Elsewhere, Bucky and Diane shared the quiet of the observation deck. Her head rested against his shoulder while they watched the skyline without words.

The next day, the mess hall hummed with activity. Jim stood at the head of the long table, arms crossed, his gaze firm as the crew filed in. The strain of the smuggling run showed in their subdued movements.

When all were seated, Jim cleared his throat. "The delivery job went off with minimal blowback." His voice commanded authority, though exhaustion edged his words. "But let's be clear: the Federation will be looking for the ones who managed to escape their patrol."

Liam leaned back in his chair, arms folded. "What's the plan, Jim? They've already started sweeps. It's only a matter of time before they reach our sector."

"We stick to the plan," Jim replied, his tone firm. "We finish Gus's delivery job, he finishes our repairs. After that, we hide out at one of the unincorporated stations until the heat dies down." He scanned the room. "Until then, make sure every system is fully operational. Every bolt tightened. We're ready to launch the moment Gus clears us."

Grace leaned forward, voice low but cutting: "Captain, Gus is questionable on a good day."

Concern rippled through the room.

Seated near the far end, Mariana spoke the questions everyone was asking themselves. "What if Gus doesn't deliver? What if he's playing both sides?"

"He won't," Bucky said confidently. "He knows the stakes. He's not stupid enough to cross us."

"You know the company he keeps?" Grace asked dryly.

JT shifted uncomfortably beside Bucky. "What about the miners? Are they all staying?"

"That's their choice," Jim said. "Anyone who wants to remain behind can do so. If they stay with us, they're crew of the Argo. That means following orders, doing their fair share, and understanding that we're all fugitives being hunted by the Federation."

A low murmur rolled down the table, half the miners muttering about staying, the others nodding grimly. The Argo wasn't just split by metal bulkheads anymore; the crew itself was dividing.

"You think any of them will walk?" asked Bucky.

"There's always a chance," Jim admitted. "Some have been with us from the beginning, but not everyone signed up for this fight. Each man decides his own path."

As the crew dispersed, Jim lingered at the head of the now-empty table. The stress of the last few weeks was wearing on him. Doubt lurked in the edges of his mind, but he pushed it back.

Bucky stepped up beside him and said, "You're doing the right thing by JT and the crew. It might not feel like it right now, but you are."

Jim rubbed a hand over his face. "Because if I'm wrong..."

"You're not," Bucky said. "But even if you are, ask yourself this: who else stands a chance of stopping the Federation? Nobody. It's too late to turn back. Benjamin made sure of that."

Jim met his friend's eyes. He gave a curt nod. "Thanks, Bucky."

※※※※※

JT lingered in the cargo bay, staring at the shuttle they had used for the smuggling run. His thoughts turned over the mission. The adrenaline had long since drained away, and in its place only fatigue and pride.

"You did well out there." Mariana's voice broke through his thoughts. She crossed the hangar and stepped into the bay. She sat beside him and waited a quiet moment before speaking again. "Your father is a good man, JT. Sending you on this mission was a big deal for him."

JT's gaze shifted to her. "Thanks, Mariana. I'm starting to feel like maybe he does trust me."

"You're more like him than you realize," Mariana said. She leaned in without noticing how close she had drawn. "I can see a leader in you. Someone the crew can depend on when it matters. You've got heart, JT, and that's what counts." Without waiting for a reply, she rose and walked away, leaving JT alone with the echo of her faith in who he would become.

Later that night... Jim stood by himself on the observation deck, watching the rust-colored surface of Mars glow faintly under the starlight. The door slid open behind him. He didn't need to turn to know it was Grace.

"Can't sleep either?" she asked, stepping to his side.

"No. Too much on my mind," he admitted.

"Grace, I won't let anything happen to you or the crew."

Grace gave him a genuine smile.

Jim turned back to the Martian horizon. The truth solidified in his mind. "The Federation's closing in. It's time we strike first."

Grace studied him. She saw the steely resolve behind his weariness and didn't argue.

ΛS THE WORLD TURΠS

The mess hall was louder than it had been in weeks, filled with laughter and the clatter of poker chips on the metal table. The buzzing lights overhead nearly vanished beneath the noise of banter and the occasional cheer. For the first time in what felt like forever, the crew carved out a sliver of normal life.

Commander Buchanan sat with a mountain of mismatched chips in front of him, a lopsided grin on his face as he shuffled a battered deck of cards with the ease of a man who had lived in smoky backrooms all his life. "All right, folks, ante up," he said, tossing chips into the pot. He dealt fast and the hand began.

After a bold raise from Bucky, Liam chuckled, folding his arms. "You're bluffing already, aren't you, Commander?"

"Wouldn't you like to know, Power?" Buchanan shot back, his grin widening.

Lisa fiddled with her hand like she was plotting an escape course. "Can we just play our hands? Some of us would like to keep the game moving."

Grace laughed from her seat beside Jim. "If you're that worried, Cross, maybe stick to navigation."

"Big talk from someone who lost half her credits last round," Lisa replied, eyebrows raised.

The table broke into laughter. Even Jim cracked a smile. JT sat near the end, nursing a modest pile of chips, wedged between his father and the others. He wanted to call, but was waiting for the right hand.

"JT," Bucky nudged him, "you in or what? Sitting there hunched like a gargoyle doesn't scare anyone."

JT blinked. "Yeah, I'm in." He pushed a stack into the pot.

"Nice call, kid. Way to show some stones!" Bucky said, just before laying down his winning hand. "But not this time."

The game rolled on with cards sliding across the table, bets rising, and voices rising. Bucky pushed hard as always, bluffing with such conviction that it was impossible to know he was holding. Grace played carefully, her expression flat. Liam shifted between bold aggression and last-second folds.

Camaraderie shone through every hand. Bucky teased Lisa when she overbid trying to bluff. Liam launched into an exaggerated story about an old security detail gone sideways.

As the laughter cooled, Jim raised his hands. "Enough. Back to the game. James, what have you got?"

JT looked at his cards. His hand was strong, but his pile was weak. "I'll raise. All in." He shoved the rest of his chips into the pot.

Bucky's eyes glinted. "Bold move, kid. Let's see."

Most folded. A few called. When the reveal came, JT laid down a flush, the best hand by far.

"Not bad," Bucky said, clapping him on the shoulder. "Beginner's luck?"

JT grinned. "Or maybe I'm just a quick learner."

Before they could reset, the ship's comm crackled. "Captain Eckhart, it's Gus," the mechanic's gravel voice came through. "I've got an update you'll want to hear."

The crew traded glances, and the laughter died.

Jim stood, his face tightening. "What is it, Gus?"

"It's the Feds," Gus said. "Sweeps in the hangars. Looking for something. Or someone."

Jim looked at his crew. "That's it for tonight. Everyone back to your stations. We need to stay ahead of whatever this is."

The crew scattered. Work replaced play. Jim lingered, staring at the scattered chips on the table, a fleeting reminder of the old days, a life worth fighting for.

"Captain?" Bucky said.

Jim glanced up. "Yeah, Buck?"

"You don't have to worry so much. We got this." He held out his hand for their secret shake.

Jim smiled and clasped it. "You're right, Bucky. Let's get to work."

On the bridge, Jim stood at the central console, flanked by Grace and Lisa. They gathered as Lisa pulled up surveillance feeds from the dock's public networks. The low-quality video displayed Federation patrols moving in coordinated sweeps around the lower hangars.

"They're maintaining a tight net. It will take time for them to close in on our sector," Lisa said while zooming in on a group of Federation guards questioning dockworkers.

Grace leaned against the console, her arms crossed. "If they find her, we're finished. They'll arrest us and impound the Argo."

Jim dragged a hand through his hair. "Then we make sure they don't find her. Or us."

Lisa frowned and glanced over her shoulder. "How long can we hide here? Repairs aren't finished, and even if they were, the docks are swarming with patrols. We can't just fly out with the hangar doors sealed."

"Yes, it's a tough spot," said Jim.

The door slid open, and Liam entered. "Captain, we've got a problem. Federation officers are asking about recent shipments. Gus says it's only a matter of time before they search our sector for contraband."

Jim's brow furrowed. "Maybe they think there's a link between the two crimes and Mariana. They must have seen her on their security footage. How much time do we have?"

"Four hours before they reach this section. They're sweeping sector by sector, making sure no one slips past their dragnet."

Grace's frown deepened. "We need to hide Mariana. If they search the Argo, they'll find her for sure. Then there's nothing we can do."

"There is one thing," Jim said. "Lisa, keep monitoring their movements. Tell us if they move on our sector. Liam, gather the crew."

"What's the plan, Captain?" Grace asked.

Jim's lips pressed into a thin line. "If they find her here, they tie everything back to us, so we hide her somewhere they won't look."

The bridge buzzed with subdued energy when Jim arrived. Bucky, Karl, JT, and several others were already gathered. Their faces were set with the same grit that had carried them through every crisis so far. Mariana stood apart from the crew. Her attention was locked onto Jim as he entered through the airlock.

"What are we going to do, Captain?" Bucky asked, straightening from a crate.

Jim surveyed the group before speaking. "The Federation is closing in. If we don't act now, they'll find Mariana, and that blows our cover. We can't let that happen."

"Captain, this is desperation disguised as a plan."

"They won't find her. Not where we'll hide her," said Jim.

Liam raised an eyebrow. "And where is that?"

"In the Argo's smuggling quarters," Jim answered. "The Federation patrols will never find her there. She can lock herself in from the inside. The walls are shielded like a cloaked Faraday cage. Their scanners won't detect a thing. It's our best chance."

Liam crossed his arms. "Smart, but do you really trust her? What if next time we need to hide JT, Diane, or Raegan? That compartment is worth as much as the Argo itself."

"Would you question my decision if it was any other member of the crew?" Jim asked.

"I trust her," JT said a little too eagerly.

"I agree," Jim replied. "I believe we all do."

JT's face stayed firm, his expression even.

"Captain," Mariana said, moving closer. Her movements composed. "If they catch you hiding me, you put the entire crew at risk. Are you sure I'm worth it?"

Jim met her eyes. "You're part of the crew now. The same rules apply to you as anyone else. That makes you, our responsibility."

Emotion shuddered across Mariana's face. "Thank you, Jim."

"Comforting," Liam muttered, looking out the viewscreen. Shadows in the distant corners of the docks tugged at his paranoia.

Mariana straightened, her face unreadable. "Where do I hide?"

"Come with me," Bucky said. "Somewhere the Feds won't find you."

He led her into the captain's quarters. They walked to the back of the room, and Bucky told her to turn and cover her eyes. She obeyed. A groan of hidden machinery made her glance up just as a four-foot door slid open, revealing the smuggler's hideaway. "A small, storage-sized hole in the wall, black as space itself."

"Your new abode," Bucky said, gesturing toward the hole. "Stay quiet. Stay hidden. We'll come back for you when it's safe."

Mariana nodded. "Understood." She slipped inside, her palm brushing the data stick in her pocket. Not yet.

Bucky stepped into the corridor, where Liam waited.

"How many times has Jim hidden in there to avoid one scorned flame or another?" Liam joked.

Bucky's expression was bleak. "Let's just make sure Gus finishes those repairs. Otherwise, we're gonna wish it was just a scorned flame looking for us."

※※※※※

The bridge was a hive of subdued activity. The glow from the monitors washed the crew in hues of blue and green as Lisa reviewed surveillance feeds from the Martian docks. Each screen displayed a different angle: Federation patrols moving in pairs, questioning dockworkers, inspecting crates, and scanning ships as though they were looking for someone. They weren't specifying who, but the description matched Mariana. The reassuring thrum of the Argo's systems pressed against the strained silence.

"They're getting close," Lisa said, zooming in on one feed. The display showed a patrol officer gesturing toward a section of the docks while his partner spoke into a wrist-comms device. "Looks like they're coordinating a sweep that's heading our way."

Drone patrols flew overhead, scanning the Argo from above, but they continued their patrol.

Grace frowned at her console. "Damn it. These guys are so annoying."

"They always are. It's part of their creed." Jim stood near the center of the bridge, arms crossed as he studied the screens. His calm demeanor couldn't hide the tension in his brow.

Lisa switched to another angle that showed a group of officers gathered around a map projection of the docks. She enhanced the audio, and clipped Federation voices filled the bridge.

"Sectors 6 through 8 clear. Begin sweep of Sectors 9 through 12," one officer ordered.

Grace straightened. "Sector 12 is close. At this rate, they'll reach us long before the repairs are done."

Jim winced. "We need more time. Suggestions?"

Lisa looked up from her station, fingers drumming against the console. "We could jam their comms, but they'd triangulate the source."

"They'd track it back to us," Grace said, shaking her head. "Too risky."

Jim turned to her. "So, what do you propose?"

"We create a distraction," Grace said. "Something to pull them away from this sector until Gus finishes the repairs and we complete the delivery."

Lisa frowned. "What kind of distraction? It would have to be big enough to hold their attention."

Grace answered. Big, but not too big. Just enough to make them look the other way while we finish our list."

Jim studied them both. "All right. What's your plan?"

"It's an old favorite. Just like the time we fled Ceres after you cheated the Commodore out of that card game."

She pulled up the ship's logs. "We rig a drone with explosives. Karl creates a counterfeit clearance to get it past the guards, and it 'malfunctions' in the chemical yard. They'll think some scavenger botched a job."

Lisa's eyebrows rose. "You want to make one of our drones look like an incompetent criminal?"

"Exactly," Grace said. "We transmit a signal so it appears to come from a scavenger crew in Sector 28. The Feds will waste time tracking a phantom signal. It's not perfect, but it's our best chance to buy time."

Jim rubbed his chin. "Karl can make sure it doesn't point back to us?"

"This is Karl we're talking about."

"Do it," Jim ordered. "Keep it subtle. If it fails, it's your plan, not mine."

In the engineering bay, Karl crouched over the battered frame of one of the Argo's untraceable drones. The hull was scarred from past escapades. Karl moved with stiff joints as he programmed the operating system, while his fingers moved with practiced precision across the control module.

Grace stood nearby, arms folded. "How's it coming?"

"Almost there," Karl said without looking up. "These outdated protocols take longer to program, but it'll work."

"Make sure the signal can't be traced back to us," Grace said. "We can't afford any mistakes."

Karl snorted. "When have I ever made a mistake?"

"Do you want the list alphabetically or chronologically?"

Karl chuckled. "Fair enough. But not with my drones. Once this drone does its job, the signal will bounce through so many relays they'll be searching for days."

Grace's eyes stayed on the console. "Good. If they catch us, the captain will never let me hear the end of it."

Karl tightened one final connection and wiped his hands on a rag. "Done. Drone's ready, signal transponders set. All we need is activation."

"Perfect. Let's get it moving."

Grace waited with bated breath as Karl completed the drone's final checks. The midsize device buzzed to life. Its rotors hummed, and it lifted smoothly, hovered for a moment, then zipped through the Martian docks. It flew low enough to disappear into the shadows.

Lisa monitored the drone's progress from the bridge. The display showed Karl guiding it through the narrow alleys. Its movements were deliberate, moving as though it was on a delivery.

"It's heading for Subsector 12 now," Lisa reported.

Jim leaned over Grace's shoulder, eyes locked on the screen. "What happens when it gets there?"

"Watch and learn."

The drone glided into the supply yard once its counterfeit credentials passed inspection. Inside, its sensors locked onto a stack of volatile barrels. The drone hovered briefly before emitting a high-pitched whine that simulated a malfunction. Moments later, a sharp explosion rippled outward and triggered chemical blasts that set half the yard aflame. Alarms howled across the docks.

"They're responding now," Lisa said, sounding relieved. "Dock Control just sealed three bays. Two dockhands injured. Fire crews are stretched thin. That chaos buys us more time."

Dock loudspeakers barked evacuation orders as fire crews scrambled. Patrol chatter spiked across open comms lockdowns, reroutes, panicked requests for backup.

Lisa glanced at her console. "Karl came through. They're tracking the drone's source back to Sector 28."

Jim's eyes softened with the smallest sign of relief. "Good. Now let's finish these repairs and be ready to move."

*****

In the drone bay, Karl leaned back, folding his hands behind his head with smug satisfaction. "Told you it would work."

Grace rolled her eyes as she hugged him. "I never doubted you for a second."

*****

The crew pushed through the night without rest. Their focus sharpened by the time Karl's trick had bought them. The

Federation still loomed nearby, but for the first time in days, the Argo had a sliver of breathing room.

The Argo's dim corridors stretched quietly as Jim walked toward engineering, his boots echoing against the floor. He had just left the bridge after confirming that the distraction was successful, but unease coiled his shoulders. The Federation's presence gnawed at his patience, and Gus's patchwork repairs weighed heavily on his mind.

Turning a corner, he nearly collided with Bucky, who was balancing a heavy crate of tools in his arms.

"Captain." Bucky shifted the crate. His casual tone didn't hide the concern in his eyes. "You look about as cheerful as a man on his way to the gallows."

"Funny, Bucky. How's engineering?"

Bucky lowered the crate. "Not bad. Karl's finishing diagnostics on ventilation and containment. Grace is checking the power core replenishment progress, but she's about two breaths from strangling Karl if he doesn't quit humming that tune of his."

"Keep them working. The Federation will eventually come to inspect the Argo."

"Understood. I'll make sure the crew stays sharp."

Before Jim could answer, a comm notification cut through the ship.

"Captain to the cargo bay," Lisa's voice called. "We've got company."

Jim's annoyance flickered across his face. He shot Bucky a glance, then the two of them moved quickly down the corridor toward the bay.

The threat from the patrol had passed for now; the cargo bay swarmed with activity when Jim and Bucky arrived. Mariana, returned from her hiding place inside the smuggling compartment, lingered near the back of the cargo bay. She kept to the shadows as her eyes were fixed on the two figures flanking a cargo container. One was Gus. The other was a tall, wiry man with a clean-shaven face and Federation-standard attire, far too polished for a man in the Martian underworld.

"Who's your friend, Gus?" Jim asked.

Gus turned and wiped his hands on his stained coveralls. "Relax, Captain. This here's a... business associate. He's not a friend to the Federation, Jim."

Jim studied the stranger. "A business associate who's a Federation officer. Gus, what are you thinking?"

The man raised his hands in mock surrender. "Name's Caldwell. I'm not here to cause trouble, Captain. Quite the opposite."

"Then start talking," Jim said, his tone cold.

Caldwell glanced at Gus, who gave a small nod. "I represent certain interests within the Federation. It isn't united as people think. Half want you dead, half need you alive. You've survived out in the belt when most would fold. That makes you valuable. My allies think we share an interest in disrupting Federation plans."

"Not sure I like the sound of that," Bucky said.

Caldwell's grin sharpened. "ScarJo-9, registry tail 4A-K77. Those types of favors don't come cheap Captain."

Jim folded his arms. "What exactly do you expect in return?"

"Information. We need intel on the Federation's activities on Ganymede specifically, Project Chimera," Caldwell said. "In return, I get you past Mars Control. I have a man inside who can open the hangar doors."

"What makes you think we have that information?"

"Your navigation system shows you've been researching the fastest routes to Ganymede," Caldwell said. "My employers have eyes everywhere, Captain."

"Then they should know we don't like being spied on. What's stopping me from throwing you off my ship right now?"

"If this traces back to me, I vanish into a tribunal hole. I have no choice. It's survival. You need Gus to complete repairs, and you need me to open those hangar doors, and I need information. We're connected, whether you like it or not."

"What if we refuse?" asked Grace.

Caldwell turned. "We're on the same side, Miss Hernandez."

Jim exchanged a glance with Bucky. "You're playing a dangerous game Caldwell. If your employers think we're pawns in someone else's agenda, I'm going to disappoint them."

"Think it over, Captain. You have more to gain from this partnership than you realize."

After Caldwell and Gus left, the crew gathered in a tight circle. The good vibes earned from the drone distraction had evaporated.

"That guy's a snake oil salesman," Bucky said. "We can't trust him."

Jim rubbed his temples. "Agreed. But we also can't afford to make an enemy of them right now. We're stuck between a rock and a hard place."

"The Federation's already hunting us. Getting involved with Caldwell's conspirators will draw more unwanted attention to us," said Mariana, her arms crossed.

Grace looked at Jim. "So, what do we do Captain?"

"We finish the repairs," said Jim. "We deliver Gus's crates. Then we leave Mars. Whatever Caldwell's plan, we have to play along for now. Caldwell is right about one thing. We need to know what's there on Ganymede if we're serious about stopping the Federation. Ganymede is where we'll find answers."

The crew scattered back to their stations. Their unease was clearly written on their faces. Jim lingered, staring at the spot where Caldwell had stood moments before. The man's words echoed in his mind. Even as they fought to survive, the Federation's web stretched farther than Jim could imagine.

␡␡␡␡␡

Jim's hands rested on the armrests of the captain's chair as he watched the live feed of the docks. Lisa had programmed a rotating surveillance pattern that tracked Federation patrol movements.

"They're sweeping Sectors 13 and 14 now," Lisa reported.

"Close, but we still have time," Jim said.

Grace was wiping her hands on a grease-stained rag as she entered. Her hair pulled into a messy bun; exhaustion was written all over her face. "Power core's stable. Dampeners back at ninety percent. We're almost ready for takeoff."

"Good," Jim replied. "What about life support?"

"Dr. Inoue and Dresden are running diagnostics," Grace said. "If we're lucky, no one will die of hypoxia on the way to Jupiter."

"Let's aim for better than lucky."

Grace let a weary smile escape. "I'll check my aim, Captain."

Down in the cargo bay, the air was thick with coolant and grease. Bucky and JT worked shoulder to shoulder to fasten the last restraints on Gus's smuggled crates inside the shuttle. The boxes looked harmless enough, marked with generic supply codes, but everyone knew their contents were anything but ordinary.

"You sure about this, Bucky?" JT asked as he cinched a strap tight. "What if Caldwell's playing us?"

Bucky gave him a sidelong look. "I'm sure he is. Doesn't change the fact that we need to make Gus happy, so he helps us get off Mars. Caldwell knows it, Gus knows it, and so do we."

"So, we just go along with it?"

"For now. That's called the long game, kid. You'll learn soon enough."

JT swallowed his retort and turned his focus back to the restraints. He didn't like it, but he trusted Bucky's unbreakable confidence more than his own doubts.

In the med bay, Dr. Inoue worked at a table lined with surgical instruments and vials. Her movements were brisk and exact as she prepped a field kit. Mariana sat nearby, quietly watching.

"You're awfully quiet," Raegan remarked without lifting her eyes from the kit.

Mariana raised her hands. "Just observing."

"Observing what?"

"Your setup is very efficient."

Raegan arched an eyebrow. "That supposed to be a compliment, or are you sizing me up for something?"

"Why not both?"

The ship's comm cut in with a crackle.

"Bridge to med bay," called Jim's voice. "Dr. Inoue, status update on the crew's vitals?"

Raegan tapped the console and scanned the readouts. "Everyone's stable, Captain. Tired, but holding."

"Good. Keep me posted," Jim replied before the line went dead.

"He makes everything sound so simple," said Mariana.

"It rarely is," Raegan muttered.

The crew's collective effort was paying off. The engineering deck thrummed as repaired systems came back online, the hull plating was sealed, and power relays were rebalanced. Jim moved from station to station to check on progress, offering steady words where he could.

By the time Jim returned to the bridge, the tension had eased slightly. Lisa was hunched at her console, her eyes on the dock surveillance feeds.

"Anything new?" Jim asked from behind her.

Lisa shook her head. "Karl's distraction bought us some breathing room. Still close, though."

"Keep watching. If the Feds so much as scratch their nose, I want to know."

"You'll know," Lisa said, her fingers zipping across her keys as she adjusted the sweep.

On the observation deck, the ship's quiet hum underpinned a rare calm. Bucky and Diane sat shoulder to shoulder. The glow of Mars' nightlife hung in the viewport.

"You're pushing yourself too hard," Diane said.

Bucky leaned back, his eyes on the void beyond the glass. "Comes with the territory."

"That doesn't mean you carry it all by yourself." She rested her hand on his arm. "You don't have to do this alone."

He turned to her, his usual bravado tempered. "I know I can count on you, Diane. I'm grateful for that. But right now, there's too much at stake to slow down. We need to launch before they find us."

"Then promise me we'll take a vacation when this is over."

"I promise." Bucky's grin had a crooked edge. "We'll have a candlelight dinner, watch old movies, and then—"

"Don't you dare," Diane warned as she punched his arm. Then she kissed him.

The Argo exhaled into a fragile calm. Repairs were nearly finished. The threat of discovery had eased but worry of capture pressed on everyone.

Jim stood alone on the bridge. He gazed at the Martian docks through the viewscreen. The stars beyond twinkled, impossibly far and yet so close.

"Almost there," he murmured. Jim had a sinking sense Mars still had unfinished business with them.

08
CHAPTER

GONE WITH THE WIND

The southern docks swarmed with bodies, creating an intricate web of organized chaos. Neon lights fractured across dented steel, and the distant hum of freighters docking and departing provided an ominous score. The air inside the cargo bay was full of anxiety, the kind that crept under the skin and refused to let go.

Jim stood on a raised platform and scanned the turmoil below. His crew worked tirelessly as the direness of their situation grew with every passing second.

"Captain," Bucky's voice crackled over the comms, snapping Jim's focus from the scene below. "We've got a situation topside. Federation patrols are closing in."

Jim gripped the railing. "How close?"

"They're wrapping up Sectors 14 and 15," Bucky replied. Gus just sent word that they're getting rough with anyone who resists. Not good."

Jim eyed the sparking conduit. "How long?" Sweat ran down Grace's temple as she tightened connections on the auxiliary systems.

"How much time?" Jim asked.

"Four hours unless you like radiation chic," Grace said, not looking up.

"We don't have four hours." Jim keyed the comms. "Liam, does Gus have the drop-off coordinates for his client?"

"Gus just sent the location," Liam answered, late as always. "He's stalling the Feds for us, laying it on thick."

Jim's mind raced. The smuggling job had been a necessary evil to secure the parts and repairs they needed, but now it was turning into a game of time. If the contraband was found on board, there'd be no talking their way out. Arrest would be immediate.

"Bucky," Jim said. "Prep the shuttle in the bay. Take Liam and JT, make the delivery, and stay under the Federation's radar.

We're departing as soon as you get back. The patrols will be all over an unauthorized shuttle landing."

"Understood," Bucky replied.

Jim spotted JT securing straps on a line of crates near the shuttle. "James," he called. When the boy looked up, Jim motioned him over. "You're with Bucky and Liam on this run. Follow their lead, every order. Am I clear, Crew Member Eckhart."

JT tried to mask his grin, but excitement lit his face. "Yes, sir, Captain!"

Bucky entered moments later, his usual swagger stripped away. He clapped JT's shoulder as he passed. "Stay close, kid. You've done it once. The second time's easier."

The shuttle loomed in the corner, its matte-black hull merging with the shadows. As Bucky, Liam, and JT boarded, Jim turned back to Grace. "There's no way to hide their return without being spotted. The patrols will swarm an unauthorized landing. We launch the second they hit the ramp."

Grace wiped her forehead with the back of her hand. "We're cutting it close. Critical systems are online. No guarantees past that."

"Thanks, Grace. We're counting on you."

Above the docks, Federation patrols moved with clinical precision, their vessels casting long shadows over the bustling marketplace. Gus, smooth as ever, stood at the Sector 16

causeway and inspected a stack of crates while two officers questioned him. His face showed no fear, only the practiced neutrality of a man who lived by his wits.

"We've had reports of unauthorized cargo being transported through this sector, Gus. Fugitives from the Federation," one officer accused. "The reports also stated that you and Caldwell were tied to stolen Federation contraband."

Gus shrugged and spread his hands in a show of innocence. "Nothing unusual around here. Just another day at the docks. My business stays clean, Officer. You can inspect anything you like."

Suspicion hardened the officer's stance. "We will. If there's contraband, don't think we won't find it."

As they turned toward the crates, Gus flicked his wrist to activate his comm. "Captain, move fast. The Feds are sniffing around Caldwell's cruiser. We tipped them off about contraband there, so they'll tear it apart, but once they figure out that it's a bogus tip, they'll be pissed, and you're coming up soon."

"Understood," said Jim. "Bucky's team is already on the drop. Keep them distracted while we slip the shuttle around their patrol."

"They'd better succeed, Jim," Gus replied. "Otherwise, we all end up in a Federation penal colony deep in the belt."

The channel cut, leaving only the rising hum of the docks and the weight of time running out.

Inside the shuttle, JT adjusted his harness with deliberate care. He felt steadier than he had during his last away mission. Liam sat across from him, calm and resolute. Bucky occupied the pilot's seat. He ran through pre-flight checks with practiced ease.

"You good, kid?" Bucky asked without turning.

"You betcha," JT said. "Ready to get this done."

Liam leaned forward slightly. "Just like last time. We get in, make the drop, and get out. No improvising. No hero stuff."

"Got it," said JT.

Bucky powered up the shuttle's internal systems. "All right, fellas. They're pushing us past the patrol, then we lift off. The minute we're square with Gus and Caldwell, we're off this rock."

Behind the shuttle, the crew heaved in sync, steering the shuttle resting on top of a maglev transport toward Sector 17. They timed their movements with Gus's distraction to slip past the Federation patrol. Gus counted them down on comms. Caldwell spooled his cruiser's impulse coils. A moment before the shuttle took off, the flare cooked local thermals, and sensors temporarily overloaded. Bucky flew on muscle memory as they ran dark past the patrol.

Jim watched from the platform as the shuttle disappeared into the shadows. Pride and unease battled inside his mind.

"Looks like it worked," Jim muttered. "Godspeed." He turned back to the task at hand.

The shuttle slipped through the docks, its matte hull blending with the neon-lit shadows. Bucky guided it with calm precision. He alternated between screens to ensure they weren't being followed. The thrusters filled the cramped cabin with their steady whine, broken only by the occasional crackle of the comms.

Liam scanned the area, his voice low. "Hopefully Gus's contact doesn't bring a welcoming party this time."

"Let's not stick around long enough to find out," Bucky replied. He glanced back at JT. "Keep the comms scanner hot. Tell us the second someones' on to us."

JT nodded, his fingers poised over the console. Determination edged past his nerves as the grid pulsed across the display.

"This subsector is a mess of alleys and blind corners," JT muttered. "How does anyone find anything here?"

"They don't," said Liam. "That's the point."

The drop point came into view: a narrow alley squeezed between towering stacks of containers. The overhead lamps stuttered, pulling laddered shadows up the ribbed walls. Bucky switched to backup lights that threw twenty feet of clarity ahead and behind the shuttle while the rest of the alley sank into darkness.

"We're asking to get mugged landing here," JT said.

"Smugglers don't work in the open, kid. Speed is what keeps you from getting arrested." Bucky eased the shuttle down. "That means all hands on these crates. Grab one and stick close." He cut the engines. The silence settled around them. "Stay alert. We don't know who's waiting."

The ramp lowered with a hiss. Cold, metallic air swept in from the sector. Bucky stepped out first, wearing his trench coat. He moved with precision. Liam followed, his hand close to his holstered sidearm. JT trailed. His eyes were wide as he tried to take in everything at once.

A lone figure emerged from the shadows. His jacket was weathered, and his cap was pulled low, but his sharp gaze betrayed a man who trusted no one.

"Let's move this quick before someone notices," he said. His voice was all gravel.

"That's the plan," Bucky answered. "Got the payment?"

The man jerked his chin toward a steel door. "Payment's right here, if you've got the four crates Gus promised. Drop them just inside the door here."

He pulled a case from his jacket and tossed it to Bucky, who caught it with ease. A faint glow lit his face when he cracked it open before snapping it shut again.

"JT, Liam, let's unload," Bucky ordered.

JT hesitated for only a second before he stepped forward. He hefted a crate, his muscles straining, and carried it to the door. Liam and Bucky joined him. Each moved with clipped efficiency. One by one the crates disappeared into the ware-house, until JT returned with the last and stacked it inside.

"Pleasure doing business," the man said. "If I were you, I'd move fast. Federation patrols are crawling through this sector. They're hunting some renegade science officer. Must know something she shouldn't."

"We've heard the rumors. Don't worry about us. Worry about yourself," Liam snapped. He turned on his heel, heading up the ramp with JT close behind.

Off in the distance, small lights began to flicker.

"We've got company," said Bucky. "Those are rifle-mounted flashlights coming down the alley."

"Federation?" JT asked.

"Who cares," Liam replied as he drew his sidearm. "Let's not stay long enough to find out."

The crew prepared to launch in record time. Bucky slapped the control panel, and the ramp sealed with a hiss. "Strap in," he barked as he sprinted toward the cockpit.

JT barely made it into his seat before the shuttle roared upward, its engines thundering to life. The narrow alley sank below them as Bucky hauled the vessel into open air. The glow of the docks shrank below.

"These aren't just security drones," Liam warned, eyes locked on the scanner. "There's a Federation patrol ten klicks out, and they're gaining."

"Not for long." Bucky's hands moved across the controls. "Hold on."

The shuttle banked hard left and skimmed close to a towering stack of containers. The pile toppled with a thunderous crash. JT clutched the edge of his seat. His stomach lurched as the vessel threaded the labyrinth of the Southern Sector's streets.

"They're closing fast," Liam said. "Two signatures on our tail."

"JT, take the turret!" Bucky ordered. "Liam, plot us a course out of here. Find us some cover. Pick something that doesn't get us killed. I'll keep us airborne."

JT scrambled to the rear. His hands shook as he dropped into the turret seat. The controls felt alien, but he forced himself to focus. He steadied his breathing while adrenaline surged through him.

"Got a lock. They're closing," JT said, his voice firmer now.

"Targeting jitter," JT muttered. He killed the auto-assist, thumbed to manual. "I've got it." He squeezed the trigger. The turret flared, lighting the darkness in violent bursts. One of the pursuing patrol ships swerved, but the second pressed closer. Plasma cannons spit fire that streaked past the shuttle's hull.

"Anytime now, Liam," Bucky growled as he pushed the shuttle dangerously close to the merchant canopies. The blast of their thrusters ripped several canopies apart.

"Dock Control flagged them on open channels. Fines queued, citations confirmed. But it bought them precious seconds."

"Working on it," Liam shot back. "There's a maintenance tunnel half a klick ahead. Let's dare them to follow us inside. They'll be ducks in a barrel."

"That tunnel is extremely tight. What about us?" Bucky quacked.

"JT handled the transport tunnels on our last run," Liam fired back. "Afraid we'll find out he's a better pilot than you?"

Bucky pretended to clutch his chest as if Liam's jab had hit home, "JT, be ready. This is gonna be a shoot-out in a phone booth." He adjusted their course and angled the shuttle for the tunnel entrance. JT kept firing, with a quizzical look on his face, scattering the formation before they regrouped.

"Brace yourselves," Bucky called as the shuttle plunged into the tunnel. The walls blurred in a dizzying rush. The tight confines left no margin for error. The ships followed pursuit into the tunnel as their pilots moved to single file to fit the entrance.

"Come on," JT muttered, his finger tight on the trigger.

The lead ship entered the tunnel, plasma fire striking the cargo bay. JT's next shot clipped its engine, slamming it into the tunnel wall. The impact turned the ship into a fireball that flooded the tunnel. The trailing ship was unable to stop before crashing into the wreckage.

"Nice shot, kid," Bucky said at last. "That was an impossible shot."

JT exhaled, the tension draining from his shoulders. "All those mission-sim hours finally paid off."

Liam said, "Thermals show a void mid-span. We slingshot off that pressure vent on exit. Marking it."

The shuttle burst out of the far side of the tunnel and climbed into open air again. Neon advertisements washed the skyline in lurid color. Liam leaned back. Relief flickered across his face.

"We're clear," he said. "For now."

"Let's not test that theory," Bucky replied. He set a course for the Argo. "Good work, team."

As the shuttle streaked away, JT felt like one of them at last. He no longer felt like he was an anchor. He actually made a difference. His pride swelled, and a tear slid down his cheek. He wiped it away quickly, hoping neither Bucky nor Liam noticed. But both men were too busy scanning for patrols.

*****

The shuttle docked with a loud thunk as hydraulics lowered the hatch. The team moved briskly. JT stepped off first, his shoulders squared, his smile unshakable. Bucky scanned the bay for danger as the cargo doors sealed behind them.

"That was close," JT muttered.

"Welcome to the big leagues," Bucky answered, clapping his shoulder. "You kept calm and made the shot when it mattered. Your dad would be proud."

"Let's get the Argo ready for departure." Liam gestured toward the crates. "We don't stop until we're ready to launch."

"Great job, team. Uneventful, I hope?" Jim's voice came through the comms.

"Just another day in the office," Bucky answered.

"Federation patrols will be here soon. Get moving."

"On it, Captain," Bucky said. He signaled the deck crew to hustle.

▚▚▚▚▚

Supply crates slid onto mag-lev loaders and vanished into the secure storage bays.

Moments later Jim entered, his face carved in stone. He scanned the bay, assessing every detail. Satisfied, he gave a nod. "We launch in ten minutes. Grace, status report."

Her voice came through the intercom. "Main systems online. Dampeners stable. Gravity assist system passed diagnostics run. Stabilizers secure. Power core topped off. Containment sealed. She's ready to take us to Jupiter and back."

"That's as good as it will get." Jim turned to Bucky, who was directing the final preparations. "Are we clear on the delivery job for Gus?"

Bucky paused before saying, "He's satisfied. Gus nearly danced and was gone with the Martian wind the moment after. We never got the full rundown on those crates, and that's probably for the best. We're square with Gus, and Caldwell's happy too. He promised he'll get us out of the hangar and past the Feds."

"If he's genuine, his contacts should authorize our launch credentials and make sure the hangar doors are open when we lift off. We'll need to time it perfectly. They won't keep those doors open long."

As the crew performed final checks for launch, an alarm shrieked through the cargo bay.

Lisa activated the ship-wide comms. "Captain, we've got trouble. A Federation patrol spotted the shuttle docking with the Argo. Three minutes to the cargo bay airlocks are secured."

A wave of dread swept through the bay.

Jim tapped his comm. "Lisa, broadcast our credentials to Mars control and prep for immediate launch. I want full thrust the moment we clear the hangar doors."

"Understood, Captain," Lisa replied.

Jim turned back to the crew and spoke. "Engage."

The Argo's thrusters powered up with authority, and vibrations shook the deck plates. Jim strode onto the bridge. His presence was commanding while he dropped into the captain's chair. The viewscreen showed the sprawling Martian docks, a tangle of ships and scaffolding bathed in artificial light. Federation patrol ships overhead scanning the docks. Their searchlights stabbed through the haze.

Hunched at the navigation console, Lisa kept her eyes on the readouts. "A patrol is closing fast. They're moving to block our departure. If we don't launch in sixty seconds, they'll pin us down."

"Then we won't give them the chance," Jim said. "Grace, how's the engine room?"

"Engines online," Grace answered over the comms.

"We launch hard, finesse later." Jim replied. "Lisa, take us out."

"Impulse engines increased to fifty percent, Captain," Lisa announced.

The patrol ships repositioned and tightened their net, but the Argo surged forward, slipping past a split second before it closed. The patrol ships lost distance as they course corrected.

"Keep us steady until we clear the doors. Let's not give them extra cause for suspicion," Jim ordered.

The southern hangar doors groaned open to reveal the red-orange Martian sky. Patrol vessels loomed far off. Their lights cut through the dust.

"I'll be damned," Jim muttered. "Caldwell pulled it off."

The Argo eased forward. Thrusters rumbled as they crawled toward the sky. Outside the domes, Federation patrols shifted position. Their movements were calculated and deliberate.

Lisa warned. "They're hailing."

"Send the ScarJo-9 launch credentials," Jim said. "Stealth on standby for post clearance and prep evasive maneuvers."

The Argo roared through the widening gap in the hangar doors. Acceleration pressed the crew into their seats. The hull groaned as the ship clawed its way into the Martian atmosphere.

On the observation deck, JT gazed at the shrinking domes of Mars. The sight both thrilled and unnerved him.

"Federation ship locking onto us," Lisa reported. "They've corrected course to intercept."

"They've deployed drones," she added. "Four of them, armed and fast."

"Bucky, get to the turrets," Jim ordered over the comms. "James, go with him. Grace, keep a tight watch on the engines. Report any power fluctuations."

The crew scattered into motion. Bucky and JT reached the weapons station and activated the controls. Plasma fire raked the starboard fin. Warning klaxons stabbed the air. "Sensor B just went blind," Lisa snapped.

"Rerouting," Grace said.

"Ever run one of these?" Bucky asked, flicking switches.

"Only on the shuttle," JT admitted.

"Lead by a length. Breathe, now relax, and you're ready."

The Federation drones closed in on the Argo. Their sleek frames sliced through the thin Martian atmosphere. The Argo banked sharply to the left as it accelerated and narrowly avoided a volley of plasma fire.

Inside the weapons station, JT clutched the turret controls. His eyes were fixed on the targeting display. "Got one in my sights." His finger rested above the trigger.

"Then fire, kid," Bucky ordered. His own turret fired in rapid bursts.

JT fired. The energy blast streaked across the sky and tore into the nearest drone. It erupted in a burst of flame, sending shards scattering in every direction. A brief cheer came through the comms, but it ended abruptly.

"Three more inbound," Lisa warned. "They're closing fast."

"That's what they're designed for," Bucky muttered, squeezing off another round. His shot clipped a drone's wing and sent it spiraling out of control.

As the Argo climbed higher, the atmosphere gave way to the cold expanse of space. Federation patrol vessels lingered far behind. Their pursuit faltered as the Argo's thrusters roared. The stealth systems engaged, masking their telemetry and preventing a lock.

"We're almost clear. By the time they adjust and match our speed, we'll be out of range," Lisa said.

JT tracked another drone and fired again. His blasts struck the mark and sent the target into a death spiral. The last drone fell back, too far away to engage or strike effectively. A collective exhale rippled through the crew as the scanner cleared.

"Good shooting, both of you," Jim said. "Now focus on putting distance between us and them. We're not clear until we pass the Mars stations."

The bridge grew quiet. The only sound came from the ship's environmental systems as it adjusted to the coldness of space. Jim leaned back in his chair. The tension in his shoulders eased only slightly. The escape had been too close, and the weight of his choices pressed harder than ever.

"Status report," he said.

Lisa glanced up from her console. Her hands moved over the controls with speed and precision. "We've cleared Mars airspace. Stealth systems engaged. Course locked for the asteroid belt. No immediate threats, Captain."

"Your debt's been noted, Captain," Caldwell crackled over the comms. "Get us the data on Project Chimera and we'll call it even."

"I know what the deal is, Caldwell, we'll contact you from Ganymede." Jim turned to Grace, who stood at the engineering console near the rear of the bridge. "Engines holding?"

"Better than expected. Gus really came through," Grace answered. "But the stabilizers need to be replaced, not overhauled at some point. The stress from departure caused minor damage to life support and gravity assist. A repair team is already on it."

Jim nodded. "Good idea to keep the crew working. Idle hands are no use. We need the Argo in top form when we reach the belt."

"Already in motion," Grace said as she turned to leave. "But don't expect another miracle. You've already maxed your quota."

"Captain," Mariana's voice broke in, "we should keep stealth protocols active all the way to the belt. Patrols could still be nearby."

"Agreed. Lisa, alter our course every four hours. I don't want them predicting our heading. Grace, I need a full systems report within the hour."

The Argo pressed forward. Its path was lit faintly by the distant glow of Jupiter magnified on the viewscreen. The danger was ever present, but for the moment, they had managed to slip past their nemesis. Still, Jim knew the reality was that they were outlaws from the system. It was kill or be killed.

The crew gathered in the mess hall, still buzzing from their narrow escape. "What's our heading, Jim?" Grace asked, arms crossed.

"Toward the belt for now," Jim said. "Once we clear the belt, we press on to Ganymede. That's our only lead to find the answers we need to unravel this mystery of Project Chimera."

Mariana tapped the memory device. "If I can crack this encryption, maybe we can find something we can use against the Federation."

Jim gave a curt nod. "Then that's our next step. Back to work."

The crew gathered in the mess hall, still buzzing from their narrow escape. "What's our heading, Jim?" Grace asked, arms crossed.

Jim stood alone at the viewport. The stars stretching endlessly before him.... It was full of dangers already faced and possibilities not yet named. The door hissed open behind him, but he didn't turn.

Grace stepped inside. "You should be resting."

"So should you."

Grace joined him at the glass. She studied the stars before speaking. "The crew is holding together as well as can be expected but they're scared."

"We're all scared, Grace. Even me."

"We believe in you, Jim, even when you doubt yourself."

He exhaled. "Thanks, Grace."

"Don't thank me yet. You've still got time to muck it up."

They went quiet. The space between them closed. The stars were the only witness to their embrace as they readied themselves for what lay ahead.

The Argo's thrusters pulsed with an even rhythm while the ship settled into the stillness of deep space. The strain of escape was replaced by uneasy calm. On the bridge, the crew moved deliberately, but their thoughts wandered toward the future.

Sitting in the captain's chair, Jim's hands gripped the armrests as he studied the navigation display. The asteroid belt loomed ahead. It was a restless field of rock and ice that promised both shelter and peril. It would be their first shield from pursuit.

The mess hall buzzed with the rare sound of laughter. The crew, frayed by weeks of tension, reveled in the comfort of familiar walls and banter.

Bucky leaned back in his chair, his boots planted on the table, much to Grace's annoyance. "Well, Mars was fun," he drawled. "What's Jim got planned next? A joyride through the asteroid belt, dodging raiders with the Feds at our heels?"

"Don't encourage Jim's lunacy," Raegan said as she stirred her tea. "We've had enough excitement for three lifetimes."

JT looked up from his plate. "What's the plan once we're in the belt? Do we hide forever?"

"Not forever." Mariana sat opposite him. Her eyes were locked onto his. "The belt buys time, nothing more. The Federation won't stop until we're all captured."

Grace leaned forward. "What about the device? We risked everything for that data. It better be worth it, or we'll have nothing to show for all those risks we took."

Mariana noticed Jim stepping inside. "I've only been able to partially decrypt it," she admitted. "From what I see, it holds details on the Federation's mining operations involving the organic compound. But there's more. Something hidden."

"Like what?" Bucky asked. His boots thudded to the floor.

"I don't know. But whatever it is, they'll kill to keep it secret." She paused. "Captain, the file name was 'For Mariana.' Someone meant for me to find it."

The room fell silent. As Jim moved to the head of the table, his presence commanded attention.

"Whatever the device holds, whoever left it, it's our only chance to uncover the Federation's plans. For now, we focus on getting through the belt. That's all. Back to work."

⟋⟋⟋⟋⟋

Jim and Grace stood together as the shifting rocks of the asteroid belt drifted past the viewport. The Argo glided through an empty corridor, but the asteroid belt pressed ever closer.

"You're pushing them hard." Grace sounded concerned.

"The work keeps them focused," Jim replied. "It stops them from dwelling on the situation."

"They're not invincible. Neither are you."

Jim turned to face her. "They need to think I am. If I falter, they lose faith. Without that faith, we don't stand a chance."

"Just remember that they have limits. They're tired, even if they won't show it. You're tired too. I can see it in your eyes."

"I just don't have the luxury to be tired. Not now."

⟋⟋⟋⟋⟋

In the crew quarters, Bucky and Liam faced each other in a makeshift poker game. The small table between them overflowed with ration packs and mismatched poker chips. JT sat close by, looking amused and fascinated.

"You're bluffing again." Liam's eyes narrowed as he tried to read Bucky.

Bucky shoved every ration pack he had into the pile. "Am I? Call me and see."

JT leaned forward, curious. "What happens next?"

"Depends." Liam answered without looking away from his opponent. "If I call and he takes me down, he gets my lunch for the whole week. If I fold now, he only gets bragging rights until tomorrow."

"What if you win?"

"Bucky takes my shifts in maintenance for a week," Liam said.

"I call," Liam announced as he slid his last few chips and ration packs into the pot.

The tension climbed as Bucky flipped his cards onto the table to reveal a full house. "Looks like I'll be eating well." He laughed. He reached for the pile and then tossed a packet to JT. "Here, kid. Freeze-dried banana split, courtesy of Chief Power."

Their laughter echoed off the metal walls. JT let it wash over him. The darkness around them remained, but in that moment, the crew bathed in a sliver of warmth.

At the edge of the asteroid belt, the crew manned their stations. Their eyes were fixed on the viewscreen as massive rocks drifted closer. The Argo loomed against the threshold. It was a fragile speck poised to enter a shifting sea of stone and dust.

"Everyone ready?" he asked over the comms.

"Ready as we'll ever be," Lisa replied from navigation.

"Lock our course," Jim ordered.

Lisa's hands moved expertly, and the ship's path lit up across the display. The Argo surged forward as they plunged past the outer rim of drifting giants. Its steel frame stalwart as it entered the maze of uncertainty. The crew braced themselves, all aware that survival depended on precision, courage, and lots of luck. They were pressing deeper into the Federation's web, and none of them pretended otherwise.

Jupiter's faint glow crept up the glass. Jim set a palm to the rail. "Project Chimera, Ganymede. And the end of running."

DANCING WITH THE STARS

The *Argo* moved through the asteroid belt at cruising speed. The sprawling field of tumbling rock stretched in every direction. Some asteroids were the size of tall buildings, and a few were large enough to swallow cities. The ship's external lights struck the jagged surfaces to create an eerie shimmer that shifted with each rotation. Inside the bridge, the crew was focused.

"Midpoint of the belt, Captain," Lisa announced. She fine-tuned their trajectory with deft movements.

The belt's twisting corridors and hidden hazards made this one of the most dangerous regions to navigate. "Good. Be prepared," he said.

"Always am, Captain." Lisa adjusted the course with practiced precision.

Karl broke in over comms. "Drones in position. Scans coming through now, Captain."

"Good work, Karl," Jim said. "Patch to nav."

The main display rendered a live map. Hazards flagged, marking a safe corridor pulsing ahead.

"We've got a path opening ahead," Lisa said. "We can slip past this cluster and avoid any major impacts."

"Do it." Jim looked toward engineering. "Grace, how is Engineering?"

"Engines steady, but let's skip the stunt flying today, Jim."

"Noted." Jim glanced at Lisa. "We'll keep out of harm's way."

At the rear of the bridge, JT leaned against the bulkhead, his arms crossed and his face betraying a mix of awe and nerves. The asteroid belt had always fascinated him. As a kid, he had heard the stories of city-sized asteroids hurtling endlessly through space, fragments of a world that never formed. Seeing them up close always left him speechless.

"Hey, kid," Bucky said as he entered the bridge.

JT tried to sound confident. "Hi, Commander."

Bucky dropped into a chair. "After me, Lisa's the best naviga-tor on Mars. But ask her, and she'll say in the system."

Lisa smirked. "Nice to know someone in here notices talent when they see it."

The bridge laughter died as the console tone cut sharp through the air.

"Captain, we've got a problem," said Karl.

Jim straightened. "Report."

"One of the drones picked up an unregistered vessel that course corrected. Decommissioned ships don't course cor-rect."

"Then it's probably a raider scout," said Jim, his eyes nar-rowed.

Bucky shrugged. "So much for good luck. We've gone weeks without a mishap. Guess the belt wanted to shake things up."

"Options?" Jim asked.

Lisa studied the holographic map, her brow furrowed. "We can alter course and try to shake them. It'll take us deeper into the belt, but it adds a week to the journey."

"What if we stay on course?" JT asked.

"If we don't, they'll call in reinforcements," Lisa said. "If a raider fleet is nearby, they'll chase us down. We can't outrun them."

Jim weighed the options for a moment. "Lisa, change course. Karl, send the compromised drone away from our heading.

Let's not lead them back to us. Keep the others in formation, scanning ahead. Report any signal the moment it shows."

"Yes, Captain." Lisa adjusted the nav controls.

"On it," Karl confirmed, his fingers already rewriting the drone's orders.

The Argo shifted course as its side thrusters fired in short bursts. Lisa threaded the ship deeper into the asteroid maze. Six massive bodies drifted in slow rotation. Their shadows blotted out the sun as she steered through the gap with practiced control.

The only sounds were the random pings of sensors updating and Lisa's quiet comments to herself. Jim kept his eyes locked on the display, while Bucky leaned back. His casual posture was undercut by the gravity of the moment.

"Have you ever been this deep in the belt before?" JT asked at last.

Bucky glanced at him as if recalling an old tale. "Once or twice. It's not my favorite place to be. Too many ways to die out here with no one around to help, at least not before we all starve."

JT's gaze returned to the viewscreen. The asteroid belt stretched outward, a vast expanse of chaotic beauty. For all its danger, it had a mesmerizing allure.

The Argo jolted without warning. JT spotted it first. "Starboard collision in three!"

Lisa yanked the controls, saving them from a direct hit. Even so, a glancing blow sent a shudder through the deck.

"Minor impact clipped the starboard hull. No structural damage," Lisa reported.

"Nothing to worry about!" Jim barked. "Keep us on course."

The crew resumed their duties while the Argo pressed deeper into the belt. The signal Karl had flagged was long past, and there were no threats visible on the scanners.

"Nav settings updated. Two weeks to clear the belt," Karl said.

"Good work. Lisa, set the course."

The ship's frame thrummed as micro-impacts ticked the hull, like dry rain on tin. A proximity tone chirped; inertial dampeners lagging half a heartbeat before correcting.

The darkness thickened as they neared the outer rim of the belt. Colossal rocks drifted in lazy rotation. Their craggy faces caught faint flashes of light from the distant sun.

"Any signs of activity?" Jim asked. His eyes locked onto the holographic map above her console.

"Scans show metallic debris consistent with a ship destroyed in battle off the starboard bow."

"That means raiders have a base of operations somewhere nearby." The captain turned toward Liam at tactical. "Chief Power, bring weapons online and raise shields. I want them ready if we need them."

"Aye, Captain." Liam's hands moved with expert efficiency as power redirected to the Argo's defenses. The deck plates trembled slightly under the load.

At the secondary console, JT squinted at the sensor readouts. He stayed silent, but the rapid tapping of his fingers on the panel spoke to his nerves.

Bucky leaned against a bulkhead, his posture casual. "This stretch has a reputation. Some say it swallows ships whole. Crews wander in and never come out. Like the Bermuda Triangle back on Earth."

"Not helping," Grace snapped. Her focus was fixed on the engineering readouts.

Bucky leaned closer, his voice lower. "If we disappear in here, no one ever hears the truth about Project Chimera."

Lisa rolled her eyes. "Keep talking and you're going to disappear from the bridge."

The crew chuckled. Jim allowed the moment, but it vanished when Karl's urgent voice cut through.

"Captain, drones picked up movement. Three signatures, closing fast."

"Raiders?" Jim asked, though he already knew the answer.

"Almost certainly," Karl said. "Light scouts. Fast, armed, and approaching from both port and starboard. If we don't outrun them, they'll either disable us and board or slap a tracker on us so their flagship can finish the job. If they're this far in, they're hunting more than cargo. They're chasing the same secrets we are."

"Red alert. Lock down in thirty seconds!" Jim commanded.

The lights dimmed and crimson strobes flashed through the corridors.

"Lisa, evasive maneuvers. Liam, turrets online. Karl, can the mini-drones intercept?"

"Already deploying," Karl said.

Outside, flares burst from the Argo's hull, scattering into the void. Mini-drones streaked among them. Each one broadcasting the Argo's signal and wired to detonate on contact. Two raider scouts peeled off, avoiding the false targets. The third kept its course, locked onto the real ship.

"One ship still tracking," Lisa reported as she threaded the Argo between massive rocks. "They've locked onto us."

"Liam, fire as soon as they're in range," Jim ordered. "No more trackers planted on our hull."

The rear turret roared and spit streaks of energy into the dark. The raider scout danced behind a drifting asteroid, using the rock as cover. Liam cursed as his shots went wide.

"They're good," Liam growled. "But not good enough. Time for them to feel the Power."

Jim allowed himself a thin smirk. "Any excuse to use that phrase. Cut them down, Power Bucky, get to the secondary turret and box them in."

Bucky bolted from the bridge. His boots pounded the deck as he sprinted to the weapons station. Moments later his voice came through the comms.

"Secondary turret hot, Captain. Give me a target."

"Lisa, slow the starboard engine and swing us around. Line Bucky up for a clean shot."

The Argo banked hard. The maneuver slammed the crew into their seats. JT clutched the console as the raider ship appeared on the viewscreen.

"Bucky, now!" Jim shouted.

The turret fired, its blasts cutting through the void. The raider tried to evade, but Bucky's aim struck true. A direct hit tore through the main hull, causing the ship to spin out of control. Internal explosions lit the dark before the wreck vanished into the shadows of the belt.

"Got 'em!" Bucky crowed over comms.

Cheers burst across the comm, but the triumph lasted only seconds.

"Two more ships closing from port stern," Lisa announced. The Argo shook under a barrage of plasma fire. "They didn't like losing their friend."

"Shields?" Jim asked.

"Holding, but at fifty percent," Grace replied.

"Lisa, give me an exit path. Karl, what about the drones?"

"Nothing online that can make a difference," Karl said. "Our only option is to fly our way out."

"Then we fly our way out." Jim pounded his fist into his knee. "Grace, send every spare watt to the engines. Lisa, take us through that cluster ahead," he said, pointing at the holo display. "Let's see if these raiders are bold enough to follow."

"Bold enough, or stupid enough," Grace muttered.

The Argo surged forward. Asteroids of every shape filled the viewscreen as the ship wove through them with uncanny precision. Raiders kept pace; missile trails glowed white across the darkness. Their warheads impacted against an asteroid as they continued firing, nearly striking the Argo's hull before Liam and Bucky's turrets cut the enemy formation apart.

"They're dropping formation." There was excitement in Lisa's voice. "If we push through this next gap, we can shake them."

"Punch it, Lisa. Like we got credits on the line." Jim commanded.

The thrusters flared, and the ship shot forward, skimming within meters of an asteroids' surface. The raiders scattered in confusion. One broke contact and vanished into the belt. The other, unwilling to attack alone, sent a broadcast most likely to the nearby raider armada, and it pulled away to regroup.

"They're gone. At least for now," Lisa reported. "That transmission will bring more unwanted attention here."

"Good work, everyone," Jim said, exhaling. "Grace, run a full diagnostic and give me the power core readings at once. Lisa, plot our course to Ganymede, let's skirt the Trojan Belt for cover. And thank you, all of you. That was calm under fire, the mark of a crew worth its steel."

"That's how the Argo flies, Captain," Bucky boasted.

The ship cleared the last of the belt. Jupiter's vast storms filled the horizon.

"Jupiter," JT whispered, eyes wide as the planet swelled on the screen. The storms churned like living oceans, dwarfing even their impossible victories. "It's incredible."

Jim stepped up beside his son. "It's beautiful, James." His voice faltered. "I don't say it enough, but I'm proud of you. I love you more than you know."

JT hugged him tight, his hero in his arms. "I love you too, Dad."

The crew let out a collective sigh of relief. The belt lay behind them; the unknown stretched ahead.

※※※※※

For weeks, the Argo pushed through the black. Its scarred hull was a testament to the fight they had survived. Jupiter dominated the viewscreen, swelling larger with every passing day, a giant alive with storms and secrets.

"Status," Jim said, arms crossed as he stood on the bridge. He stared at the giant planet, his posture steady for the sake of the crew.

"Engines are optimal," Grace replied from engineering. "But to be sure we make it back to Mars, I'm easing the load, routing power back to internal systems."

"Do it," Jim said. "Lisa, course?"

"Course set," she said without looking up. "Ganymede via skirting the Trojan Belt to avoid detection. Four weeks to arrival."

Jim's brow furrowed. He turned to Liam. "Long-range scans?"

"Nothing out there," Liam said flatly. "Empty space."

"Stay sharp. Bucky, crew morale?"

Bucky leaned against the bulkhead. "They're tired, cranky, and hungry for real food, but still holding. Miners don't break easy."

"Good. Keep them that way. We'll need everyone sharp when we reach Ganymede."

At the rear console, JT stood silent, arms folded. His thoughts raced. His mind was filled with images of raider fire and near death.

"You're quiet, JT," Bucky said. "That's not you."

"Just thinking."

"That's a bad habit to get into."

Lisa chuckled.

JT's eyes narrowed. "I'm serious. This crew is risking everything. And for what? A long shot at survival, just to get crushed by the Federation?"

Jim spun. "That's exactly what we're risking it for, James. A shot at success, a future free from the Federation's tyranny. We need leverage to balance the scales. Without it, they'll arrest us on sight, and their plans will move forward unchecked."

"What if it's not enough?" JT's voice rose. "What if we're outnumbered, outgunned, and outmaneuvered every time?

We can't keep counting on a miracle at the last second. When do we stop and admit this is beyond us?"

The bridge fell silent.

Jim studied him for a long moment before answering. "The Federation will erase us on site to keep their crimes hidden. There's no surrender, and we can't hide forever. We have to reach Ganymede to expose their plans. We have no choice."

JT nodded, his eyes down.

Bucky flicked his ear. "Don't worry, kid. Your dad's got a solid plan. It'll hold."

"Captain, this is Diane. I've finished reviewing the geo-sensor data. You'll want to see this."

"Bring it up. What are we looking at?"

"Unusual energy readings near Ganymede," Diane replied. "And a deposit of the compound buried under the ice. The energy signature matches what we've been tracking, but it isn't Federation tech. It's different."

Jim narrowed his eyes. "Different how?"

"Hard to say," Diane admitted. "We'll know more when we're closer. But there's something else."

"What is it?" Jim asked.

"The second compound signature leading out of the Trojan Belt is near our current position. Just inside the belt here. We could reach it in six days."

"You're kidding," Bucky groaned. "No more rocks, please."

"If it's a Federation black site, it's far smaller than any Ganymede outposts. It looks desolate and lightly defended. We could learn what they're doing much sooner, with less risk of running into a patrol."

"Understood. Send it to Lisa's console."

As the comms clicked off, Jim faced the viewscreen. The mysteries around the compound seemed to deepen every other day.

"Jim," BK said cautiously, "Diane's right. There's a faint energy signal inside the Trojan Belt, must be a black site. What do you want to do?"

Jim frowned in thought, then answered. "If we can uncover answers in six days instead of a month, we take the risk. It's our best chance to stay ahead of the Federation. Adjust course into the Belt." The Trojan graveyard would decide their fate, and if the Federation wanted war. The Argo would be the spark.

Uneasy glances rippled through the crew, but no one spoke. They were loyal, even as uncertainty spread through their ranks.

That night, the mess hall was quieter than usual. The crew picked at their food. Their minds still turned over the day's revelations. JT sat across from Mariana, his plate nearly un-touched.

"You need to eat," Mariana said. "You'll need your strength."

JT poked at his food. "How do you stay so calm? Everything feels one step from falling part."

Mariana studied him before replying. "Second-guessing the captain doesn't help anyone. Strength is contagious. Show them you can be trusted when it matters, and they'll follow. That's called true leadership, JT."

JT sat up straighter in his seat momentarily looking bewildered, "I guess you're right. We're all in this together. Thanks, Mariana."

Across the table, Bucky arched a brow. "Didn't think I'd live to see the day someone shut JT up."

She smiled. "I have my moments."

As the crew finished their meals and drifted away to rest, Jim stood unnoticed in the doorway watching them go. They were tired, anxious, and staring down impossible odds. But they were still in the fight. That was the best they could hope for, at least for now.

THE TROJAN REVELATION

The *Argo* traveled through the darkness of the Trojan Belt, a region thick with drifting debris and jagged asteroids condensed into a narrow region of space. The Trojan Belt was both a navigational nightmare and the perfect hiding place for anything meant to stay hidden.

Jim sat in the captain's chair, gripping the armrests as he stared at the forward display. The ship's lights swept over looming asteroid formations. Their fractured edges shifted as they tumbled slowly through the void.

"This place looks like a minefield waiting to explode," Bucky muttered. Lisa gave him a long-suffering glance before turning back to her console. He leaned in anyway, watching her sensors trace the safest route forward.

"The orbits aren't right. Something's pulling the asteroids into formation, like marionettes," she concluded.

Jim turned. "How?"

His eyes focused. The Federation had a long history of unsanctioned black projects. The failed ones were buried and forgotten until some unfortunate crew stumbled across the wreckage. He glanced at Grace, who was already cross-checking the engineering diagnostics.

Bucky leaned over his console, muttering, "Hell of a place to hide a fleet. You sure we're not flying into an ambush, Captain?"

Then Lisa's console beeped.

"There," she said, pointing at the display. "A faint organic signature. Almost undetectable, but it's there. It matches what we've been following."

Jim rubbed his chin. "This has to be it."

Lisa magnified the scan. At the heart of chaos, a structure resolved itself, concealed by jagged rock.

"Son of a gun," Bucky whispered. "You were right, Jim."

A hidden facility emerged, scarred and abandoned, but it was unmistakably Federation.

"Detecting weak power readings," BK said to everyone. "No one's responding to my landing request."

Jim turned to Mariana. "Thoughts?"

She hunched over the readouts. Her expression was tight. "I'd say this site was constructed five years ago at most. Maybe less. Evidence points to it being abandoned recently, judging from the ice growth."

Lisa nodded. "We would have missed it altogether if we weren't scanning for the compound. Whatever happened here, they wanted it erased."

Grace folded her arms. "And here we are, ready to knock on the door."

Jim tapped his fingers against the chair. The risks were obvious, but so was the reward. "Prep an away team. Bucky, Liam, Grace, James, and Mariana... we're going in."

JT's head snapped up. "Me?"

"It's time. Gear up. You've trained for this, but I want you by my side. Don't wander off."

JT hesitated, then saluted. His father finally gave him his opportunity, and he wouldn't waste the chance.

The shuttle's thrusters fired and guided it through a jagged wasteland of fractured rock. Bucky piloted with steady hands while Liam tracked their path. Jim and Bucky wore their heavy trench coats, weapons secured beneath. They were more than gear; they were armor, ritual, the mark of men leading the way to danger.

"Frost halos on the hull, shields up," Jim ordered.

"This place makes my skin crawl," Liam muttered as he watched the derelict station loom into view. Half-buried in an asteroid, the structure looked devastated.

The outer plating was scorched. Jagged rooftops exposed collapsed corridors.

"This looks like a war zone," JT whispered. "What happened here?"

Bucky gave a low whistle. "Looks like one of the Federation mistakes went tragically wrong."

A faint pulse flashed ahead, nearly lost in the haze of radiation.

"Mariana," Jim said, catching the shadow across her face. "What do you make of it?"

"It shouldn't have power. If they abandoned it, they would have disconnected the cores. Somehow it feels... familiar."

JT shifted in his seat. "What do you mean, familiar?"

"I'm not sure," Mariana replied.

Jim sighed. "We're going in. Bucky, Liam, Grace, James, you're with me. Mariana, hold the shuttle and monitor our video feeds. We may need your help getting out quickly if things go sideways. Let's get inside before the radiation levels pick up again."

"I don't like it," she said.

"Neither do I," Jim admitted. "But if the Federation went to this much to build this place here in the Trojans, it must be related to Project Chimera. It's worth the risk, we're going in."

Liam checked his rifle, then exchanged a look with Bucky. "Hope you packed extra charges."

Bucky struck a dramatic pose. "I always pack extra charges for when you spray and pray. You know that."

Grace accessed the control panel outside the facility entrance. "Odd, someone locked the door from the outside," she said. "I can open it from here."

The airlock cycled the door open with a deep groan, releasing a wave of cold, stagnant air that pressed against their space suits.

As soon as they stepped inside, JT felt something was wrong with the place. The corridors were covered in ice. Weak lights cast the faintest glow.

Bucky scanned the walls. "This place is giving me the heebie jeebies."

Grace ran a gloved hand across a console, clearing away frost and grime. "Systems are still active," she murmured. "The environmental controls are running, but I'd recommend keeping our face shields up in case the air is toxic."

Jim motioned them forward, his rifle raised. They advanced carefully. Boots clanged against the metal floor; every step echoed with an unnerving hollowness.

JT spotted a row of terminals along the far wall. Most were dark, and their glass was frosted over. Hoping for access to the central system, he wiped one screen clean.

Grace joined him. The screen flickered and sputtered to life to reveal a camera feed from deeper in the base.

Something moved in the corner of the display, shifting in the shadows before disappearing.

※※※※※

Bucky and Liam took point as the team pressed deeper into the black site. They followed the faint signature. Mariana monitored the video feeds from the shuttle. They rounded a corner and froze. The emergency strips throbbed once, faintly out of rhythm with the reactor's hum, like a pulse trying to sync and failing.

The far wall was lined with glass chambers, each coated in frost. Jim swiped back and forth with his rifle butt to clear the ice. Inside there were people. Or what had once been people.

JT's stomach knotted. The shapes inside looked almost human but twisted. Skin had discolored and pulled tight across exaggerated features, veins were black and swollen, eyes were hollow and sunken. Their mouths gaped wide showing long canines, their enlarged, bald heads terrifying.

Liam clasped his hands. "Jesus help us. They're all in Federation attire. Are they test subjects?"

Jim swallowed. "We don't have much time. Let's find what we came for."

Bucky stared, unable to look away. The sight would haunt him in every dark moment for months. "These people's faces are all wrong, they look like something out of an old horror movie. You know the one, Jim."

Jim's eyes remained fixed on the pod. "Sometimes you scare me, Bucky," he muttered. "You need to get out more."

Bucky held his ground. "You got the reference."

Grace pushed closer to a nearby console. Her fingers flew across the cracked interface. The data was fragmented and corrupted, but enough remained to piece together a story.

"The Federation injected their test subjects with an experimental strain of the compound," Grace said.

Jim asked, with a note of admiration. "They turned people into these... ghouls on purpose?" Taking a cue from Bucky's horror movies.

Watching through the feeds, Mariana had a sudden moment of déjà vu. "I'm remembering now. The Federation was trying to stabilize the compound. If they had succeeded, they could have reshaped warfare with these creatures. A long pause ensued, "They have no conscience."

JT shivered. "Did they succeed?"

Grace kept her eyes on the console. "Pulling up the results."

The logs told of disaster after disaster. Subjects lost their minds, their bodies warped, with many turning into violent cannibals.

Then she reached the last entry. "Project Chimera – Subject twenty-two... classified 'Stable. Experiment successful.'"

Grace whispered, "No. This can't be right."

JT's frown lines deepened. "Stable? As in... it worked?"

"Subject twenty-two, that's me," Mariana's voice shook. "I remember now. I was here before, with Elijah. He injected me with the compound and implanted me with cybernetics, but I'm not sure why he chose me. Or why he designed them to look so natural. It's like he wanted to conceal them." She suddenly realized she could control them all along as she activated them, her bionics glowing for the first time.

Everyone froze. Suddenly a deep metallic groan rolled through the facility. A warning klaxon blared, and the containment chambers' lights shifted from green to red.

JT's heart pounded against his ribs. "Uh, guys..."

The figures inside twitched once, twice, then their eyes snapped open. A wet, gurgling, inhuman screech erupted from the pods.

The lights flashed and cut out, leaving only the emergency strips for light in the room.

The crew looked on, unable to move. The sounds started deep and low, like metal tearing under terrible strain, then rose into a howl that no human throat could produce.

JT stumbled back as the glass splintered. Cracks spread like a spider's web across the pods' glass until the farthest chamber shattered open by the punch of a gnarled fist.

A figure lurched out. Its limbs jerked unnaturally. Dark veins pulsed under pale skin. Its eyes were pitch black, as though every trace of humanity had long been removed.

JT's stomach turned. "Oh, hell no. We must have tripped a system reboot when we accessed the system."

Grace groaned, "Of course. Reboot auto-cycles containment. We basically rang the dinner bell."

Jim shoved JT back. "We're moving! NOW!"

Glass exploded as more pods burst open, shards scattering across the deck. The ghouls spilled onto the floor moving in broken, unnatural jerking rhythm.

Jim raised his plasma rifle and fired. The crackling bolt struck center mass, knocking the first monster back as black blood exploded from its chest. It staggered, shook violently, then started forward again.

A second blast tore part of the creature's shoulder away, the wounds taking their toll as the ghoul collapsed but kept crawling, slowly pulling itself back to its feet.

The creatures accelerated, their grotesque forms blurring with unnatural speed. In an instant, they were on the crew.

JT barely ducked before one lunged at his chest. Its claws gouged the wall, leaving four deep slashes in the metal.

Grace wasn't as quick. One seized her waist, and its claws scraped across her chest plate sending sparks flying, knocking her to the floor.

Grace snarled, yanked her sidearm, and jammed it under the monster's chin as it approached. "Eat this," she pulled the trigger two times for good measure.

The rounds blew through its skull. The ghoul convulsed and shook its head, falling on top of her with its eyes still open, barely moving.

"Oh, come on!" Grace struggled to free herself.

Jim charged and slammed into the creature's side, sending the ghoul sprawling across the floor. Liam pulled her to her feet. "Move it!"

"Center mass and head shots aren't doing it," Grace snapped. "Neuromuscular control is distributed. Take the joints out!"

"Mariana! What's our best exit?" Jim shouted.

"Back the way you came is blocked by a horde of ghouls coming your way. There's a secondary launch bay, but—"

"I don't care about the 'but.'"

"You'll have to cut through the reactor wing. If containment failed, there could be radiation leaks."

Bucky spat a curse and said, "Perfect. Just what we needed."

More ghouls poured from shattered pods. Limbs jerked as they picked up speed.

JT fired at their legs, joints crackling as they snapped into. "It's working."

Another creature's knee burst apart, and it slammed to the floor.

"Take their legs out! Fire!" Jim yelled.

Firing in unison, they shredded the creatures' limbs, dropping them to the floor; the damage forcing the monsters to crawl in pursuit. Their advance slowed, unable to keep up.

The team bolted down the maintenance corridor. Behind them, the creatures dragged themselves along as they bled out. The horde overtook the legless ghouls without a moment's concern for the fallen and was closing fast on the crew.

JT glanced back. "Nope. Nope. Nope. I hate this."

"Keep running, kid," Liam growled.

They pounded through the hallway and turned into a massive chamber. The ceiling rose several stories above them.

The reactor core loomed ahead, dimly lit by backup systems. A frozen display flashed: "OVERHEAT; COOLANT PUMP FAILURE."

Grace skidded to a stop at the base of the reactor column, her eyes wide. "The only way through is the catwalks! Keep going while I activate a coolant purge to slow them down."

Jim gritted his teeth. "I'll cover Grace, everyone else take the catwalks."

Bucky shot JT a look. "You see those?" He gestured toward the collapsed floor and the chasm below. It was filled with sparking electrical cables on the ground. "One bad step and we're Jed's Famous Fried Protein."

JT peered down at the deadly drop. "So, our choices are death by cannibals, or death by the glowing electrical pit of doom?"

Grace skidded into the access panel at the base of the reactor column and hammered it with her rifle's butt, then sifted through the wires inside. She twisted a pair of wires together activating the purge. A milky sheet of contaminated coolant fanned across the deck, hissing where it hit exposed metal and raising a bitter vapor. Grace climbed the ladder to the catwalks with Jim right behind her.

Behind them, the monsters howled like banshees. Their twisted silhouettes spilled into the room, screeching as the coolant burned their bodies.

"Keep moving! Hurry!" Jim barked.

Their boots clanged on the metal. The catwalk groaned under their weight; sparks rained from above as the failing structure shuddered around them. The station was falling apart while they made their escape.

The ghouls closed the distance, climbing up the stairs with inhuman speed.

Bucky laid down suppressive fire as he brought up the rear. Energy blasts lit the chamber and ricocheted off the catwalk's frame. "They're gaining!" he shouted.

Two round bursts from Bucky's rifle ripped through a ghoul's knees and elbows.

Jim ripped open a rusted emergency panel. Inside was a manual override lever, frozen over with a thick crust of ice.

"Hold on to something!" He braced himself; teeth clenched and yanked the release free.

The entire catwalk lurched. Metal screamed as the railing tore away, sending half a dozen ghouls plunging into the coolant below.

Their advance halted only for a moment. The survivors snarled, black veins bulging like cords under their skin. Overhead, the emergency lights flared in sync with their cries, pulsing brighter as if the creatures' fury bled into the station's systems.

Grace muttered, "That's not a glitch. They're creating bioelectric spikes that are bleeding into the systems."

Surprised, Jim said. "That's new."

The survivors clawed forward again, rage feeding the glow until the chamber throbbed crimson.

Liam shoved JT forward. "Go! The airlocks are straight ahead!"

They sprinted across the trembling walkway toward a reinforced hatch with blinking green lights on the far side of the reactor chamber. Jim slammed his fist against the panel, and the doors hissed open.

The crew barreled through. Bucky and Grace covered the rear with bursts of fire. Jim hit the emergency seal again and again until the airlock clamped shut.

The first creatures smashed into the door with bone-snapping force. Horrifying screeches reverberated through the chamber as cracks spread across the reinforced plating.

JT staggered back. His breath ragged, he said, "We need to leave. Immediately."

"Agreed." Jim's voice was clipped.

Bucky wiped sweat from his brow. "Zero out of ten stars. Would not recommend."

Liam gave a snort of laughter. "Let's get the hell out of here."

*****

As the shuttle lifted off, the black site shrank in the viewport. JT caught one final glimpse of failing emergency lights before the ruin vanished into darkness.

"You all good?" asked Bucky.

Jim exhaled. "Define good."

Grace sagged in her seat. "Let's just say we have a lot to talk about." And what the hell was with the lights syncing to their screams? That wasn't a systems glitch."

Jim's jaw tightened. "Whatever it was, those things are almost unstoppable."

JT silently stared down at his hands. His heart still fluttered in his chest. The things they had seen...the truth about Mariana...and worst of all, the Federation's experiments weren't all failures. They had succeeded once. Their proof was sitting among them on the shuttle.

The thrusters whined as the shuttle docked with the ship. Magnetic clamps engaged with a heavy metallic thud, which was followed by the hiss of depressurization.

JT sat frozen, his mind replaying the horrors of the black site. The ghouls, their screeches, the way they clawed forward even after what should have been kill shots.

Jim unbuckled and stood, his eyes sweeping across the crew. "We need a debrief. Now. I'm sorry, but it can't wait."

Bucky groaned as he stretched. "Good job down there, JT?"

"Kid held his own. I say we let him pick the next shift assignments."

JT blinked. "Uh... sure?"

Grace chuckled. "Let's just get inside before something else tries to kill us."

They moved through the airlock into the dim corridor where the rest of the crew waited. Lisa, Chief Samuel, Diane, Raegan, Karl, and BK.

"What the hell happened down there?" asked Lisa.

Jim rubbed his face.

"Captain Eckhart?" said Mariana.

Jim drew a long breath. "We just saw what the Federation is doing with the compound."

Raegan frowned. "Meaning?"

"There's a reason that black site was abandoned." Grace cut a glance at Mariana. "And it had your handiwork all over it."

Mariana's face stayed neutral, but JT noticed the defensiveness in her stance.

"So, what does that mean for us?" asked Liam.

"We thought we were just running, trying to shake the Federation off our backs. But this isn't about us anymore," said Jim.

The room fell quiet.

"They're experimenting with technology they can't control," Jim continued. "They're turning people into monsters. If we don't stop them, they'll destroy everything we know. Their lust for power has crossed into madness."

"So, what's our move? Do we take the fight to them?" asked Lisa.

Jim steadied himself. "First, we clear the Trojan Belt. Then we figure out our next step. Ganymede may not be worth the risk after what we saw. Once Mariana cracks that message, we'll know how deep this runs. Until then, we stay alive and keep moving."

Mariana sat alone in the central comms room. The dim glow of the screens threw shadows across her face. A decrypted data file was open in front of her. The author was Elijah Ember himself. His warning was at last revealed.

> The words froze her blood.
> Mariana, if you are seeing this,
> it means I have failed,
> and that I am most likely dead.
> They are coming for you next.

Project Chimera is the Federation's attempt to control this alien technology, but they can't. The organic compound was never meant for human integration without understanding its implications first. This isn't just about space travel or the ultimate weapon. It was about the ones who left it behind. They left us a warning about their mistakes so we wouldn't repeat them.

Mariana's breath caught in her throat. There was more: coordinates for Ganymede. Then the final message. She pressed play.

Dr. Ember's voice crackled through the speakers, warped and unsteady with age.

Captain Eckhart, if you are listening to this message, it is up to you and your crew to stop the Federation's plans to perfect these enhanced humans. The answers you seek are on Ganymede, buried deep in the ice. You must stop Project Chimera at all costs.

A cold chill climbed her spine. She reached for the comm panel and opened a channel. "Captain. You need to hear this."

The Argo's thrusters roared. Vibrations rattled through the deck as Lisa and Bucky prepared for the speed jump.

JT, Mariana, and the captain moved quickly through the corridors back toward the bridge to debrief the crew on the decrypted message. Mariana said, "There's more to decrypt as well, Captain."

"This changes everything," said Jim. "James, do you want to take the lead and explain Ember's message to the crew?"

JT stopped and turned to his father. "I'm ready."

Jim put a hand on JT's shoulder. A faint grin broke through the tension. "Then show me."

Jim stared at the holographic projection that showed Elijah Ember's final words. Ganymede loomed on the display beside the message. The frozen moon's background consumed by the storms of Jupiter's atmosphere. They were headed straight into the abyss.

JT stepped forward. "We've all heard Ember's warning, and we all agree the answers we're seeking are on Ganymede." His voice was steady. "The Federation has left us no choice. This is our only chance to uncover their plans and stop them. That's the key to unraveling this mystery and finally getting the Federation off our backs, for good."

Jim studied him. JT stood taller now, sharper, more confident than before. "Son," Jim said, "I think we passed the point of no return a long time ago."

Bucky chuckled from his station. "Too late to ask for a refund?"

Lisa flipped switches as the engines powered up. "Not unless you want to take the Scarlett back to Mars."

Jim turned to the crew, smiling. "Ganymede it is. Let's finish this."

The Argo surged forward, accelerating toward destiny on Ganymede, toward the truth.

Most of the crew shared the captain's resolve, but the look on Grace's face told Jim that she wasn't convinced. She dragged a hand through her hair.

"We're already in over our heads," she said. "Now you want us to chase some half-baked conspiracy to Ganymede? Based on what, a corrupted data log and a cryptic warning from a dead billionaire?"

"We can't ignore this, Grace. If the Federation is tampering with forces they don't understand, this isn't just about what they'll do to us anymore."

"Since when did we become the guardians of the solar system?"

"When Mariana came aboard," said Jim. "We already kicked the hornet's nest. If we walk away now, it's only a matter of time before they find us again, and next time we're the ones who get stung."

Bucky rubbed the back of his neck and sighed. "He's not wrong, Grace."

She threw her hands up. "Fine. But when this explodes in your face, I get to say I told you so."

"Duly noted," Jim replied.

"At least we're heading to our original destination. How long until we reach Ganymede?" asked Liam.

Lisa tapped out the figures. "At cruising speed? A month."

A collective groan rolled through the bridge.

"Another month in deep space?" JT muttered. "That's going to be rough."

Jim exhaled. One month until they reached Ganymede, until they uncovered the Federation's truth. Or proved themselves wrong in the worst way.

The Argo had barely cleared the black site when an alert lit up Lisa's console.

"Captain," she called, "we've got incoming, a Federation ship, closing fast."

Jim had feared this. Their proximity meant only one thing: the Federation had been watching the site the whole time.

Bucky leaned over Lisa's console. "What are we looking at?"

"An interceptor," Lisa answered. "And it's far too fast to outrun."

"Bring it up on the holo-display," said Jim.

The readout appeared on the viewscreen. "Signature matches a Federation assault interceptor," Lisa confirmed.

Silence swept across the bridge. They were the hunted, and the Federation wouldn't stop until Mariana was in their clutches.

Grace whistled low. "Guess they didn't like us poking around in their little lab of horrors."

"Distance?" Jim asked Lisa.

"They'll be in weapons' range in five minutes. If an interceptor is here, there's a flagship not far behind."

Liam crossed his arms at the tactical station. "We can't outgun them."

"So, what's the plan then, Captain?" Bucky asked, cracking his knuckles.

Jim's eyes narrowed. "Then we outsmart them with a few mining tricks they won't see coming. Lisa, get us out of here."

The side thrusters engaged, and the ship pivoted, showing its agility in the narrow confines as it plunged deeper into the density of the Trojan Asteroid Belt. The crew braced against the sudden inertia as the Argo wove between immense asteroids drifting through the void.

The Federation ship followed. Its sleek hull maneuvered with precision through the same field.

"Evasive maneuvers, Lisa!" Jim ordered.

"You should hold onto something," she said switching to manual controls.

Lisa worked the controls in rapid succession as the Argo spiraled between two massive asteroids skimming so close that dust and rock fragments scattered in its wake. The ship lurched as it clipped the edge of a smaller asteroid.

"Easy, Lisa!" Bucky called from his station. "Let's not make this a salvage operation."

"Next time, you can fly," she shot back.

Jim studied the sensors. "They're gaining."

Liam leaned over the tactical readouts. "Interceptor's weapons systems are online. If they get a lock, we're finished."

Jim's mind calculated the odds. "We have the Trojan Belt all around us. Let's use it to our advantage."

Lisa nodded. "Diane, find me a big asteroid with high gas content close to the surface."

Diane scrolled the scans. "Found one. A thousand meters wide, with an iron-ore vein under the crust and gas pockets surrounding it. The perfect storm, waiting to blow."

Jim's thoughts hardened. They could never win a straight fight, but they might trick the interceptor into a fatal mistake.

"Take us around it. Bucky, fire the harpoons when we're close. The inertia will give us the momentum we need to reach our mark."

Lisa swung the Argo around the asteroid. Its thrusters strained as the ship arced. "Bucky, now!"

The harpoons launched and struck deep into the jagged rock. The sudden force hammered the crew with crushing G-force. The hull groaned in protest as the ship changed direction.

"Detach anchors!" Jim barked.

The ship skimmed the surface, sending plumes of dust erupting behind them. The added momentum and the cloud of debris bought them breathing room to set the trap.

Liam's eyes never left the weapons board as they approached their mark; the interceptor recovering quickly. "Just give me the cue to blow it?"

"Yeah," Jim said. "Buckle in. This will be rough."

Diane locked her eyes on the geo-console. "Now!"

Liam unleashed a volley of plasma bolts into the weak point Diane had marked. The gas pockets ignited in a thunderous eruption. The blast hurled thousands of tons of debris into space. A colossal slab of iron sheared free and barreled straight into the interceptor's path.

The Federation pilot barely had time to react. Iron shards peppered the hull like shrapnel, thousands of impacts in seconds, before the massive slab crushed its starboard side. The vessel spun helplessly, smashed into a large asteroid, erupting in a storm of fire and twisted metal.

The crew erupted in cheers. Against all odds, they had survived again.

"Lisa, set course for Ganymede. Let's clear this sector."

The wreck faded from the scanners, left behind in the graveyard of the Trojan Belt, taking its next victim.

Bucky whooped and threw his arms skyward. "Now that's how you make it happen, Cap'n!"

"I need a drink," said Lisa, her voice shaky.

Grace dropped into her seat. "I need a double."

Jim said nothing. He only stared at the viewscreen, Jupiter's storms a dim glow far ahead. Ganymede loomed in their future; the real fight waited there.

The Argo coasted into relative quiet. The immediate threat had passed, but the ship bore the scars from its close encounter. The explosion rattled its framework and stressed its systems, triggering damage reports to stream in from across all decks.

Jim leaned against the command console and drew a steady breath. His body ached, his mind burned, but there was no time for rest. The crew wanted answers, and he had none, at least not yet.

Grace's voice cracked over comms.

"Engineering to bridge, we're running on hopes and dreams right now. Can you stop breaking things faster than we can fix them, Captain?"

Jim rubbed the bridge of his nose. "Give it to me straight."

"Engines at sixty percent. The port stern is damaged. Another maneuver like that and the outer plating will fracture. On top of that, the power core's coolant system is leaking. We'll be glowing soon if we don't fix it fast."

"Stabilize the coolant first," Jim said. "Then patch the stern plating. I want thrust integrity before we touch anything else."

Jim turned to Bucky, who was scanning the sensors. "You heard her?"

Bucky nodded. His grin was long gone. "Yeah. If we don't get repairs underway soon, the Argo will be little more than scrap metal long before we reach Ganymede."

Lisa spun in her chair. "That's reassuring."

"I need manpower," said Grace. "JT, Karl, and anyone else not flying the ship."

Jim nodded sharply. "Liam, go help Grace. James, you too."

JT straightened. "On it, Captain."

"Try not to get radiation poisoning," said Lisa.

JT wrinkled his nose as he followed Liam out.

The bridge thinned out, leaving Jim, Bucky, Lisa, and Mariana.

"I gotta say, Cap," Bucky started, tossing his poker chip into the air and catching it with one hand, "that was one hell of a gamble, even for us."

"Agreed. That was way too close for comfort," said Jim.

Bucky scoffed. "Really? You think so?"

"This doesn't make any sense." Lisa shook her head. "Since when are we heroes? We're a mining crew, albeit a damn good one."

Mariana, silent until now, said, "It's not about being heroes. It's about stopping the Federation to protect our way of life. If they succeed, it's only a matter of time before they unleash those enhanced humans on anyone who opposes them, and that includes us first."

The room fell silent.

Mariana fixed her gaze on the display. "The files we pulled show the Federation is testing new weapons technology. They're trying to control the gravity fluctuations caused by the FLS drive, turning it into a weapon capable of conquering the system. Something went wrong, and they buried the evidence."

"That sounds a lot like zero-point energy theory. And what did you mean when you said you were Subject Twenty-Two?" Jim asked. "You said that place felt familiar."

Mariana rubbed her temple. "I didn't know because Mc-Connell erased my memories, but when I saw the black site, they came back. The Federation kidnapped me and kept me as collateral against Elijah. I don't know why I'm different from the failed experiments, why I didn't turn like the others. McConnell was already searching for a new source of the compound, so they hired you to explore the belt. They knew he would arrest you once you outlived your usefulness."

Her eyes betrayed the pain of her memory. "I began piecing together his lies. I saw his cruelty when he thought I wasn't watching. Then I met your crew. You fought a lot, but you always had each other's backs, like family. I can't explain it, but I felt like I could trust you, Captain Eckhart."

Bucky flipped his poker chip one last time and caught it with a slap to his palm. "That's terrible, Mariana. I'm sorry you went through that."

"We can't let the Federation harm anyone else with this technology," Jim stood resolute. "We're in this to the end. There's no turning back."

Tears streamed down Mariana's cheeks as she bowed her head. "Thank you, Captain, for treating me like family."

Jim gave her a reassuring look, then turned to Lisa. "How long until we reach Ganymede?"

Lisa checked her console. "A little under a month at current speed. If we add a third engineering shift, maybe three weeks."

Jim stared at the stars on the viewscreen. "A month of repairs, and for Mariana to work on Ember's secrets, and to process her revelation."

While Jim was distracted, Bucky pulled Diane aside and leaned over to whisper in her ear. "How's the little one?"

Diane became visibly agitated, "You could have died, Bucky. I thought I lost you."

Bucky gazed into her soul, "Moments like that make you realize what's important. It's always been you, Diane."

"Bucky, maybe it's not the best time for that conversation seeing how things are going."

"Maybe that makes it the perfect time," Diane stared back for several long seconds before Bucky averted his eyes. "Let's talk about it later."

Jim stood and spoke to the bridge. "All right, everyone. Get some rest. We have work to do before we reach Ganymede."

Lisa, Diane, and Bucky left the bridge, leaving Jim and Mariana alone. Mariana stood with her arms crossed and her eyes locked on the screen.

"Something's bothering you," Jim said.

Mariana nodded. "That message from Dr. Ember. 'The answers you seek are on Ganymede, buried in the ice.'"

"You think he was warning us about what you'll find there?"

"Yes. I believe Ember left the key to the Federation's plans for us on Ganymede, but if we're not careful, it could become the final resting place, for all of us."

Jim said nothing. He turned toward the stars, staring into the endless black. Whatever waited for them on Ganymede was the key. He closed his eyes and prayed that they got there first."

THE COST OF SURVIVAL

T he *Argo* cruised on its set course toward the frozen moon, taking the safest path to avoid the radiation levels of Jupiter, but more importantly the Federation outposts on Callisto. They were far enough from the last battle to catch their breath but never far enough to feel safe.

Jim stood at the center of the bridge; eyes fixed on the data scrolling across the console. The ship's hull had taken a beating. They needed a plan, and fast.

Sensors reported no Federation ships in their vicinity, but Jim knew better. The Federation would be sweeping every corridor of space between the Trojan Belt and Ganymede by now.

"Okay, Raegan," Jim said, his voice rough. "Give me an update on the crew's injury log."

Dr. Inoue, stationed at the environmental console, skimmed through a list. "Still treating some for minor injuries, but nothing serious."

Jim nodded, relieved. At least there was that.

Bucky rubbed his temples, reminiscing about their escape. "I still can't believe we pulled that off, Captain."

Liam snorted and turned to Bucky. "It's like Jim doesn't even know what he's going to do until it happens."

"Seriously, Liam. They'll be waiting for us at Ganymede. We know it's a trap, so why go there?" Grace muttered.

"The only reason we're still alive is because they want their prize: Mariana;" BK said. "Let's not kid ourselves."

Jim's gaze shifted to Mariana. She had been withdrawn since the battle. "What's the status on decrypting the rest of the message from your device?"

She blinked as if she was pulled from a distant thought, then straightened. "I'm working on the next file. This one is difficult."

"Time's not on our side," Liam said.

"I'm aware," Mariana shot back.

Standing off to the side, JT spoke up. "Mariana is doing the best she can."

"Let's think it through," said Jim, refocusing the group. "Everything we've uncovered—the black site, the anomalies, the Federation's obsession with the compound—Ember's riddle. It all leads to Ganymede. We know it's a trap, but it's also where the answers are."

Lisa pulled up the solar map on the viewscreen. The trajectory glowed across the dark expanse. "It's a straight shot from here to Ganymede. What's the play, Captain? We need to move soon, otherwise the Federation patrols will be on top of us."

He gave her a tired look. "We can't go back; our only choice is to find evidence on Project Chimera and get it to Caldwell."

"Have Karl deploy drone decoys, BK, transmit false telemetry, and Lisa, set our heading," said Jim, patting her shoulder. "Let's keep them guessing. Bucky, check on Chief Samuel and the crew, have them start repairs and inspect the hull."

Jim turned to the crew. I'll think up a plan for when we get there. Rest while you can."

JT couldn't sleep. He wandered to the med bay, where he found Mariana hunched over a console. Her face was lit by the pale glow of the screen.

"Still no answers?" he asked.

Mariana barely looked up. "I'm close," she said, eyes never leaving the code."

"Are you okay?"

She finally met his eyes. "They used me... tortured people. The experiments changed them somehow. I don't know what it means yet."

JT's throat tightened. "No one deserves that, Mariana. Especially you."

She sighed and rubbed her temples. "I found a text file about the organic compound, and the enhanced human project." Their failed enhanced human experiments may be linked to the gravitational anomalies.

"What, how can that be?" JT asked, leaning forward, his mouth open.

A shiver crept through him, but he forced some bravado for her sake. "Then we don't have a choice. We must find a way to stop them."

"I haven't got a clue how," Mariana admitted. "But no matter what it takes, we have to connect the pieces."

JT shook his head. "We must tell my dad. He'll know what to do."

"Hopefully before the Federation finds us," she said, her voice soft now.

Something in her tone made JT's stomach twist.

A notification alert flashed on the console. It was a transmission from Mariana's science bay, routed to the bridge crew only. Jim tapped the interface, and Mariana's voice filled the room.

"I've decrypted more of Ember's files."

Jim steadied himself. "Tell me what we're dealing with."

"The Federation combined the compound with their next-gen FLS drive and then used the test subjects as the control unit. The gravitational anomalies are the scars of those failed experiments.

The crew froze, silent and unmoving.

Jim turned in his chair. "Wait. You're saying... people were turned into those...enhanced humans as part of the Federation's effort to build some new FLS technology, and it blew up in their face, so they said, hey let's try it again?"

Mariana's reply came back cold and certain. "Correct. These enhanced humans are the key to controlling the FLS drive."

Jim's knuckles whitened as he gripped the table. "You mean the Federation used people as some kind of biological interface?"

"Exactly," she said. "The compound allows test subjects to be conditioned to endure prolonged exposure to the core. But for how long who knows? There's more to it I'm sure, Captain. I'll keep working on the files."

"The Federation in a nutshell," Liam said with exasperation.

Jim drew a long breath. "All right let's break this down. What were they after? A fleet of ships with this new FLS tech and enhanced soldiers both infused with the compound, with the aim of conquering the system?"

"Yes. An army of these enhanced humans could literally overrun Mars in a matter of weeks."

Bucky shook his head. "I really hate to think of more of those popping up in unexpected places."

Jim paced the bridge. "If the compound creates these enhanced humans, and if that's somehow connected to these gravity fields, then..." He stopped and turned to Mariana. "How does this all tie back to you? What's their end game?"

Grace shoved back from her console. "This is too much. Now with Ember gone, they'll have to take even bigger risks."

Jim rubbed his temples. "That's all the more reason to stop them."

"We know one thing. If they had perfected this technology, we'd already see their fleet marching across the system right now."

Jim grunted as he considered her words.

"There are pieces missing," she said firmly. "Let's hope Ember was right, and the answers are buried in the ice on Ganymede."

"Captain, what happens if we get there and it's worse than the Trojan site?" asked Liam.

"Then we do what we always do. We improvise, and we find a way to win. Together," said Bucky, leaning back in his chair. He sounded unusually serious.

"Exactly," said Jim.

Lisa pulled up the solar map showing their position near Jupiter and adjusted their trajectory for Ganymede. "If we stay on this course, we'll reach Ganymede in three weeks. That's not much time to figure out our next move."

Jim looked around the room. "We've made it this far by trusting each other. The only way we can beat the Federation is if we stick together. Now let's get back to work."

The crew dispersed to their stations, but as Mariana turned to leave, Jim called her back.

"There's something you're not telling me," he said.

Mariana hesitated, then glanced around to make sure they were alone. "The reason the Federation wanted me is because I'm like the enhanced humans. When the FLS coils discharge, my pulse syncs to it. Promise me that if I endanger the crew, you'll stop me."

Every instinct screamed to demand answers, but his crew needed a rock, not a storm. Jim held her gaze. "That won't happen. We don't trade lives on the Argo."

As she left the bridge, Mariana looked back with admiration for the captain, who stood alone, watching Jupiter swell larger in the viewscreen.

◥◥◥◥◥

Jim called a meeting before the next cycle. The crew lazily assembled, some looking more rested than others.

"We're at cruising velocity, several weeks out from our destination," said Jim, his eyes weary. "The plan is to stay off the Federation's radar. Once we arrive, we land quietly, enter the facility, uncover whatever Ember wanted us to find out about the Federation's plans, and get out before they respond. Any questions?"

No one spoke.

"Good. Back to work," Jim ordered. "Lisa, monitor our trajectory. BK, keep a lookout for any Federation activity. Bucky and Grace, service the weapons systems. Liam and JT, do the rounds."

Mariana fought to suppress the guilt she felt for pulling the Argo's crew into her efforts to stop the Federation's schemes. They had to be stopped at all costs.

Jim noticed her expression drift as if she were caught in a daydream. When he dismissed the crew, he pulled her aside. "Something's bothering you."

Mariana hesitated. "Well... I shouldn't be here."

"What do you mean?"

She met his eyes. "You know exactly what I mean. I'm risking everyone's safety by being here."

Jim knew she was right, though he hated hearing it said aloud. "The time to worry about that was before you boarded the Argo. It's too late for second guessing."

Mariana didn't look convinced.

Jim forced himself to stay strong. He needed to convince Mariana and the others there was still a sliver of hope. They needed time to close in on the truth.

The Argo drifted through the vast emptiness of space for weeks, a solitary speck against the looming bulk of Jupiter. The gas giant's storms swirled across the viewports, its gravity already tugging at the ship's trajectory.

Hoping to avoid detection and capture, they kept the ship as dark as they dared. Jim sat in his chair while JT sat across from him, his fingers laced together as they studied the solar map hovering above the table. Their course was locked on Ganymede.

The Argo's mess hall had seen its share of slapped-together meals, late-night planning sessions, and miners collapsing into chairs after brutal shifts, but tonight wasn't one of those nights. Strings of lights turned the steel mess hall almost warm. Tables were jammed together, crates served as chairs, the kitchen crew went all out, and Jim brought out his good whiskey, saved for a special occasion.

The close calls of the past few weeks weighed heavily on them. Brushes with death, the Federation hunting them at every turn, and the creeping sense that they were flying straight toward doom. But tonight, for one night, they allowed themselves something rare: a taste of normalcy.

Bucky stood at the center of the mess hall, looking down at Diane, who sat in her usual spot with shock and joy frozen on her face.

"Diane," Bucky said, softer than anyone was used to hearing from him. He took a breath and dropped to one knee.

The room fell into silence. Jim, mid-sip of whiskey, lowered his glass.

Diane's hand flew to her mouth. "Bucky... what are you doing?"

Bucky reached into his pocket and pulled out a simple metal band with a small diamond. "I thought about planning something fancy. A candlelit dinner maybe. But we're living one explosion away from oblivion to the next, so I figured, why wait?" He sank to one knee, "Diane, will you marry me?"

A murmur rolled through the crew, raw with emotion.

Tears welled in Diane's eyes. "You are crazy."

"That's a yes, right?" Bucky teased.

She grabbed him by the collar and kissed him hard enough to draw whistles and cheers. "Yes, Bucky! A thousand times yes."

When they broke apart, he slipped the ring onto her finger. "I should've done this a long time ago, Diane, I want to spend the rest of my life with you."

Jim stood and raised his glass. "I knew this day was coming from the moment Bucky first laid eyes on Diane inside Ruby's spaceport. One thing's for sure, since he met her, he's been a hell of a lot more fun to be around!"

The crew stomped their feet and hammered the metal tables, creating a roar of applause.

"Enough from me," Jim said, grinning. "Let's get this party started. Congratulations, Bucky and Diane."

The mess hall erupted as Bucky kissed Diane again. Jim clinked glasses with Grace, JT sprayed champagne across the table, and the crew shouted themselves hoarse.

As the celebration surged on, Jim clapped Bucky on the back. "For a guy who's followed me into a lot of bad decisions, this is one of your best ever?"

Bucky smirked. "This moment sure takes me back to the day we first met."

Jim nodded, and they shared something unspoken. Moments like this were rare, and happy endings even rarer. "I'm happy for you, brother."

At the far end of the table, JT sat beside Mariana, watching the joy unfold. He swirled the amber liquid in his glass, feeling warmth spread through him. The Argo was his home.

"Are you thinking about how much that whiskey will give you a terrible hangover tomorrow?" Mariana asked, raising a brow.

JT snorted. "Something like that." He leaned closer. "You ever think about what comes after all this? If we make it through?"

Mariana didn't answer right away. She watched Bucky and Diane dancing, whispering, hands intertwined. "I used to think I didn't have an 'after this.' Lately though... I'm not so sure. Maybe there's something waiting for us after all this is over."

They shared a brief, awkward silence before looking away. JT wanted to tell her what he felt but was sure it was the whiskey doing his thinking. Instead, he tapped his glass against hers. "To not being so sure."

Mariana smiled faintly and clinked her glass to his. "I'll drink to that."

Jim eventually rose and cleared his throat. The crew quieted, and their attention shifted toward him. He wasn't one for speeches, but tonight it felt necessary.

"We've been through a lot together over the years," Jim began, rolling his glass between his fingers. "We don't know what tomorrow brings. Every day is a mystery." His eyes moved across the room and stopped on Bucky and Diane. "No matter what happens, I know I can count on every one of you to have my back, just as you know I will have yours. And we all know why. Because the crew of the Argo is family. Whatever lies ahead, we'll face it as one."

"To the Argo!" the crew shouted together, raising their glasses.

"To family," Jim added.

"To family!" they echoed.

The warmth of the moment wrapped around them like a blanket, a brief escape from the shadows chasing them. As the party wound down, the crew scattered through the ship. Some headed to bunks, but others lingered, clinging to the last spark of celebration.

Bucky remained at the main table, finishing his drink when JT approached, shifting awkwardly.

"You, uh... finally did it? Congratulations, Matthew," JT asked.

Bucky chuckled at the use of his real name. "Marry Diane? Yeah." Then in earnest said, "What's really eating at you, kid?"

JT shook his head. "I mean—" he hesitated, then pushed forward. "After tomorrow, everything changes. I wonder if we'll ever get a moment like this again."

Bucky sighed and ruffled JT's hair like he had when he was a young boy. "James, moments like this don't come often. Never take the opportunities life gives you for granted. Life is full of unknowns, and Diane is the best thing that's ever happened to me." He slid off his trench coat and handed it over.

JT frowned, looking at the worn leather. "What's this?"

"What does it look like, kid?" Bucky said. "Your dad and I have been wearing coats like these since I was younger than you. It'll bring you good luck tomorrow."

JT turned it over and ran his hand over the inside pockets and the hidden holsters. "I thought you didn't believe in luck."

Bucky shook his head. "Maybe not, but I believe in you. You've got heart, JT. You just need to believe in yourself the way your father and I believe in you."

JT swallowed hard, his throat tight. He wanted to tell Bucky to keep it, to hold onto the coat that clearly meant so much. Deep down, he knew this was Bucky's way of saying how much he cared. But instead, he curled his fingers around the lapels and said, "Thanks, Bucky. This means the world to me."

"You don't need to thank me," Bucky replied. "Just take good care of my coat. You earned it, kid."

He ruffled JT's hair one last time before walking off, leaving JT standing alone with the coat around his shoulders. The leather felt comforting, warm against his skin and warm inside his chest. JT felt that he was exactly where he belonged.

12

BECOMING A LEGEND

The shuttle slid through Ganymede's thin air too easily. That smooth approach only deepened the knot in Jim's chest. He, JT, and Bucky wore their leather coats, a small tradition on big days. JT's grin said the rest; he wasn't a kid anymore.

Ganymede loomed below, its icy surface reflecting Jupiter's eerie glow like a frozen wasteland locked in perpetual twilight. The largest of Jupiter's moons looked desolate except for the Federation's nearby presence, which had long ago scarred its untouched beauty.

Jim had chosen his boarding party: Mariana, Liam, JT, Bucky, Grace, and himself. On the Argo's bridge, the remaining crew stood watching as Navigator Lisa Cross guided the ship into its final approach vector.

Jim took a steady breath. "Mariana, what's the latest on the scanners?"

Mariana, seated at the shuttle's main operations hub, said, "The facility is the source of the signal we've been tracking. It originates from deep underground, directly beneath the station. I'm picking up a compound deposit larger than anything I've seen before near the same location, but the surface appears abandoned. No heat signatures, no lighting, no signs of life. Looks like nobody's home."

Jim nodded toward Bucky. "It's true then. Imagine what the Federation could do with that much of the compound. Put us down just outside the entrance. No pings or movement below. Keep our profile dark."

"Understood," Bucky said, adjusting the trajectory.

The shuttle touched down on the frozen terrain with a soft thud, its landing struts skidding against the ice.

Chief Security Officer Liam Power carried his rifle at the ready as the group trudged through knee-high frost toward the looming structure. The facility was massive; an old Federation research station built into the glacial ice. The metal doors stood frozen shut. Ice crept over their hinges as if nature itself was reclaiming what the Federation had abandoned.

"This has serious haunted space station vibes," Bucky muttered in his best spooky voice.

"Keep helmet comms open," Jim said. "We get in, find what we need, and leave before anyone—or anything—knows we were here."

Mariana melted the ice from the control panel with a pocket torch and plugged in a datapad. The cracked screen flickered with garbled code.

"This system was wiped clean. No logs, no trace of who was stationed here or why." Her fingers glided across the controls. "Once inside, I may be able to recover something from the backups. If they didn't erase everything."

Liam shifted his grip on his rifle. "Or we listen to the warning signs for once and don't go inside."

"Too late for that, Chief," JT said, pointing at the terminal.

The screen flickered again before stabilizing. A new message glared in bright red: "Enter Access Code."

"I'm seeing a spoofed derelict beacon and scrubbed logs. Someone wanted the base to look deserted."

Mariana tapped in a command. "Good news, I can hack the lock. Federation security hasn't been updated in years. Bad news, there's a reason for that."

Bucky let out a low whistle. "That's reassuring."

Mariana's eyes narrowed. "I'm not here to reassure you, Commander."

The door groaned and stopped halfway. Ice cracked and broke away, but the passage remained blocked.

Jim studied the frozen entrance, then scanned the tundra behind them. No movement. No sound. No patrols. The ease of their approach was too clean. It screamed trap.

"We're going in," Jim said, ignoring the alarm bells in his head. "Someone built this enormous facility for a reason. If the Federation worked with the compound here before moving to the Trojan black site, then we may finally find the answers we need. Let's move."

Grace looked skeptical. "Of course we're going in. No active emissions. But, still, keep face shields up."

Mariana overrode the controls, and with a mechanical groan, the doors opened wider. Ice shattered and fell in heavy chunks as a stale, frozen gust seeped out, like the breath of something long buried.

JT hesitated at the threshold. "Yep. Definitely haunted space station vibes."

Bucky clapped him on the shoulder. "You first, kid."

JT glared at him, then stepped inside.

The corridors stretched before them. Walls were coated in frost. Jagged icicles dangled from the ceiling. Emergency lights flickered weakly and cast pale illumination across the sterile, frozen halls. The air carried a metallic tang, but underneath it was a scent that had no business existing. It was something alien, something wrong.

They advanced with weapons raised, their flashlight beams cutting through the gloom. Their footsteps crunched on the frost-covered floor.

"I don't like this," Liam muttered as he swept his rifle toward a branching passage. "Too quiet."

Mariana checked her datapad. "Central research lab is deeper inside. If anything survived, it'll be stored there."

They pressed on, pushing farther into the heart of the facility. When they reached the central lab, the doors were already open. Ice climbed up the edges like jagged scars.

Inside, consoles and research terminals lined the walls. They were covered in a thick layer of frost but appeared to be operational. At the center of the room stood a row of containment pods. Their glass exteriors were cracked and fogged with ice.

Jim scraped the ice and peered inside the nearest pod. His gut twisted at the site of more ghouls. Even if they were frozen solid.

Frozen inside was a bizarre looking humanoid figure. Its features were grotesquely distorted, its skin was mottled with dark veins and unnatural patches of bioluminescent color. Its eyes stared lifelessly, but its expression suggested it had died in agony. The canines had lengthened into enormous fangs, and its mouth hung wide open, stretched far beyond human limits. It looked like an earlier, more primitive attempt at creating the ghouls from the Trojan black site.

Mariana accessed a terminal. "Logs confirm early human trials—radiation resistance, strength, heightened cognition—plus some kind of electro-magnetic manipulation. Subjects overpowered staff. This was the prototype that led to the Trojan site.

"You're right, Jim. Something went horribly wrong here. These look like aliens from that other horror movie." Bucky started into an impression before Liam grabbed his shoulder.

"Don't you dare say it, Bucky."

Mariana glanced at the frozen corpses. "As crazy as that sounds, yes."

Mariana frowned at her screen. "Looks like the enhanced human's used their strength and intelligence to overwhelm the scientists." After a moment, she added, "There's more. Reports confirm localized gravitational anomalies caused by their failed experiments."

She turned to Jim. "Captain, this entire site was built to study the compound's effects and weaponize them with the next-gen FLS drive, but the question is, where the hell is everybody? There aren't any signs of life."

Jim studied her. "Why did they leave? Where are they now?"

Mariana's eyes fixed on the console. She tapped a command, and the login screen appeared. She looked at Bucky. "If Elijah left us anything, he would've left it here. Maybe he kept my credentials active, somehow."

Bucky smirked. "These ghouls are dead. No harm in rebooting the system?"

Mariana typed her credentials. The system paused, then unlocked with a dull chime.

"We're in," she said, louder than intended. "Dr. Ember tied my login to his. He gave me access to his hidden projects, the ones he kept from the Federation."

"Now we're getting somewhere," Bucky said, unrestrained enthusiasm spread across his face. "Let's see what our dead friend was up to."

Mariana opened a folder labeled "For Mariana," Wait... he must have found this back door before he died, and sent me a message to retrieve the files here on Ganymede. That's why he couldn't include them in the Mars transmission. The encryption wouldn't have fooled Federation techs."

She clicked the folder. A message flashed across the screen:

"DOWNLOAD THESE FILES. THEY ARE THE KEY
TO STOPPING THE FEDERATION."

She plugged in her memory device. Together she and Bucky watched the readouts. The files chilled her to the core. The first contained blueprints for a next-gen Federation destroyer, marked "Above Top Secret." The design showed a fully operational next-gen FLS drive with a secondary containment system for an enhanced human interface. A strange symbol marked the control slot where the Enhanced being would connect with the FLS drive.

Bucky shook his head. "No way a normal human lasts long in there. Not with that kind of radiation."

Two more files followed.

"Here, an Ember-designed EMP system," Mariana said. "It's modified for the Argo. He hid a kill switch inside his Federation ship designs without their detection. A direct hit to their FLS drive disables their ships temporarily."

Bucky whistled. "Can't wait to try that bad boy out!"

The final file contained blueprints for McConnell's Mars research base.

"This is their most top-secret site," Mariana said. "Buried in Olympus Mons. Dozens of floors deep, with the control room at the base. Ember marked a path through the maze of lava tubes for someone desperate enough to infiltrate the control center. He wants us to shut it down from the inside."

The screen flickered again, and a final message appeared:

"IF YOU'RE READING THIS, THEY KNOW YOU'RE COMING. ESCAPE NOW!"

A pressure alarm chirped. An iris hatch yawned below the lab—but not from their accessing the system. Mariana's eyes widened. "Remote trigger on the service network. Someone just opened that hatch from orbit."

Before Mariana could speak, a heavy clang echoed through the facility. She ripped the memory device free and turned toward the sound.

"Uh, guys?" JT pointed toward a pair of twin doors hidden on the far side of the lab. "I think the trap part is happening."

The doors slid open, revealing a chamber beyond with walls covered in glowing alien glyphs. They were runic-hieroglyphic markings that none of them recognized. Lights stretched downward into a vast structure hidden beneath the Federation lab.

The Federation had built this site atop something ancient, far older than humankind.

"So, the plan was to mine the compound from this alien structure below and haul it up here to conduct their experiments," said Grace.

"If those ghouls have been feeding on the compound down there all this time—what do they look like now?" said Jim, his voice low and grim.

From somewhere deep within the alien structure, a low, unearthly rumble rose into a guttural speech. Then movement.

The shadows in the corridor shifted. At first, it looked like a trick of the failing lights, but figures emerged.

Three humanoid figures lurched forward. Gaunt, bioluminescent veins coursed under cracked skin. Their hollow eyes seemed lit from within. Their jaws hinged too wide. Cords of warped muscle drove them forward at terrifying speed. Human once. Not anymore.

"They're coming out of what looks like an alien base under the station," Jim said grimly. "What are they?"

Project Chimera's leftovers," Bucky said as though it was obvious. "Then they're Chimerans."

Jim barked an order. "Someone opened the access hatch. Everyone move! Hurry!"

Liam fired first, his rifle blasts filling the corridor with blue light as the Chimerans sprinted toward them. The nearest creature staggered but didn't fall. It lunged, closing the gap in an instant.

JT shoved Mariana aside just before the Chimeran's claws ripped across his side. He cried out and crashed against a console, blood soaking his suit and trench coat. Grace rushed to him and slapped a sealant wrap over the torn fabric so the suits' emergency systems could close the breach.

"JT!" Mariana scrambled toward him, but Grace yanked her back.

"No time. Move!" Jim shouted, firing his rifle, the blasts hitting center mass as he pulled JT toward the exit.

He fired two more shots, slamming into one of the Chimerans. Once Jim was clear, Mariana slammed the door controls. The door sealed. A heartbeat later the creatures hammered it, buckling the frame. Their strikes echoed through the chamber. Metal warped then claw marks began tearing through the door.

Liam and Bucky unleashed plasma fire, shredding the corridor in bursts of light, while the rest of the group bolted for the main hatch.

They burst into the frozen air outside. Lisa's voice snapped through comms. "Captain, incoming! Federation heavy cruiser dropping from low orbit, fast!"

Jim gritted his teeth. "Now we know why the Federation abandoned this site. Same reason we're leaving. Get to the shuttle. Now!"

The crew sprinted across the ice. Jim carried JT up the ramp, his son half-conscious and bleeding.

As the shuttle lifted, Jim stole a glance back at the black facility entrance and remembered the words that had flashed on the terminal:

> "THEY KNOW YOU'RE COMING. YOU MUST ESCAPE NOW."

Liam pushed the shuttle's throttle to maximum and raced for orbit. Grace pressed bandages into JT's wounds, but the gashes were deep, and the blood loss was catastrophic.

Once docked, the med bay became chaos. Raegan barked orders while her team scrambled to stabilize JT and seal the wounds. Blood pooled beneath him and soaked his trench coat. His skin was chalk-white, his breaths were shallow, and his forehead was slick with sweat.

Grace stood frozen near the door. Mariana hovered at the bedside, panic overtaking her usual calm demeanor. Jim loomed over Raegan, his fists clenched tight.

"Vitals are crashing," Dr. Inoue snapped. She scanned his wounds and cursed. "The lacerations tore through vital organs. He's losing too much blood. Even with the wounds sealed, he needs a transfusion right now or he won't make it."

Jim stepped forward without hesitation. "Take mine. Whatever it takes."

Raegan shook her head. "Not compatible. JT's blood type is rare. There isn't a match on the ship."

Lisa and Liam exchanged stricken looks, but Mariana broke in.

"You haven't checked me yet. I looked at his file. We're a match. Use my blood."

Raegan frowned, already knowing the problem. "Mariana, your blood's been altered by the compound."

"I know exactly what's in my blood," Mariana shot back. "The compound could help him heal. Or we just watch him die."

Jim's chest nearly seized. "Are you sure this will work?"

Mariana's eyes burned. "Do we have another choice?"

Bucky stepped forward. "Jim, if we use her blood, we don't know what it'll do to him," he said, his voice low. "This isn't something you can take back."

Mariana looked down at JT's pale, broken body. His chest rose and fell in uneven bursts. Seeing him like that caused a wave of emotion to overwhelm her senses.

Jim's shoulders sagged. "I'm not letting him die." He gave Raegan a single nod. "Do it."

Dr. Inoue worked fast. Tubes linked Mariana and JT, and the IV filled with her blood. She barely flinched; her eyes locked on him.

At first, nothing changed. The monitors droned, steady but faint. Minutes dragged. Suddenly JT convulsed. His chest heaved as he sucked in air. The monitors spiked, and his heart pounded erratically, wild and unstable, before leveling into a repeating rhythm.

"Neurological activity surging way above baseline," Raegan called out. "His system's responding, but..."

JT gasped. His eyes snapped open, his pupils wide.

Every light in the med bay flickered. Instruments rattled on trays. The deck itself groaned under some invisible force. Then silence.

"Spikes match adrenaline surges. Bioelectric bleed over coupling into the ship's power grid. He's causing energy fluctuations with the internal systems."

JT blinked rapidly, struggling upright. His breaths came short, but he was alive. Confusion spread across his face. He turned toward Mariana. "What just happened?"

Jim stepped closer. His shoulders trembled, as if a tidal wave had finally broken. "Easy, son. Don't tear open Dr. Inoue's good work. She fought hard to patch you up."

JT's thoughts reeled. His body felt different, supercharged. The med bay seemed sharper, too bright. Every detail pressed in on him. He flexed his fingers and frowned. Even that simple movement felt foreign, like his body was responding in ways he didn't fully understand.

Across from him, Mariana sat with the IV line still running between them. "You almost died."

JT swallowed. "Yeah, I gathered that." His throat was raw, and his voice rasped. He rubbed his face, then froze." Weak from blood loss, he asked, "Why does my skin burn?"

Dr. Inoue scanned him again. "Because at the cellular level your body is adapting. The compound in Mariana's blood is intertwining with your DNA."

JT turned toward Mariana. He felt something beyond words, as if her blood had carried not just life but a memory of her into him. A new understanding stirred, though he couldn't name it. He looked stricken. "What happened to me?"

Mariana's voice was sober but heavy. "Your injuries were fatal, JT. We had no choice but to give you a transfusion. My blood was the only match on the Argo."

JT stared at her. He wasn't angry. Or grateful. He was just overwhelmed.

Jim stepped forward and embraced his son gently. His tears spilled freely. He pulled back and searched JT's face, as though afraid the vision would vanish. His voice broke. "Thank God you're alive. I'm so sorry I let you down. It was my—"

"Dad, it wasn't your fault," JT interrupted. "I made my choice. I'm fine with it. We saved lives, didn't we? And thanks to Ember's message, we might even stop the Federation." He let the words sink in before adding, "Besides, it's what you would've done, Captain."

Jim's pride swelled. He nodded slowly. "I'm just thankful you're still with me, son. Mariana was right. You're alive because of her." He suddenly swept Mariana into a bear hug, lifting her clean off the floor. "I can't thank you enough."

Embarrassment colored her cheeks, but there was warmth too. She hugged him back, stammering, "You're welcome, Captain. It was the least I could do after the kindness you and JT have shown me."

Jim set her down and regained his composure. "James, stay here with Raegan. The rest of us need to get to the bridge."

"Why?" JT asked. His hair was soaked with sweat.

"Because the Federation just hailed us," said Bucky."

JT blinked. "That's bad."

"Yeah, kid," Bucky said flatly. "It's bad."

Jim, Bucky, and Mariana raced down the corridor toward the bridge. JT remained in the med bay with Dr. Inoue, weak and woozy but alive.

When the others entered the bridge, Lisa and Liam were already at their stations.

"The F.S.S. Aegis has a weapons lock on us," Lisa reported.

Jim sank into his chair. The holo display flickered to life. He saw Admiral Kepler, his crisp uniform and cold expression radiating Federation authority.

"Captain Eckhart," Kepler said smoothly. "You've become quite the nuisance."

Jim clasped his hands together. "Nice to be appreciated."

Kepler ignored the quip. His gaze landed on Mariana, and his expression sharpened. "I see you still haven't returned our property. We'll need her to reestablish our base on Ganymede." His lips curled. "You don't understand what you're involved with. Stand down now, and perhaps I'll let your crew live."

Jim chuckled. "Yeah, thanks for the offer but we're good here."

Kepler's smile vanished. "Then you leave me no choice. We'll take what belongs to us, then destroy your ship with you, and your crew in it."

The transmission cut.

"They're charging weapons, once they're within range, they'll use harpoons to board us, Captain." Liam said, hands flying over his console.

Jim glanced at Bucky. "You thinking what I'm thinking?"

Bucky cracked his knuckles. "Oh yeah. Time for the Gauntlet Run!"

Jim gave a short nod. "Same as the unsanctioned belt races, where we skimmed asteroids for credits. Only now, it's a Federation destroyer."

Liam groaned. "I always hated the Gauntlet."

"The blueprint I pulled shows the Aegis is a prototype heavy destroyer," said Mariana, her voice low. "Once they have me and the Federation retakes Ganymede's compound source, they'll destroy the Argo and use me to power their prototype. They wanted us to come here because I'm the key to their plans. I've endangered all of you."

Jim met her eyes. "It doesn't change anything. We run straight at them. They'll assume we're plotting an escape vector. That hesitation is our opening."

"Do they really think you're not that reckless, Jim?" Grace muttered. "Because anyone who knows you knows you're insane."

Bucky barked out a laugh. "And being insane is why we're still alive."

Lisa swiveled in her chair. "Captain, if we're doing this, it has to be now."

Jim scanned the faces of his crew. They weren't just miners or family anymore. The were the rebellion, and they were at war. If they failed, the Federation would unleash an armada that could overtake the solar system, destroying everything he loved.

He looked back at the viewscreen. Jupiter loomed, its storms swirling like gods of war, setting the background as the Aegis waited, guns primed.

Jim rolled his shoulders. "On my mark: camo flare array and drones in front of the bow. Lisa, lock onto their bridge and accelerate. We're not a faster ship, but we can outsmart these Federation cowards."

The Argo surged forward, its thrusters blazing hot against the frozen backdrop of Ganymede. The F.S.S. Aegis, a towering Federation warship, loomed in the distance like an iron colossus. Its targeting systems locked onto the approaching mining vessel.

On the bridge, Jim braced against the captain's chair, eyes fixed on the holo display projecting their trajectory.

"This is outrageous," Mariana muttered from her station. "Even for you, Captain Eckhart."

Bucky stood beside Jim, arms perched on the console, a wicked gleam in his eye. "You call it outrageous. I call it the stuff of legends."

Grace shot him a glare. "You would."

The comms lit up as Admiral Kepler appeared. "Captain, I'll give your crew full marks for bravery, but if you keep bearing down on us, we'll open fire." His tone was sharp. "It's only a matter of time before we reclaim what belongs to us."

"Jim, we can't outrun that ship, and we don't have weapons strong enough to knock out their power core," Bucky whispered to Jim. "If this goes sideways, I've got the Scarlett prepped for departure. One play left."

Jim gave him a quick glance while he weighed the truth of it, but he only said, "No Bucky, there's always another way."

Just then, Lisa called from navigation, "Flare array countdown beginning now."

Jim's voice cut sharp. "Time to run the gauntlet." He turned toward Karl. "You got that ace up our sleeve ready to go?"

Karl cracked his knuckles. "Locked and loaded, Cap."

"Good. When I give the signal, unleash the package. Make it look like the Fourth of July. They'll think we're masking an escape burn, not driving straight at their command tower."

Karl grinned. "I'll make it a light show to remember."

"Three minutes!" Lisa shouted.

Jim's gaze locked on Bucky. The two men shared a look that needed no words. Both knew the truth. Even with Karl's fireworks and the surprise feint, the Argo wouldn't reach the asteroid belt alive before the superior vessel ran them down.

Jim exhaled. "All right, people. Let's make this convincing."

After slipping off the bridge without a word, Bucky headed for the cargo bay. Under the tarps and crates was his shuttle named the Scarlett, his contingency plan. He had already wired it with a crude but powerful explosive device, too heavy for any drone to carry. If the Argo had any chance of escaping, the Aegis's next-gen FLS drive had to go offline. This was the only way.

He rubbed the wedding band Diane had slipped onto his finger only hours before. A hollow laugh escaped him. "Well... guess I'm gonna miss that candlelit dinner." He climbed into the Scarlett. The engines coughed to life. Behind him, the cargo bay doors sealed; the ship's systems would betray him soon enough.

On the bridge, Jim's resolve held firm. The Aegis had them in its sights, plasma cannons primed, but they were holding fire. They wanted Mariana alive.

Admiral Kepler's voice thundered across comms. "This is your last chance, Eckhart. Surrender or be destroyed."

Jim smirked. "We'll take Option C."

He slammed his hand on the console. "Karl, deploy counter-measures."

From the Argo's stern, thousands of flares exploded outward and filled the void with a chaotic storm of blinding light and static interference. Karl's drone swarm followed, diving in kamikaze runs toward the Aegis.

The Aegis's targeting systems faltered, thermal sensors over-loaded.

On the other end, Kepler sneered. "They're covering a retreat vector with flare arrays. Watch out for the drones."

Exactly what Jim wanted him to think.

As the flare storm reached its pinnacle, the Argo cut through the haze, bearing down on the Aegis's bridge. The drone swarm led the charge, slamming into the warship's hull with blinding precision. The Argo's incalculable run caught the superior vessel off guard. Kepler saw the approach and panicked. "Full evasive maneuvers, now! He's bloody crazy!"

The Aegis engaged its advanced warning systems. The pris-tine hull twisted aside as the bridge veered away from the Argo's course.

The instant Jim knew the ruse had worked, he barked, "Now, Lisa!"

The crew braced for impact. The Argo lurched hard to star-board as the two ships collided. Outer plating splintered from both hulls, littering the void. A shockwave slammed through the mining vessel. The screech of tearing steel made Jim feel as though the ship itself was being ripped apart.

At last, the vessels broke free of each other, leaving behind a massive debris field, hundreds of shattered panels and twisted fragments drifting in silence.

"Jim, you've gone fully off the deep end," Grace said, deadly serious.

The crew gaped at the viewscreen, stunned by how close their gamble had come to annihilation.

"Yeah, maybe that was a little closer than I thought," Jim admitted. "But it should keep the Aegis busy for a while." He forced confidence into his tone, but he knew the truth. The Federation destroyer would correct its course, and then in days—perhaps weeks—it would hunt them down, destroy the Argo, or worse, drag them away in chains.

From the cockpit of the Scarlett, Bucky saw Jim's unimaginable gambit. It had bought him his opening, but it wouldn't last. Only Jim and Bucky truly understood how desperate their situation had become. This was the only way.

Lisa's eyes widened. "Unauthorized launch from the cargo bay!"

Jim froze.

Liam shot to his feet. "Who the hell?"

Jim's heart dropped. The chair beside him sat empty, only a poker chip left behind. His fingers closed around it, hard. His stomach turned. "Bucky," he muttered under his breath.

"Sorry, brother," Bucky murmured as he throttled the shuttle straight at the Federation warship. The Scarlett burst through the flare-lit chaos, like an arrow trained on the Aegis's main hull. Bucky tapped the screen, voice dry. "You always said I had to be the center of attention, Jim."

"Bucky! What the hell are you doing?"

Bucky's voice came smooth, cocky, almost casual. "Becoming a legend."

Jim's chest locked tight. He shouted. "Get your ass back here, that's an order!"

Bucky laughed, light and easy.

"Sorry, Jim, you know that's the one order I can't follow. We'll never outrun this monster, and you know it."

Jim gritted his teeth. "Don't do this, Matthew. We always find another way!"

Bucky's tone softened into something Jim had never heard before, sincerity unshaken by bravado. "You have to get them safe, Jim. For Diane, for JT, for the crew. It's the only way. I'll need you to help Diane keep an eye on our boy. Treat him like your own."

"Bucky—"

"Tell JT he's ready. He's the best of all of us. I'll see you in another life, brother."

Bucky banked the Scarlett across the Aegis's hull, his hands steady on the controls. The comms cut out.

At that moment the admiral realized his mistake. "Evasive maneuvers! Turn to port, immediately!"

Bucky flew with nerves of steel. He slipped the shuttle under the warship's belly and locked on target.

The Scarlett struck the Aegis's FLS engine.

The explosion was blinding. The shockwave enveloped half the ship in fire. The destroyer lurched as secondary detonations tore through its hull. Blossoms of light consumed steel in every direction.

On the Argo, astonishment reigned. The Aegis lurched off course. Debris scattered from the impact, and the destroyer spun as its crew scrambled to regain control.

Inside the bridge of the Argo, Jim stood frozen. Bucky was gone. No more banter, no more miracle escapes, no last-second ace up their sleeve. Just reality.

"Captain... we have a clear path to the asteroid belt," Lisa said, her voice trembling.

Jim couldn't breathe.

"Jim," Grace whispered, touching his arm. "We have to go."

He forced himself to move and swallowed the grief lodged in his throat. "Get us out of here," he whispered. The words felt like they belonged to someone else.

The Argo hurtled away from Ganymede. Her hull ravaged, shuddered under the strain of rapid acceleration as she raced to escape before more Federation ships arrived. The Aegis, now nothing more than wreckage, drifted in Jupiter's immense gravity well. Its once-imposing frame was reduced to a monument to Bucky's sacrifice.

The victory felt hollow. There was no celebration. Not a word passed between the crew. Each member was too stunned to speak. No one moved.

Jim sat in the captain's chair, elbows braced on his knees, staring at his bloodied hand. The poker chip Bucky had left behind clenched in his fist. Its edges dug into his palm. His face was stone, but his grip told the truth.

"We're in the clear," Lisa said, as if waking from a trance. "No pursuit from the Aegis. No other Federation vessels detected in our vicinity."

Jim didn't look up.

Liam exhaled and rubbed his face with a hand. "Yeah. No pursuit. Because Bucky..." He stopped. "Because Bucky made sure of it."

Diane sat at her station. Her eyes were locked on some distant point. Her hands drifted to her stomach as if to comfort her unborn son. "I can't believe he's just gone. Is he really gone?" She turned to Grace for an answer.

Grace wrapped her arms around her and held her close. Her eyes lifted toward Jim. "Captain?"

Nothing.

The crew exchanged uneasy glances.

Then Mariana, who had been standing at the entrance of the bridge, stepped forward. "Jim."

He remained statuesque, unflinching.

She touched his arm. "Bucky did what he did because we were his family. Just like you, he'd do anything to protect us. We owe it to him to stop the Federation. You saw how far they're willing to go. They built a Federation base on top of that alien structure to run experiments on innocent people. They knew a higher intelligence couldn't control the compound, but they continued their experiments anyway, hiding it from everyone. Whatever McConnell is planning on Mars will be far worse. We have to see this through."

Jim finally raised his head. His eyes were dark and stormy. "Finish what, exactly?" His voice carried too much raw emotion. He stood there searching for the strength to stay in control, suppressing the rage clawing beneath the surface like a dangerous predator waiting to be unleashed.

The anger in his tone made the crew tense, but Mariana met it head on. "The fight against tyranny. The fight for freedom. It's still up to us, or they win."

Jim looked around at his crew—his family—and saw the loss carved into every face. Somehow, they were still alive. Because of Bucky's sacrifice.

Jim exhaled. His fury eased as he settled back into the captain's chair. "Lisa," he said, his tone heavy. "Mariana's right. We honor Bucky's sacrifice. Plot a course through the asteroid belt for Mars. We take down McConnell. For Bucky. For the future."

Lisa hesitated, then nodded. "Aye, Captain."

The crew returned to their stations. Their movements were lethargic.

Grace lingered nearby, watching Jim. Concern etched her face. "I know how much Bucky meant to you... to all of us. I'm truly sorry, Jim. I'm here if you want to talk."

Jim didn't answer. He feared that if he spoke, the dam inside him would break. Instead, he turned in his chair and stared at the viewscreen as Jupiter shrank behind them.

Grace sighed but didn't press. "I'll be in engineering if you need anything. They needed me there ten minutes ago." She turned and left.

Jim closed his eyes. He hadn't felt this alone since his father's disappearance.

In the med bay, JT began to panic after hearing the news of Bucky's death. His mind refused to accept that Bucky had sacrificed himself to save them all. He heard screaming, but it took him several moments to realize the sound came from his own throat. JT lost control. Energy surged around him as he sobbed. The pain was more than he could bear.

The lights of the med bay flared, sparks burst from overloaded circuits. The effects rippled throughout the ship's systems. Jim hailed Dr. Inoue. "What the hell is going on down there?"

Dr. Inoue's reply came fast. "It's JT, Captain. He's overcome with grief, and he's losing control of his new... abilities."

Mariana rushed into the med bay. She saw JT crying. His sobs echoed off the walls. Her cybernetic implants surged brightly, the pain almost overwhelming. The lights pulsed in rhythm with his outbursts.

Without hesitation, she grabbed JT, pulling him into a frantic embrace, burying his head against her shoulder. "It's all right, JT. You're not alone. We're here for you... I'm here for you."

His sobs quieted, and his body slowly stilled. The ship's systems returned to normal. They remained that way for a long while, neither of them needing to say another word.

Later that day, Diane sat on the edge of her bed, staring at nothing. The wedding band on her finger felt heavier than it should have.

She had spent most of her time weeping since they left Ganymede. Her mind had refused to accept reality. Even when Jim called the crew together to honor Bucky's sacrifice, Diane just kept asking Karl where Bucky was, even though he had already told her twice that he was gone. She had seen the explosion herself, but she still couldn't to accept it. Bucky was gone, just like that.

She longed for one more chance to speak with him. No goodbyes. No last words. Just gone.

Her trembling fingers reached for a small holographic recorder on her bedside table, one that hadn't been there before. She activated it, and Bucky's voice filled the room.

"Hey, sweetheart. If you're hearing this... well, that means I probably did something stupid, and I'm gonna be late for that candlelit dinner I promised you."

Her breath caught.

The recording continued. "I'm not giving you some 'don't be sad' speech, because I know how I would feel if I were you, instead of me. Seriously, Diane, I'm sorry I had to be the one to make the sacrifice. If it wasn't me, it would have been all of us. I know you're gonna miss me almost as much as I'm gonna miss you, but there is one thing I need you to do for me."

Tears began to pour.

"Live, Diane."

She closed her eyes, her vision blurring.

"Live for me. Live for our son. I'm sorry I won't get to watch him grow up with you. Just know I'll be watching. Don't forget to tell him how much I love him!"

The tears fell faster.

Bucky chuckled faintly in the recording. "And, hey. Don't let Jim get too moody. You know how he gets. Someone's gotta keep him in check."

A broken laugh escaped Diane, half-sob, half-chuckle.

"I love you, Diane. From the first moment your eyes locked onto mine. Always will."

Diane covered her mouth. Silent sobs wracked her body. She didn't move for a long time.

In the med bay, Dr. Inoue completed her last scans on JT. Her face was tight with concern.

JT sat on the exam table, rolling his shoulders. He felt unsettled, though he couldn't say why. "What's the verdict, Doc?"

Raegan frowned at the screen. "Your wounds are closing at an impossible rate. Your reflexes and strength are way above normal. I can't believe it, but your vitals are stable."

JT narrowed his eyes. "Sounds like there's a but in there?"

She hesitated, then turned the screen toward him. "But your neural activity is off the charts."

JT blinked. "How so?"

Raegan sighed. "Your neural network is building new connections with a complexity I can't explain. It's as if your brain's electromagnetic field is interacting with energy from the environment. For example, the EMFs from the electronic equipment here in the med bay. How's your pain level?"

JT flexed his fingers. He had sensed a shift in his mind's awareness since the transfusion, though he hadn't focused on it until now because of his exhaustion and wounds. "Far better than they should be." He felt stronger with each passing minute, though he had no idea how.

He turned to Mariana, who had been standing quietly at the door, watching him with unreadable eyes. "You knew this might happen." It wasn't a question.

Mariana nodded. "I suspected there could be side effects, but we had no choice. You were dying, JT. I couldn't let it happen. I..."

JT shook his head and waved a hand. "I know you did what you had to do, and I'll be thankful forever, but I'm a science experiment now, aren't I?"

Her lips twitched. "Technically, we both are."

JT let out a short laugh and shook his head. For the first time since Bucky's death, he felt something besides grief. He felt changed. Older somehow, wiser.

As the Argo sped toward Mars, Mariana sat alone in her quarters, decoding the last fragments of Ember's message.

Her fingers worked over the screen, piecing together the final sequence.

Then, without warning, the message unlocked.

Mariana's breath caught as Dr. Ember's voice. His real voice filled the air.

"This message is just for you, Mariana. The Federation has started their plans, and time is short."

She froze, and her heart hammered in her chest.

"You must understand. What you carry inside you was meant to be a bridge for humanity's evolution. You are the key."

Mariana's head spun. The room tilted out of focus.

"Soon you will discover who you truly are..."

The message cracked apart. Static swallowed the words. But then one final sentence broke through: "You are not alone."

Mariana stared at the screen, pulse racing.

Not alone?

She drew a shaky breath, and her thoughts reeled. She had to tell Jim. Immediately.

13

CHAPTER

STORMING THE CASTLE

As the *Argo* pressed forward, Jupiter's immense silhouette shrank in the viewports while the crew steadied themselves for the long journey home. Mars waited, and so did their confrontation with McConnell.

With the ever-present hum of the bridge in the background, Captain Jim Eckhart stood at the command console, staring at the decrypted file Mariana had worked on for what felt like an eternity. The final data fragment from the Ember file was ready at last.

He had no idea what to expect.

There was something in Mariana's manner—the way she sat perfectly still, her eyes unblinking—that told him she was holding something back.

Jim tapped the ship-wide intercom. "All hands, report to the mess hall. We need to talk."

⸻

Jim stood at the head of the table, the entire crew looking at Mariana and waiting. Lisa and Raegan monitored her datapad. Karl rubbed his bald forehead without realizing it, and Grace sat rigid, muscles coiled. The rest of the crew leaned close. Each wanting to ask a hundred questions.

JT sat beside Mariana, feeling a strange weight in his chest. Ever since the blood transfusion that had saved his life, his body had grown stronger. But he pushed the thought aside. This wasn't the time to discuss what was happening inside him.

Diane sat quietly with her hands resting in her lap. The absence of Bucky beside her was a wound none of them could ignore.

Mariana gathered her thoughts, then activated the holo dis-play to replay Ember's message. The final words of Elijah Ember flickered to life.

A grainy, distorted version of Ember's face appeared. It was older, weary, desperate.

> "Captain Eckhart, you and your crew are my last chance to stop the Federation's plans, which means their push to take Mars has already be-gun."

The crew exchanged uneasy glances. Jim stood stiff, his arms drawn tightly across his chest.

> "I designed the next-gen FLS drive to free hu-manity to explore and colonize the galaxy be-yond our solar system, not this madness. The Federation has created a weapon that could bring horrific destruction upon the entire sys-tem. McConnell's base on Mars is their most advanced research station. Once they succeed, they'll unleash their assault on the colonies. I've given you the tools to stop McConnell. It's up to you now.

Jim was silent. He had suspected as much all along.

"When I left Earth, I knew I had to hide my greatest breakthrough from the Federation. So, I left it... in Mariana."

The holo display zoomed in, and suddenly Mariana's face stared back at them.

Gasps rippled through the room. Mariana froze in place.

"Mariana Kade wasn't just a scientist working for the Federation. She was my greatest achievement. A human enhanced with cybernetic implants, capable of direct communication with machine AI systems through the electromagnetic spectrum. My formula gave her the genetic traits needed to interface with the next-gen FLS drive prototype without suffering the horrific side effects of the earlier human experiments. That makes Mariana truly one of a kind."

The crew sat transfixed by Ember's words. Humanity's golden goose had entrusted his last creation—Mariana—to the crew of the Argo.

JT's thoughts spun.

"She is what the Federation has been trying to create with the organic compound. I kept them from succeeding until now. With me gone, they will stop at nothing to take her back. She is paramount to their plan's success. She is the link between organic and artificial intelligence. She is... the key."

Mariana's breath hitched. For an instant she couldn't feel her own hands. The room seemed to tilt, and she fought the urge to push away from the table.

The message cut out; Mariana shut off the holo display and turned to face the crew. For a long moment no one spoke, as if they all needed time to absorb the meaning of Ember's words.

Jim let out a slow breath. "So, that's it, then?" His tone came out harsher than he intended. "You're not just some scientist running from the Federation. You're their greatest military asset."

Mariana balled her fists at her sides. "I didn't know." Her voice drifted as if caught in a memory. "Hearing Ember say it was like unlocking part of my mind that was always there."

JT felt a surge of empathy for her. "Ember said you were his greatest breakthrough. What does that even mean?"

Mariana's demeanor shifted. "It means I was never meant to have an ordinary life." She met Jim's gaze. "It means the Federation will never stop hunting me no matter what happens. Elijah must have planned my escape from them all along."

"Wait a minute," Lisa said. "He's telling us you're a cyborg? You've got, what... a motherboard in your chest? A CPU in your brain?"

Grace raised an eyebrow. "That's enough Lisa?"

Mariana gave her a flat look. "I'm not a machine. I'm human, just different. Enhanced in ways I don't fully understand, yet."

Grace looked unconvinced. "Well, that's not a lot to go on." She rubbed her temples. "So, what have we learned so far? The Federation's endgame isn't just mining this organic compound to take over the system using enhanced humans, and advanced ships. They're using Mariana to recreate the spark for their new technology. To lead their enhanced army.

"That tracks with everything we've uncovered," Jim said.

"If Mariana was their perfected version, why didn't they just make more of her?" Raegan asked.

Mariana hesitated. "Ember already answered that." She lowered her eyes to her hands. "I wasn't built with Federation technology. I was built with Dr. Ember's formula derived from the compound. He kept his greatest discoveries hidden from them... in me."

JT's pulse quickened. Her blood had saved him, but he still didn't know what it had done to him. He had no implants like her, so the compound's effect on his body was still a mystery.

Jim studied her for a long moment. "Well, that explains why McConnell wants you so badly. The Trojan site was an attempt to perfect their formula from what they found on Ganymede. But once Ember set off the self-destruct, the enhanced humans—those Chimerans—overran the black site, and the Federation fled without their research."

JT felt the mess hall tilt around him. His head swayed as he pressed his hand to his temple. He nearly passed out before he shook himself hard, trying to clear his thoughts.

Mariana turned toward him. Concern showed in her features. "You don't look so good, JT."

"What's happening?" Jim asked.

JT gritted his teeth. "I don't know, but it feels like my body's working overtime to heal my wounds. It's like I can almost hear someone trying to talk to me." A tingling spread through his hands, as if energy in the room coursed beneath his skin. The metal cup on the table rattled, then shook harder.

Lisa pointed. "Uh, what is that cup doing?"

The cup vibrated off the edge of the table. Before anyone could move, JT darted forward and caught it. His hand moved in a blur, crushing the metal without effort, bending it in half.

The crew stared in shock, their faces lit with astonishment at his sudden display of strength and reflexes.

Jim fixed his gaze on JT. "How is that possible? The compound in Mariana's blood has made you faster and stronger. Let's make sure you're not having any adverse side effects. Go see Dr. Inoue in the med bay and have her run a full scan for any side effects from the compound's healing properties. Just as a precaution, James."

JT glanced at his trembling hands. He remembered the surge of power when Bucky died. Was this the same storm, lurking inside, waiting to break loose again? JT placed the mangled cup down and nodded. "Yeah, maybe that's a good idea."

Jim walked with him toward the med bay, already preparing to brief Raegan on JT's latest episode.

＼＼＼＼＼

The Argo traveled for weeks through the asteroid belt without encountering a single raider scout ship. The captain wondered why. Was something larger happening within the independent factions? Was the Federation setting the way for another trap? There was no way to know for certain.

Now they were in open space, beyond the safety of the belt. Their destination was Mars. The weeks passed as the crew busied themselves with repairs and final preparations. They whispered about Ember's revelations in hushed tones during off-hours.

JT spent his free time attempting to reignite his brain's ability to interact with electromagnetic fields, but nothing. His body grew stronger and faster, but the spark had vanished. It felt as if the power needed tragedy to awaken, like when Bucky died. Mariana became the only one willing to train with him since his changes began. Even Liam could no longer match him in hand-to-hand combat.

The days blurred into whispered debates about Ember's message. But as Mars swelled larger in the viewports, the crew's unease sharpened into purpose.

Captain Eckhart and the senior crew worked toward finalizing the attack plan for McConnell's base. Mars now loomed on the viewscreen. Its rust-red disc swelled larger with every passing hour.

Jim gathered the crew. His presence manifested calm certainty. "You all know the plan. No mistakes. Team One makes the push to the base. Team Two buys us the window. Once we have McConnell's confession, we collapse the caldera and bury his base for good."

His eyes strayed to Bucky's empty seat. The ache of his absence pressed down on him until he drew in a breath and steadied himself.

"If anyone wants to back out, now is the time to speak up. No one is coming to save us. There's no cavalry if we fail. But I won't turn my back on Bucky's memory. He'd want us to see this through, not only for the Argo's crew, but for the entire solar system. This fight is for every soul who deserves a future free from Federation tyranny."

JT locked eyes with Mariana. His skin tingled, and his pulse thrummed with urgency, something he couldn't explain. He knew one thing with certainty: he was finished running. Fear no longer held sway. Only a determination to stop the Federation and protect Mariana, and his father.

It was at that moment that JT admitted to himself what he had tried to deny all along: he had fallen for her. He set it aside. There was only room for McConnell. JT decided he must be the one to make him pay. But could he make his father understand? He chuckled at an inward thought: How was I ever afraid of the truth?

The Argo crept through space like a silent assassin. Mars dominated the forward view.

From orbit, the planet looked tranquil. Dust storms churned beneath its thin atmosphere. The sprawling domes and underground cities remained invisible from this distance. But Jim knew better. This was McConnell's domain, and they were about to willingly enter. Would Ember's plan hold them through?

In the makeshift war room, the giant volcano, Olympus Mons, dominated the holo display, its ancient lava tubes webbing beneath the caldera straight into McConnell's command center.

The aureoles of Mars — or lava tubes — sprawled for hundreds of kilometers, the volcano rising and stretching across the surface.

"With the element of surprise and Ember's help, we can end this before it starts." He tapped the panel to zoom in on the access points. Mariana reviewed Ember's stolen blueprints. She studied every corridor.

McConnell's base was no mere bunker. It was an impenetrable fortress.

"From here, McConnell could take over the system," said Jim. "Mars is the crown jewel. Control it, and you control the trade lanes."

"Defenses are going to be heavy," Grace said, her arms folded. "What's your plan to get past them?"

Jim gave a hard nod. "We hit the base head-on, draw their attention, and keep them focused on us while the shuttle flies into the abandoned mining cave entrance that leads to the lava tubes."

JT frowned. "The abandoned tunnels? You know they're abandoned for a reason, right?"

Jim ignored the remark. "The lava tubes connect directly to these tunnels. They were mined during early colonization, abandoned since, but Ember says there's still an uncharted opening."

Liam studied the projection with a skeptical look. "That's one hell of a gamble. If those tunnels collapsed, the plan dies with us. Or worse, they collapse while we're inside."

Jim's face hardened. "Get us out if you can. If not, save the Argo." Jim turned to the crew and set his shoulders. "The Argo draws fire with Ember's EMP, my shuttle team will infiltrate, plant the explosives, force the confession, get the hell out, and collapse the caldera."

"The whole operation depends on Ember's EMP." He added a wink.

Grace replied with pride. "We moved three turrets into the expanded bay, rewired them in parallel, and rerouted the power grid. We had to shut down power to several lower decks, but Ember's design is almost online."

"Good thing Ember was ahead of his time," Jim said with approval.

"So basically, we use Ember's weapon to make ourselves the biggest Federation target in the system, just so the shuttle team can slip past?" said Lisa.

"Yes. That's exactly what we're going to do." Jim scanned the room. "Liam and Mariana are coming with me on the shuttle."

The moment Jim said Mariana's name, JT sprang to his feet. His voice rang with defiance. "No. You're not leading the away mission. I am." All eyes turned.

Grace gave a sharp snort. "You're not serious, are you, JT? Those abilities only get you so far, it's your decision-making that's lacking."

"She has a point, James, why should you lead the mission?" came Jim's reply.

JT faced his father directly. "Because if something goes wrong, I'm the one best suited to deal with it. My wounds should have killed me, but Mariana's blood saved me, and now I'm stronger and faster than any of us. If we're serious about winning, the Argo can't survive this fight without her captain on the bridge, and I won't let others risk their lives to protect me when I should be protecting them."

He took a breath. "I know you're afraid you'll lose me like you lost Bucky." His voice softened. "Be honest with us. You know it's the only way." They stood in that moment, eyes locked onto each other, the crew mesmerized. "Mariana knows it too."

Eyes moved to Mariana.

For a heartbeat, Mariana saw both father and son staring at her, waiting. The weight of their auras pressed harder than any implant ever could. She studied them all before answering. "It's a slim chance but he's right, though calling it that is generous. It feels more like a suicide mission."

JT turned back to Jim. "Dad, you know I'm ready. The question is, do you trust me?"

A tear slid down Jim's cheek. "Bucky was right..."

JT looked puzzled. "What do you mean?"

Jim pulled him into a tight embrace. "You really are the best of all of us."

JT hugged his father back with equal strength. Father and son wept, then they began to laugh through the tears.

Diane and Grace rose and joined the embrace with the crew following close behind.

Mariana stood frozen at the periphery until the crew turned to look at her. Jim called out. "In this family, no one passes on group hugs. Get in here, Mariana."

Mariana rushed forward and the crew engulfed them all in one massive embrace.

"'For Bucky!' JT shouted.

The crew thundered back.

JT lowered his voice. 'For you, Dad.'"

Jim smiled and spoke softly, "All this time I've been trying to protect you, James. But now you're the one protecting all of us. I'm so proud of you."

Jim rubbed his eyes and turned the crew's focus back to the plan. "All right, James. You lead team one into the mining caves here. Fly the shuttle inside as far as possible. Land here, then move on foot to the lava tube entrance at this intersection. The tubes will take you under the command center."

He pointed to the schematic. "Diane has marked your wrist displays with prime spots for explosive charges. Plant them along the way. Follow the blueprints and they'll take you beneath the command center. Your objective is to reach McConnell, force a confession, and use their communications tower to broadcast the Federation's plans to the entire system."

His voice dropped, and he added, "Once you're clear, we blow the charges. The explosions will collapse the tubes and rupture the magma chamber. That will trigger a volcanic eruption powerful enough to bury the base. Then it's over, and we figure out what comes next."

∧ DEBT MUST BE P∧ID

G race began her protest. "Jim, this is even more insane than your Gauntlet Run."

Jim shot back. "Come on, Grace, unpredictability is the only way we survive. Our best option is to take the fight to them, before they can use their numbers against us."

Lisa rubbed the bridge of her nose. "Are we really sure about this, Captain?"

Jim smirked. "Sure as I was about the Gauntlet Run," he said with a wink.

Lisa muttered under her breath, but the faint grin gave her away.

Liam checked his weapon, then turned toward JT. "You ready for this?"

JT flexed his fingers. The strange energy under his skin pulsed stronger. "Ready as I'll ever be."

Liam nodded. "Then let's get to it."

The ship vibrated as they entered the Martian atmosphere.

Lisa gripped the panel. "Two Federation ships inside the crater. They're climbing fast to clear the summit."

Jim adjusted his harness. "McConnell knows we're here." The hull rattled as thin wisps of atmosphere whipped past the Argo's shields, the red planet swelling in the viewport like a rising tide.

Lisa accelerated. The thrusters threw the Argo into a hard bank. The Martian sky burned red behind them, the thin atmosphere flowing around the hull as they made their final descent.

Karl's hands moved with precision over his console. "Ember's EMP countermeasures are online. A direct hit should disable their defensive measures for thirty seconds at most."

Jim grinned. "That's all we need."

Grace eyed him warily. "Let's hope you're right, Captain."

In the lower decks, JT, Mariana, and Liam sat in the shuttle, waiting at the cargo ramp. It lowered with a hydraulic groan. The shuttle plunged from the Argo's bay. For a breathless moment, the shuttle felt weightless, then gravity seized it, hurling them toward the mountain's shadow.

They descended into darkness, stealth systems engaged, their floodlights dead, throwing no signs of their passing into the Martian sky.

The Argo blazed across the night. Its exterior lights struck jagged rock spires below masking the shuttle as it flew into the hidden opening, landing minutes later on the flat cavern floor. The insertion team unstrapped and prepared to disembark.

JT's heart pounded, not from fear but from exhilaration. Something inside him felt close to awakening.

Mariana adjusted her weapon. "You good?"

JT exhaled. "Yeah. I'm ready."

Liam checked his comms. "All right. Let's move."

Boots struck the cavern floor. JT steadied himself and scanned the dark. His patched leather trench coat hung heavy. He had sown the gashes closed, but the stains of his blood were impossible to hide. Mariana glanced at him and felt uneasy. The fury radiating from him burned hotter than the sun. Maybe McConnel was the one in danger. Would JT lose control and try to kill McConnell in a rage or complete the mission? She wasn't sure.

The team lit their exo-lights.

"Stay close," Liam ordered.

The caves narrowed. Their walls were cracked and unstable. Each step left a deep mark in the soil.

Mariana checked her pad. "The lava tube that leads to McConnell's base lies about a klick east of here."

Liam gave a low whistle. "Then let's not keep the bastard waiting."

JT's skin prickled again. He searched for a word to capture it. "Awakening" maybe.

High above Olympus Mons, the Argo roared through the emaciated atmosphere and descended toward the crater's lip. Below, the Federation ships flared their thrusters, burning white-hot against the red planet as they climbed to intercept.

Inside the cockpit, Lisa pulled the ship into a wild roll. "It's time, Captain. Let's bring the noise."

Jim strapped in. "Karl, send them a hello for me."

Karl laughed and slammed his hand on the controls. A barrage of EMP blasts erupted from the reworked turrets, spiraling in dazzling arcs of light that would have made the Northern Lights look pale.

The Federation base's anti-aircraft defenses lit up the sky. Their sensors scrambled to lock on to the Argo. The ground fire had little effect on the EMP wave as it struck the base with a direct hit and shut down the turrets one by one.

"Here they come," Grace called from tactical.

A squadron of Federation gunships appeared, closing on McConnell's base. They broke formation and accelerated to intercept. Their thrusters screamed as they cut through the sky.

Jim braced himself. "Lisa, evasive maneuvers."

She activated the maneuver. The Argo's thrusters lit up; g-forces crushing the crew into their restraints as the ship weaved through the turret fire and skimmed the volcano's outer wall. Lisa's hands never faltered as she pulled them level again.

Plasma bursts hissed past the hull, the Federation gunner's aim faltered. The Argo's surprise EMP attack kept them off balance.

Karl fired again. The EMP blasts spread wide, striking an Interceptor. The explosion of light turned into a blinding corona across its hull; the vessel staggered, engines useless as it dropped toward the surface.

The gunship slammed into the ground with a rolling fireball that lit the Martian night. Jim slapped the comms. "Liam, you're clear. How close are you to the base?"

Deep beneath Olympus Mons, JT, Mariana, and Liam pressed through the lava tubes with weapons raised. Their shadows flickered across ancient rock as they set charges along the walls just as Diane had instructed. They pushed deeper into the maze until the tunnel opened into a cavern where red emergency lights painted the metallic walls of a hidden Federation entrance.

"Hold," Liam whispered, raising a fist.

Ahead, two guards slouched near a security checkpoint. Their rifles dangled carelessly.

JT's skin tingled, and the vibrations beneath it grew stronger. His breath caught as the lights dimmed, then flickered violently.

One guard clutched his head. "Do you feel that?"

JT realized that the interference was his doing. He had focused his mind on the guards, disrupting their thoughts.

Liam seized the chance. His rifle barked twice, and both guards dropped.

Mariana hurried to the terminal. Her wrist display mapped their position. "The command center is down this corridor. The guards at either end are blind to the entrance, so once we cross, we'll have a straight path to the entrance."

Liam's face hardened. "Then let's find McConnell."

They advanced through the steel passage, deeper into the bowels of the base. When they reached the control room junction, no guards stood watch.

The motion sensors triggered. The doors hissed open.

Dozens of screens cast a cold blue glow across the command room.

At the center stood McConnell, flanked by five technicians focused on their stations.

The team stormed inside with rifles raised. Liam barked at the techs, "Face down, hands behind your heads. Move and I'll drop you where you stand."

The terrified techs obeyed without argument. Liam bound them quickly and took position to cover JT and Mariana. Mariana accessed the command uplink into the Mars open net—open station bands—anything the Federation would struggle to control.

McConnell, however, seemed amused. "I was wondering when you'd arrive."

The admiral wore an advanced exo-frame suit, its dark plating laced with glowing conduits. Cybernetic implants pulsed beneath his uniform and crawled across his body. His face a twisted, reptilian cast.

Usually stone-faced in firefights, Liam flinched at the sight, as if McConnell had become something inhuman.

JT stepped forward. "We know what you've done. You'll tell the system what the Federation is planning or we start shooting." His voice was sharp.

McConnell chuckled and folded his hands. "Is that so? You don't understand at all." His eyes cut to Mariana. "But you do. Don't you?"

Mariana froze. "What are you talking about?"

He stepped closer. "No, you don't remember who you really are; interesting."

"I know exactly who I am." Her voice caught.

"No," McConnell whispered. "You only know that you were made in a lab. Just like the others."

She shook her head. "You're lying."

McConnell smiled faintly. "Am I?"

JT's blood boiled. His hands clenched on the rifle as McConnell's words rang in his ears.

"Enough," Liam snapped. "Start talking."

McConnell sighed. "You want the truth? The truth is you're all inconsequential.

Liam pointed his barrel directly at McConnel and said, "Start talking, or I start shooting."

"You're nothing more than Eckhart's lapdog, but fine. Project Chimera was never about creating a new FLS drive. It was about conquest, an army of enhanced soldiers powering Federation destroyers to break the system. I'll use Mariana to lead the enhanced humans, and they'll answer to me alone. Mars will be mine, free of Earth's committees.

"She's the key, but Ember hid her too well. I pushed the Federation to move her to the belt, leverage to keep Ember compliant. Then Eckhart safeguarded her on his ship, and we've been hunting you down ever since. After she vanished, Ember blew the Trojan site, the test subjects broke loose, and the Federation scientists regrouped here.

"Now that you've brought Mariana back to me, I'll finish the work Ember began. There's your confession."

The weight of his words made JT stagger backward.

"Jesus help us," said Liam.

McConnell smiled. "But here's the best part. You'll never leave this base alive. Welcome home, Mariana."

JT's fists clenched. He felt the room's currents, the exo-frame's rhythm. Micro surges riding each wave. He pushed the current field that made him faster.

Chaos erupted. McConnell lunged at JT, his exo-frame blurring with unnatural speed. JT barely reacted before a plated fist slammed into his gut, launching him across the chamber. His rifle was sent flying as the blow knocked the wind from him.

He crashed into the wall. Pain flared through his ribs. Before he could recover, McConnell was already closing the distance.

Liam fired, but McConnell wove through the shots as though he could see them coming. His movements were too precise, too quick.

"You're all so predictable," McConnell sneered. His implants glowed brighter as they came fully online.

JT groaned as he forced himself upright. His vision sharpened. The air around McConnell rippled. JT felt the distortions in the energy currents pulsing across the room.

It struck him all at once. McConnell was relying on his cybernetics to manipulate the electromagnetic fields. But JT could do it without them.

He tried to focus on the sensation, but McConnell pressed again.

Mariana intercepted him. Her own reflexes matched his. Their strikes blurred in a storm of fists and parries, a deadly dance of speed and precision.

McConnell roared as he slipped past her guard and clamped a hand around her throat. He lifted her with ease, his eyes gleaming with arrogance. "I should have known. You're just another failed experiment. It doesn't matter that you've begun to remember. You're too late to stop me."

Mariana clawed at his grip, gasping for air.

JT felt the energy inside him surge. He didn't think. He reacted. A wave of power tore from his chest like a battering ram that slammed into McConnell.

The admiral staggered, eyes wide. "What are you doing?"

JT advanced, unaware his hands were extended wide in front of him.

McConnell stumbled again. Sparks ripped across his implants, chattering out of sync as JT's interference desynchronized the exo suit's control system. He clutched his head, and his knees buckled.

"What... are you doing to me?" he gasped.

JT steadied his voice and held back the rage. "Kicking your ass, Admiral. Just like my dad did. You owe my family a debt, and now it's time to pay. This is for Bucky."

Alarms screamed through the base.

"They know we're here!" Mariana shouted.

At the comms, Liam had already uploaded McConnell's confession. He cast JT a hard glance, then slammed the transmit button. "Time to go." Within seconds, the confession was trending on miner boards from the Valles to the Southern colonies.

McConnell writhed on the floor, his implants sparking violently.

JT hesitated for a beat, a moment of composure, then he turned and ran.

Above Mars's surface, the Argo banked hard and fired the EMP weapon once again, while simultaneously dodging a fresh wave of plasma fire. The Federation ships attempted to outflank them.

Jim hit the comms. "Liam, where the hell are you?"

"Mission successful, Captain!" Liam reported back over the comms. "We transmitted his confession. Meet us at the extraction point!"

JT and his companions raced through the lava tubes as fast as the non-enhanced Liam could run.

Jim's lips tightened. "Lisa, bring us in closer for extraction."

Lisa altered the ship's direction and dropped altitude toward the mining cave entrance.

Karl launched another round of EMP blasts to keep the Federation ships at bay and buy them precious seconds to reach their pickup coordinates.

JT and Mariana sprinted toward the shuttle bay door and dove inside. JT headed directly for the controls before the others had time to lock into their seats. Minutes later the shuttle shot out of the mining cave entrance. Thrusters blared behind them.

Karl opened the cargo bay doors.

The shuttle barreled into the cargo bay on a dangerous trajectory slamming hard against the maglevs.

Karl sealed the cargo bay doors. Without confirmation, Lisa punched the engines into action.

The Argo rocketed upward through the Martian atmosphere, leaving McConnell's base to burn.

Behind them, a series of explosions began. The charges blasted through dozens of meters of solid rock.

The fractures caused the volcano's inner walls to fall into the caldera. Pressure from the magma chamber tore through the side wall of Olympus Mons.

Sections of the Federation base broke apart and sank into the magma. Toxic gas plumes burst through pressurized vents all throughout the base. McConnell's failed empire sank into the magma, buried forever inside Olympus Mons.

The Argo roared through the Martian sky. Its thrusters screamed as it dodged incoming plasma fire from the last of the Federation gunships. A final volley of EMP blasts forced them to scatter for fear of falling out of the sky.

With masterful control, Lisa navigated the Argo away from the relentless pursuit of the Federation's forces.

"They're not letting us go that easy," Grace broadcast from her station as she adjusted the shielding levels.

"Why would they?" Jim growled. His eyes fixed on the warning lights flashing red across the displays. "We just exposed their plans to the entire solar system. They'll be coming for their pound of flesh."

"Yeah, well, let's piss them off just a little bit more before that happens," said Karl as he launched a last volley with his best defensive measures.

The rear turrets spat out a barrage of counterfire. Highly explosive flak rounds detonated midair and created an impenetrable wall of shrapnel behind them.

The two nearest Federation destroyers weren't fast enough to evade the blast field. Their hulls punctured, cores burst into fire, as shockwaves spread through the thin Martian air.

Lisa hammered the controls to avoid the worst of the explosions, deftly guiding the Argo out of harm's way.

"We need to make our move before they regroup and give chase."

                        \\\\\\

The carnage below was surreal. Olympus Mons split open, spewing fire and stone high into the Martian sky. Lava surged across the crater rim as shockwaves rolled out of the giant's heartbeat.

The colonies nearest the volcano stood watching the on-slaught. Ash clouds turned daylight to dusk. Protective domes cracked beneath the rain of molten rock, alarms blar-ing as emergency crews scrambled to hold them together. In the distance, Valles Marineris trembled with quakes, its cities shrouded beneath the spreading dust. For hundreds of miles, Mars itself seemed to cry out.

Somewhere under the rolling ash, thousands of colonists clung to survival; their fate changed with a single gambit.

Jim exhaled. "Then let's get to it. Lisa, punch it." He opened the comms. "Liam, James, status?"

In the lower decks, Liam helped JT limp to a nearby seat so he could take a load off his battle-worn body. "JT is stable," Liam said. "Barely."

JT's face was pale as he tried to sit upright. The strain of using his abilities had drained his body. "I'm fine."

"You're about fifty shades of not fine," Liam snapped. "Lay down before I duct tape you to the table."

JT grumbled but obeyed. Exhaustion pressed on him after the battle with McConnell, a strange sensation like static electricity rippled through his body.

Raegan stood nearby and tapped her console. "He'll need real medical attention soon. That blood transfusion did something to him no one has ever diagnosed before."

"Understood, Doctor. Get strapped in, everyone. Looks like we've worn out our welcome," said Jim.

As the Argo passed Mars' space stations, the Federation ships far below tried to regroup, but they were too far behind to catch them. The stress of the ordeal began to lift from the bridge.

Jim stood at the command station, staring at the red planet shrinking in the viewscreen. The Federation ships vanished from sight.

Grace rubbed her forehead and laughed morbidly. "Holy shit. We actually pulled it off."

Jim formulated his reply slowly. "I don't know," he countered. "Feels like someone let us go."

Liam dusted himself off and frowned. "What we did was impossible, Jim. Don't be an ass. Take the win."

Mariana, who had stayed silent since leaving the base, finally spoke. "There's... something else."

Jim looked at her.

She continued. "A hidden message unlocked. I have no idea how Elijah managed it."

Jim's brow furrowed. "What did it say?"

Mariana braced herself and played the recording again.

A holographic figure flickered above the command console: Elijah Ember. His face looked worn with age, and his eyes were full of regret.

"Great work, Captain Eckhart. If you're hearing this, then you've beaten McConnell, and you've earned the right to know the truth, so listen carefully. McConnell was never the mastermind of the enhanced human program. He was only a puppet. The true architects are forging ahead with their plans to retake Ganymede, to restart Project Chimera."

"Your journey is just beginning. You'll have to continue on your path to uncover the truth and stop this evil from overtaking the system. You are humanity's last hope."

A set of coordinates appeared on the display. The message ended. Silence filled the bridge. Jim gripped the console's edges.

Liam let out a slow breath. "So that's it? We fought through the impossible, and now we have to do it again, or something worse will take McConnell's place?"

Mariana closed her eyes. "Looks like it."

JT, still weak but recovering, spoke from the doorway. "We can't quit now. We have to make a plan and stop them."

Jim turned.

JT stood unsteady, but his spirit burned. "We finish this," he said. "No matter what it takes."

Jim studied him for a long moment. Finally, he made his decision. "We'll set a course for one of the independent space stations for now."

Grace exhaled and shook her head. "What about those coordinates Ember left us?"

Jim turned to Mariana.

She brought up the final set of coordinates from Ember's message, "Not sure yet. Let me map it's trajectory first, but it's way out in the system, beyond our reach."

Back in the crew quarters, JT sat on his bunk, staring at his hands. The room was dim, shadows stretched by the soft glow of the ship's lights. The energy stirred inside him. He heard the hum of the ship's systems, but it was more than sound. He felt them, almost as if they were speaking.

The electromagnetic fields around him seemed alive, a web of invisible forces flowing through the air and pulsing under his skin.

Mariana stood at the doorway, watching him.

"You feel the compound changing you, don't you?" she asked softly.

"Yeah." His eyes never left Bucky's trench coat. The thought that he and his dad would have to confront their past without Bucky there to confide in pressed at the front of his mind.

Mariana stepped closer. "You're going to be okay, JT."

JT slumped, his shoulders deflating. "What am I turning into?" he asked.

"Something new. But still you, JT. You're not like the others. My blood is different. Ember made sure of that."

JT stammered. "Yeah, but I don't have your cybernetic implants. I'm different? What if I turn into one of those monsters that tried to kill the crew, Dad, or worse, you?"

JT's fingers curled into fists. Mariana placed her hands over his, softened his grip, and slid her hand into his. She looked into his eyes with a concern that revealed true feelings for him.

"Then we'll find out what this means together." JT swallowed hard, eyes drifting to the battered trench coat in his lap. Bucky had worn it like a second skin, a reminder that strength meant sacrifice, not power for its own sake.

The thought struck him cold. What if his father looked at him now and saw a weapon instead of a son? The Argo drifted through the vast emptiness of space, the red glow of Mars fading behind them.

On the bridge, Jim sat in the captain's chair, spinning lazily. Grace leaned on the engineering console and rubbed her eyes. Mariana worked at her station, searching for any last clues to Elijah's message. JT stood at the viewport on the observation deck, staring into the endless void.

They survived the battle, but their war with the Federation was only beginning.

A soft beep from Mariana's console broke the silence.

"I've mapped it out," she said.

Jim turned. "The coordinates?"

Mariana nodded. Her green eyes glowed faintly as the light from the display struck them.

"They lead to an uncharted sector. Far out in the solar system, well past any known Federation-controlled zones."

Lisa frowned from her pilot's seat. "There's nothing out there. No stations, no colonies. Just the Kuiper Belt."

Jim exhaled. "Then why send us there?"

Mariana's fingers hovered over the controls. "I don't know."

JT spoke. "Maybe that's where we'll find the answers we need to stop this madness, once and for all."

Grace rubbed her temples. "Answers? We just risked everything to take down McConnell. What if there's nothing out there? And the tech to get us there and back alive doesn't even exist."

Jim regarded her with steely eyes. "He must have left a clue about how to reach the edge of the system without dying. We just have to find it."

Grace considered his words. Trust softened her expression as she nodded.

"So, what now?" Liam asked.

Jim stood, rolling Bucky's poker chip between his fingers one last time before slipping it into his pocket.

"We get off the radar. Find a place to lie low for now."

Standing by the viewport, JT felt something in his chest that constricted his breathing. It was the same sensation as before, only stronger.

Jim stood stoic while bewilderment spread across the bridge.

Lisa let out a low whistle. "This is just too creepy. A supposedly dead billionaire sending us messages from the far side of the solar system."

Jim took a slow breath and turned to her. "We stick to the original plan. That's good enough for now."

Lisa hesitated, then nodded. "Aye, Captain."

She keyed in the coordinates, and the thrusters rumbled as the ship angled toward the their destination.

As the crew settled in for the journey, Jim found himself at the observation deck.

Grace approached, leaning against the railing. "Tell me something," she said as she studied the stars. "Do you think this fight ever ends?"

Jim thought before answering. Then, he shook his head. "Not for us. But maybe someday for the kids. JT and Mariana deserve the chance for a normal life."

Grace sighed, her shoulders slumped. "Didn't think so."

"It's a race to see who gets to Ember's secrets first, and the fate of the solar system is the prize."

Grace turned back to the stars. "You're right. I just wish Mariana had ended up on someone else's ship." She slid her arms around Jim's waist and pulled him close.

⟋⟋⟋⟋⟋

JT sat in the dim crew quarters, contemplating the events that just transpired. Bucky's battered trench coat lay beside him.

Mariana entered and stopped in the doorway. "How are you feeling, JT?"

JT nodded. "Better. Thanks."

She studied him for a moment, then sat across from him. "When I first learned what I was, I felt lost, angry," she admitted.

JT looked at her. "You're not lost anymore. You have us."

She smiled and winked. "Neither are you, JT. You have me."

A long silence passed. Then JT smiled, and she wrapped him in a hug.

The Argo's FLS drive ran at maximum velocity. The power core containment unit read just inside safe levels.

Jim returned to the bridge and stood beside Lisa as she finished her calculations.

"Final chance to change your mind," she joked.

Jim gave her an amused look. "Not a chance."

Lisa studied him. "Figured." She hit the final command sequence.

The Argo surged forward, streaking into the void , toward the unknown. Ember's secrets waited.

EPILOGUE

The Shadows Move

The command deck of Outpost Epsilon was steeped in unease. No one wasted words or movements. The environmental systems seemed louder than usual as recycled air pumped into the lungs of some of the most powerful people in the Federation.

Through the high reinforced windows, the broken silhouette of the F.S.S. *Aegis* hung motionless in space. Once sleek and imposing, the ship's form had been left inoperable by the battle with the *Argo*. Half-melted plating and crippled engines bore witness to Bucky's sacrifice. Once an indomitable force, the defeated warship, now drifted as a testament to the resilience of a mining crew that should have been easily removed.

A group of engineers were assessing the damage inside the war room; the atmosphere remained cold and despondent. No one dared speak. Confusion reigned.

At the center of the table, seated in a high-backed chair that resembled a throne, Admiral Helena Drayton watched in silence. Her expression wasn't angry. If anything, she looked uninterested.

"We lost an entire black site, all our research," Vice Admiral Tobias Raines said at last, his voice sharp with restrained fury. "The Aegis, our flagship, was crippled by a freighter with an outdated FLS drive. And McConnell..." Raines shook his head. "McConnell let himself get outplayed by a crew of belt miners."

Drayton remained quiet. She continued to study the ruined Aegis, her fingers pressed together in a thoughtful pyramid.

"I don't see anything salvageable here. The High Council wants answers," Raines pressed, frustration mounting. He gestured toward the burning wreck. "This is a disaster."

Drayton finally turned to him. A sly smile cut across her lips. "Oh, Tobias." She leaned forward, her fingers tapping the table. "They're doing exactly what we wanted them to do, even with McConnell's treachery."

Raines narrowed his eyes. "How in the system was that what we wanted?"

Drayton gestured to the holo display at the center of the table. A map of the solar system appeared, marking Federation sites at Ganymede, Mars, and the Trojan Belt. One marker pulsed with urgency.

She tapped it. The map zoomed, showing the Argo's position as it unknowingly passed a Federation spy drone.

"We know where they are," she said smoothly. "Their ship is damaged, and they have limited options."

Raines studied the display, his frown deepening. "Once their ship is repaired, they'll attempt to track down the source of Ember's message."

Drayton's smile widened. "We always suspected Ember left something behind, a contingency hidden from us. So, your plan is to let them find it for us?"

The war room fell silent. Officers shifted uneasily.

"You're saying," Raines spoke slowly, "that we let them escape, with Mariana?"

Drayton's glare hardened. "No, Tobias. We're letting them lead us to Ember's secrets. When they deliver, we erase them. Permanently."

Raines turned to a tactical officer, a young woman with piercing blue eyes who monitored fleet data. "What happens if they get there before we do?"

Drayton's voice never wavered. "It doesn't matter. We'll follow them every step. Once we seize Ember's secrets, we move forward as planned." Whoever owns Ember's secrets, control's the High Council."

Raines interlocked his fingers. "You're that confident?"

Drayton turned back to the viewport. Her uniform seemed to absorb the faint light of the stars. It rendered her almost spectral. She watched as the Aegis was dragged toward its berth, its once-mighty presence reduced to a burned-out carcass.

"Without a doubt," she said with icy certainty, "I told you before that the game has just begun. Eventually, they'll think it's safe to act, and when they do, we'll be waiting."

Raines felt a chill crawl down his spine.

Helena Drayton wasn't a woman who tolerated defeat. If she had planned a contingency for this outcome, then the crew of the Argo had no idea what awaited them once their usefulness ran out.

∖∖∖∖∖∖

The air aboard the Argo was thick with mixed emotions. Bucky was gone. His sacrifice had bought them freedom, but it came at an unbearable cost.

Jim sat in his chair, the poker chip in his palm. Diane stared out the viewscreen beside him, silent.

The bridge was hushed, every eye on Jim as they waited for him to address Caldwell's message from Mars.

"We have a change of plans." His voice was rough. "We received word from Caldwell that Federation patrols are policing every station in the system, even the unincorporated ones. Caldwell says the eruption has Mars in chaos. Patrols stretched thin, riots in the colonies. He can help us slip past Mars control unnoticed, and he'll cover our docking fee. That's our best play for now. He says the Southern colonies call us heroes. The Western colonies will shoot us on sight."

Grace bristled. "It's not like we meant to cause any harm. If the Federation's plans had gone forward, the devastation would have been far worse. Why would Caldwell help us anyways? Out of kindness?"

Jim shook his head. "For the information we have about Ganymede and Elijah Ember. It's worth more to him than Gus' smuggling operation."

The veteran crew began preparations for their return to Mars. The tasks at hand gave them a welcome distraction from what awaited.

Static suddenly rippled through the ship's comms. It was a voice that shouldn't have been there, a voice that froze every breath in the room.

"You are not alone."

No one moved. No one breathed.

JT's eyes met Mariana's.

Silence.

Only the desolation of the void remained. And the war to come.

※※※※※

Admiral Helena Drayton felt a vibration through the steel floors as she thought about her plans to hunt down the Argo. She stood at the center of the war room, her gaze fixed on the tactical display. The solar system glowed in perfect detail, red markers pinpointing key locations: Ganymede, where the Argo had barely escaped; Mars, McConnell's ruined base; deep beyond Saturn, the site of a failed attempt to recover Ember's secrets.

Outside the viewport, the Nemesis loomed in the hangar, its black hull etched with crimson insignias, the mark of the Federation's Black Fleet. Sleek and spectral under the station lights, its presence was understood: to finish what the Aegis could not.

Behind Drayton, Admiral Tobias Raines stood stiff, his arms folded across his chest. The officers around the table exchanged wary looks. They braced for the clash that they knew was coming.

"This is reckless," Raines said at last, his voice nearly breaking. "You never said you were sending the Nemesis. That ship isn't even fully operational."

Drayton didn't turn. "I disagree," she replied evenly, her eyes scanning the readouts. "For our purposes, it's ready enough."

Raines' frustration boiled. "The Black Fleet wasn't meant for this. Not for chasing down a ragtag crew of miners turned insurgents. You treat them like they're a threat, a rebellion."

Drayton's lips curved into a cold smile. "They crippled our flagship. They defeated McConnell."

"They got impossibly lucky," Raines snapped.

"Perhaps." She turned, her eyes locking onto his, her stare cutting the air colder than space. "I don't make plans based on luck, Tobias. I bet on certainty. And it's certain they won't resist the lure of Ember's secrets. When they make their move, we'll be there."

She gestured toward the display. "For now, we watch and wait."

Raines said nothing more. He couldn't. Because she was right. This was their chance to reclaim what Ember had stolen from them.

Drayton turned back to the viewport. Her figure was outlined by the glow of stars as she stared at the Nemisis. "The game has only begun." Her voice was quiet, but it carried across the war room.

Raines thought only of how fortunate they were to have Drayton on their side. Her intelligence was unmatched, but she was evil in its purest form.

The command room doors slid open, and a new figure entered. A striking man in midnight-black armor with a crimson insignia approached, a helmet tucked under one arm. His presence sent fear through the officers. His eye, lit with a cybernetic enhancement with a golden glow, swept across the room.

Drayton turned to face him. "Commander Abaddon."

He gave a slight nod. "The Nemesis is ready for pursuit. Once we retake the base on Ganymede, we will wait for the Argo and its treasonous crew. When they move past Jupiter toward Ember's coordinates, we'll be ready." His voice was smooth and exact, but devoid of warmth.

Drayton's smile widened. "Don't fail us, Commander."

Jim sat deep in thought in his quarters, reflecting on how Bucky had saved them all. A knock sounded at the door.

"Come in," Jim rasped. Diane stepped inside.

Jim rose at once.

Diane shook her head. "I'm not here for the captain," she said, her voice raw with grief. "I'm here for Bucky's best friend."

Jim exhaled and sat again. Tears formed in his eyes. "Diane, I—"

"I know," she cut in. "I just... I need you to tell me this was the only way. I need to know there wasn't another path for us to survive." Her throat tightened as she whispered, "Tell me the truth."

Jim swallowed and forced the words out. "It was the only way, Diane. If he hadn't sacrificed himself, we all would have died, or worse, been taken for experiments. Bucky made his choice. Same as any of us would to save the ones we love."

A sob broke free from Diane as a single tear slid down her cheek. She wiped it away furiously. "You know what that jerk told me after we got married?" Her voice quavered.

Jim shook his head.

She forced a weak smile. "He said... don't let them name the kid after me. Too much pressure."

Jim let out a rough chuckle through the tears. "That sounds like him."

Diane's face crumpled against Jim's chest as she finally allowed herself to cry. Jim wrapped her in a tight hug.

For the first time since the escape, she accepted that Bucky was gone.

Jim stood at the head of the table in the briefing room, his hands braced against its surface. The crew sat around him, worn and bruised but alive.

Lisa tapped her datapad, frowning at the readout. "This signal…" she hesitated. "The technology needed to send it from that distance without interception is extremely advanced."

"How advanced?" Jim asked.

Lisa looked up, awe in her face. "Not invented yet."

The mood grew heavy.

Jim exhaled through his nose, steadying his thoughts. "So, what's at those coordinates? Unless Ember has another secret plan waiting for us, this looks like a one-way trip to the Kuiper Belt."

"Honestly, I don't know," she admitted. She glanced at JT, then back to Jim.

Jim continued. "These coordinates hold the key to unraveling this mystery and stopping them. We have to protect them at all costs."

Jim sat alone in his quarters. The poker chip rested between his fingers. Outside the viewport, Mars loomed, the planet they had both liberated and attacked. It had been the starting point of their journey, but Jim knew it wasn't the end.

A knock came at the door. He already knew who it was. "Come in, Grace," he said.

She stepped inside and leaned against the wall, watching him in his chair. "So that's it," she said. "We're going back to Mars? You know hiding there didn't end well last time."

Jim rubbed his jaw. "We're not hiding. We're searching for answers while we regroup and avoid prison. It's chess, Grace. If we don't outplay the Federation, it's game over, permanently."

Grace asked quietly, "You think we'll find anything out there?"

Jim didn't answer right away. His gaze stayed on Mars, jaw tight. Finally, he nodded. They shared a silent moment.

Then Grace, softer now, said, "You're right. Bucky would've wanted us to."

He turned to her. "So, you're staying with me?" His voice cracked.

She held his eyes. "What, and let you get lost in deep space without me? You'd never make it home."

Grace wrapped him in a heartfelt embrace, kissing him before pulling away. "Let's not screw this up again, Captain." She turned toward the door, stopped in the frame, and gave him a wink before leaving.

Jim looked down at the poker chip one last time. Then he stood, alone again, knowing sleep wasn't coming.

The captain stepped forward and stood in the center of the bridge. He drew a breath. "We're regrouping on Mars. Our goal is to prepare for the journey of a lifetime," he said. "We have a destination. We have a lead. I won't order anyone to follow me to the edge of the solar system, but you need to understand the dangers if you choose to remain with the Argo." He let the words hang in the air.

JT rose first. "You already know my answer," he said.

Mariana stood next. Then Liam. Then Karl, Raegan, and Lisa.

Grace rolled her eyes and folded her arms. "You really think we'd let you go alone, Captain?"

Jim felt something shift deep in his chest, a welcome warmth that spread through his body. The crew had made their choice. He nodded and turned back to the viewport, staring into the distance. "All right, then. We finish this together."

Around the table, each crew member gave a silent nod. Every single crew member met his eyes. The decision wasn't Jim's alone. It belonged to all of them.

The stars stretched out before them, an unsolved mystery, an ominous warning, a new beginning.

Lisa gripped the controls while Jim lowered himself into the captain's chair. All eyes fixed on the viewscreen. Mars dominated their view. The Argo prepared for the impossible.

Coda: Mars – Two Weeks Later

The eruption of Olympus Mons had finally cooled enough for recovery crews to land on the surface. Federation search-and-rescue shuttles touched down on the blackened crust, their landing struts hissing as heat bled from the fractured surface.

Most of McConnell's base had vanished into the molten chamber. The rest jutted from the rock at odd angles.

"Charges set," called the squad leader.

The wall blew inward with a thunderclap. Smoke and dust bled from the fracture. The first soldiers entered with rifles raised, lights cutting through the dark. What they found inside was not ash and melted steel. Blood painted the walls. Technicians had been ripped apart; their bodies shredded to pieces. Armor plating bent inward, as though something had burst out.

"My God..." one soldier muttered. "This wasn't the eruption."

A low scrape echoed. The ceiling buckled. Then it collapsed, crushing half the squad beneath rubble.

"Contact!" another shouted, but the warning came too late. Something lunged from the shadows, tearing through armor as if it were paper. One soldier screamed as talons punched through his spine and dragged him into the dark. The rest opened fire blindly, plasma bolts strobing the chamber.

Howls answered them. Shapes moved too fast to follow. One by one, the soldiers fell silent until only the Chimerans remained, twisted, half-burnt, their flesh blackened yet unyielding. They screeched and bolted through the cratered wall, sprinting into the thin Martian atmosphere with no protection, their infrasonic howls echoing against the canyon rim.

Federation Reports zero survivors from the Argo's terrorist attack

All test subjects perished in the eruption

Coda: Three Months Later – Valles Marineris

The colonies of the great canyon were still recovering. Olympus Mons's shockwaves had shattered domes and driven families underground. Overcrowding festered into riots. The Federation blamed "terrorists." Locals blamed everyone.

In the lower caverns, where even Federation patrols dared not tread, the air was sour with rust and unwashed bodies. Black markets thrived in the dark, and survival meant loyalty to whoever kept food, air, and power flowing.

Bootsteps echoed down a tunnel. A man in a tattered cloak moved with purpose, though hesitation clung to each stride. Caldwell stopped before a reinforced steel door embedded in the rock. He knocked.

Locks slid free, and the door creaked open. A figure in rags, voice rasping from severe burns, greeted him. "Took you long enough."

Caldwell entered. The cavern within was larger than expected, lit by jury-rigged lamps, server banks buzzing against stone. The air stank of iron and ozone. A shadow stirred in the corner, catching Caldwell's eye.

McConnell stepped forward. He wasn't the same man. His skin was charred in patches, one eye replaced by a crude implant that dulled and brightened randomly. Metal braces wrapped his arms, trembling as if barely containing the fury underneath. Each step carried pain, but hatred kept him upright.

"You survived," Caldwell whispered.

"Survival," McConnell rasped, "isn't the right word. I endured."

Caldwell swallowed hard. "Drayton will come for you. For all of us. She's mad."

McConnell's ruined lips twisted into something like a grin. "Then we beat her to the prize. Ember's secrets are mine to control." McConnell observed his guest. "I have the Synth you're after."

"I know it's not cheap," Caldwell said quickly, though his voice wavered. "But I can pay you, whatever the cost."

McConnell's remaining eye gleamed. "You can pay me by telling me where the crew of the Argo is hiding."

Caldwell froze. He thought of Jim Eckhart, a captain who had fought for something far greater than himself. "He's a good man," he said at last. "Leave him out of this."

"My business with Eckhart is personal," McConnell growled. "Eckhart's blood will flow over my hands, and his son's will be next. Choose Caldwell. Them... or you."

Silence stretched.

Finally, Caldwell lowered his head. "Fine. You'll have what you want."

"How many escaped with you?" he asked softly.

McConnell straightened, his braces creaking. "Enough," he said. His eye burned like coal. "Enough to finish what we started."

From the shadows, something snarled. Caldwell glimpsed twisted silhouettes crouching just beyond the glow, the survivors of Project Chimera, watching, waiting.

The Federation thought McConnell dead. The Argo thought him buried alive. But in the depths of Valles Marineris, a new war was already taking shape. McConnell's body was broken, but his hatred was whole. In the depths of Mars, he whispered a name with affliction in his voice:

"Eckhart."

www.ingramcontent.com/pod-product-compliance
Lightning Source LLC
Chambersburg PA
CBHW070055120726
47909CB00002B/399